Miss Hayward and the Earl
Copyright © 2025 by Rogue Press. All rights reserved.
Published by Rogue Press

All rights reserved. No part of this book may be used or reproduced in any form by any means—except in the case of brief quotations embodied in critical articles or reviews—without written permission.

This is a work of fiction. Names, characters, places, and incidents are products of the author's imagination or are used fictitiously and are not to be construed as real. Any resemblance to actual events, locales, organizations, or persons, living or dead, is entirely coincidental.

This e-book is licensed for your personal enjoyment only. This e-book may not be re-sold or given away to other people. If you would like to share this book with another person, please purchase an additional copy for each reader. If you are reading this book and did not purchase it, or it was not purchased for your use only, please return to your favorite retailer and purchase your own copy. Thank you for respecting the hard work of the author.

Stay in touch through the C. N. Jarrett newsletter!

MISS HAYWARD AND THE EARL

DAZZLING DEBUTANTES
BOOK TWO

C. N. JARRETT

ROGUE PRESS

To all the volunteers, recipients and family members I worked with at all those late-night interventions.

Family crises never seem to happen during scheduled office hours, do they?

Apparently, life changing decisions are inevitably made in the wee hours.

This one is for you; for believing in yourselves, believing in others, and having the courage to change.

PROLOGUE

"Wit is the most dangerous talent you can possess. It must be guarded with great discretion and good-nature, otherwise it will create you many enemies."

Dr. John Gregory, A Father's Legacy to His Daughters

∼

Miss Hayward fluttered her eyelids, her lashes a frantic mimicry of a butterfly's erratic flight.

"La, sir! You flatter me," she trilled with a simper.

Lord Richard Balfour, the fourth Earl of Saunton, resisted the urge to roll his eyes at the young lady's empty-headed flirting as he twirled her across the crowded ballroom. He had quickly discovered that his dance partner, Miss Hayward, was a proper miss—charming yet vapid. He could not be happier that this waltz was drawing to a close, as the final strains of music echoed through the gilded expanse of the Astleys' stately home on the River Thames.

She was a beautiful young woman, her red-blonde hair twisted in a coronet atop her head. Her complexion was silky and clear; her arched brows framed stormy blue eyes, and her nose was delicate and straight. Under ordinary circumstances, he might have found her alluring. However, he knew he must remain on his best behavior with innocent young ladies. Marriage was a permanent state of affairs, and he needed to be certain he could endure the presence of the woman he chose as his wife. He could not allow himself to be swayed by mere beauty. How could he consider matrimony with a woman who, however lovely, could offer little beyond rehearsed pleasantries and inane chatter?

Miss Hayward tilted her head with an expectant smile, clearly waiting for him to continue their conversation. He resisted the urge to sigh. It was a pity, truly. With her charm and grace, she might have been a promising partner—had she possessed the lively wit and spirit he had once found in another.

His expectations for marriage were not lofty, but Miss Hayward was simply too frivolous to consider as a life partner. Yet, he could not deny he enjoyed the sensation of her slender waist beneath his hand; her rosewater scent stirred an unwelcome nostalgia for the intimacy he had relinquished when he ended his last arrangement. The decision had seemed prudent—an effort to project sincerity in his courtship attempts, ensuring fathers would welcome his suit. However, Miss Hayward's slim form beneath his palm distracted his thoughts in a decidedly inappropriate direction.

The 1820 Season had officially begun, and Richard already felt the creeping weight of boredom as he contemplated the months ahead. If only his former betrothed, Miss

Annabel Ridley, had not seen fit to hare off across the country and marry his cousin, the Duke of Halmesbury, in a fit of pique. He would already be wed and expecting an heir. Instead, he was condemned to endure this endless parade of polite society, seeking a tolerable bride.

Annabel. The name echoed unbidden in his mind, though he wished it would not. She had been the spark amidst the dull embers of the *ton*—a woman who had amused him and, at times, challenged him, but never bored him. Her decision to marry his cousin had left him in this unenviable position: wading through a sea of dutiful smiles and stifling propriety.

Endless small talk, nauseating orgeat, and watered-down lemonade punctuated the monotony of a parade of young ladies, all ruthlessly molded by their mothers into paragons of demure perfection. Yet, not one had a hint of originality or wit to recommend her. That absence was why he had chosen Annabel in the first place. Was it too much to ask to marry a woman with whom he could hold an intelligent conversation?

Tonight, the prospects appeared grim. It was a pity Miss Hayward was such an irredeemable flibbertigibbet; otherwise, he might have been tempted to steer her toward the terrace to steal a kiss and briefly escape his ennui.

Miss Sophia Hayward was a keen observer of people, especially men. She had to be, to have avoided marriage for the past three Seasons—four, if she successfully traversed this one without receiving a marriage proposal. Observation was key to her plans, as her sizable dowry undermined her efforts to remain unmarried. How large her dowry was, she did not know; her uncle, who served as her guardian, was notoriously tight-lipped and protective of his family, much like her grandfather before him.

Her keen observational skills accounted for why, when the Earl of Saunton—the very wealthy but notorious rogue now searching for a wife—requested this waltz, Sophia had intuitively leaned into her silly debutante act, a persona she had honed over the past three years.

Her ingénue act involved fluttering her eyelashes, using insipid language, and engaging in dull small talk about needlework, the need for various shades of ribbon, and the fine selection of gloves at the shop she had visited that day.

For another type of gentleman—the sort seeking a docile and proper wife, drawn to such behavior—she employed her bluestocking act. This strategy consisted of sounding disgracefully intellectual, with detailed analyses of Shakespearean works, discussions about the many hues of roses yet to be cultivated, and the selection of classical literature available at the bookshop she had visited.

The two strategies were surprisingly similar, albeit on opposite ends of the academic spectrum. The art lay in knowing which strategy to employ and being sufficiently subtle to avoid her aunt and uncle hearing reports of untoward behavior from the gentlemen in question.

To his credit, Saunton was the former type of gentleman. Just when she began listing all the ribbons she had collected over the years, he desperately redirected her chatter to a discussion about horseflesh. It amused Sophia to note how his eyes glazed over and his charming smile fixed itself in place, as though painted on by an artist's brush. Clearly, he had already lost interest in her as a prospective bride, which suited her perfectly.

Sophia could not deny that the gentleman was devilishly handsome. His dark brown curls, long lashes framing distinctive green eyes, and athletic build—all without a hint of padding beneath his tailored clothing—made him the most attractive man at the Astleys' ball. His pearly white teeth and perfectly sculpted lips caused her to wonder, briefly, what it might be like to kiss him.

Nevertheless, she steeled herself against the pleasing warmth emanating through their gloves as he clasped her hand to lead her in what was, admittedly, a graceful waltz. He was the very worst of husband prospects—"devilish" being an apt description. Besides, she had no intention of marrying at all, despite her nagging aunt and persistent uncle, who believed it their duty to see her safely married. She was no fool. She had seen what marriage had done to her mother, and there was nothing "safe" about her mother's untimely demise. Sophia planned to bide her time until she could claim her dowry and live independently.

She exhaled a quiet sigh of relief as the dance ended, while Lord Saunton dropped a curt bow, visibly relieved.

Plastering a polite smile on her face, she kept her expression vapid as he escorted her back to her aunt and cousin at the edge of the ballroom. He offered her aunt a shallow bow before taking his leave.

Her strategy to dissuade his interest seemed to have worked, though she could not deny that an ill-advised visit to the terrace to discover whether his sculpted lips were as kissable as they appeared would make for a pleasant interlude. It was unusual for her to entertain such thoughts, but Saunton was an unusually handsome man with an amiable smile and playful manner that were ... very appealing.

She could also appreciate that he never gambled, drank only in moderation, and managed his estates with financial acumen—attractive qualities, given the circumstances of her papa's death. Still, he was a rogue not to be trusted, and Sophia had no intention of seeking a husband. Playing bland had been easy in his company, because he was so easy to read. All she had to do was bat her eyelashes and flirt vacuously while pretending to listen as he spoke about the weather and riding. He certainly seemed to make good use of his stables, if his conversation was any indication. She had stopped herself from displaying any useful knowledge about horses; she had no wish to encourage his attentions.

Sophia sighed, contemplating with weariness that the evening had only just begun, and hours of polite conversation and dreadful orgeat awaited her.

From their position at the edge of the ballroom, she and her cousin watched the lengthy quadrille while fluttering their fans. The room grew warmer as the mingled scents of pomades and perfumes filled the air. Even the music sounded shrill, though perhaps that was her mood. She wished she could be home with a book or enjoying a stimulating conversation with her cousin Lily in the library.

Turning to Lily, her closest friend and confidante, Sophia deliberately glanced toward the terrace. Her tiny cousin, with her enormous brown eyes and delicate, elfin face, immediately understood. Lily turned to her mother, Sophia's aunt, and prepared their escape.

"Mama, I believe my hem is coming loose. Sophia and I will find an alcove to mend it and return shortly."

Lady Moreland waved a gloved hand in assent as she continued to gossip with the turbaned Lady Astley, a haughty and unpleasant woman Sophia had no wish to know.

Breathing sighs of relief, Lily and Sophia swiftly made their way from the crowded ballroom, pushing open the fogged terrace doors. Laughing softly, they spilled out into the cool spring night.

As the doors swung shut, muting the sounds of music and chatter, the pair walked to a far corner of the grand balcony overlooking the vast lawn that stretched down to the river's edge.

IT WAS NOT SO MUCH the quadrille he had just danced as the insipid dancing partners he sought to escape that drove Richard onto the balcony, where he inhaled the cool spring air with relief.

The crowded Astley ball was the first of the Season, and so far, it had proven long and tiresome. His dances had been an unceasing procession of pretty, empty-headed misses, devoid of original thought. He just needed to find one who was ... well ... thoughtful—or at least reasonably sensible—and this tiresome obligation would be over.

He reached into his pocket for his silver cheroot case, an indulgence he rarely allowed himself, when he overheard female voices from the far end of the terrace.

"What a travesty of an evening! There is not one interesting gentleman here. Spoiled, entitled bores and rogues, every last one! I thought I might fall asleep from the tedium during one dance—not to mention I danced with at least three gentlemen who, I know for a fact, are keeping mistresses. What business do they have seeking a wife?"

Richard smiled faintly, savoring the fresh night air as he listened to the tirade and the heavy sarcasm lacing the word gentlemen. This girl sounded intriguing—one unafraid to roast an entire ballroom of peers in their absence.

"Perhaps they will reform for the right bride?" a second voice chimed in, lilting with optimism.

"Lily, you are such a naïve romantic. Polite society is hypocritical and grossly unfair to women. King George is not even cold in his grave, and his son is rumored to be arranging a trial for Queen Caroline over her supposed indiscretions—while his own are legendary."

Richard glanced around, ensuring no one else could overhear the bold remarks. The speaker would be ruined if anyone noted her injudicious opinions.

The voice continued, now lowered and husky, mimicking, *"I will be king, but you will be tried, harlot wife! Be careful not to trip over my mistress there by the door. Or the one behind you. No, no, do not sit on the bed—I will never hear the end of it if you squash Mrs. Fitzherbert."*

The second girl giggled as Richard bit back a laugh.

"Shhh, Sophia! If anyone hears you talk this way, you will be ruined."

"Oh, horrors! I will stop receiving invitations from people I do not like and be forced to live outside polite society as a spinster, with only an unspecified dowry to keep me company. Oh—wait—I cannot think of a more glorious reprieve!"

Richard smirked at the cynic's sentiments. If he must marry, it would be a relief to avoid a dull girl who could ruin even breakfast. A woman like this one might enliven every meal.

His thoughts halted abruptly when the optimist spoke again.

"But, Sophia, what of Lord Saunton, whom you danced with earlier? He is ever so handsome."

Richard started at the mention of his name. So, the satirical wit had been his dance partner?

The first girl—clearly Sophia—snorted. "You jest! Lord Richard-the-Rogue Balfour, the infamous Earl of Saunton? He might be the most faithless peer in the realm! It was all I could do to politely bat my eyelashes and smile genteelly at his banal small talk. Were I to marry such a man, I would need to hire only old, grumpy housemaids to avoid embarrassment and family drama."

Richard froze. He dropped the cheroot case back into his pocket, his breathing suddenly labored as he stepped farther into the shadows. Her words struck him like a blow, freezing the blood in his veins. Was this how people truly saw him?

The memory came unbidden, sharp and vivid.

"Lucas is such a heartless cad. Can he not respect me sufficiently to avoid breaking my heart in our home with our own servants? Perhaps I should get rid of all the attractive ones. Or the young ones. Or perhaps all the women on our staff."

He had been seven, playing with pewter soldiers behind a sofa when his mother's weeping had interrupted his game. She had spoken those words to his aunt over tea in the blue drawing room. At the time, he had not fully understood, but now, as the recollection flooded back, he grasped its devastating meaning. Weeks later, she had grown ill and faded away, as though sorrow had stolen her will to fight.

Am I a laughable caricature of my father?

Richard grimaced, recalling his own uncharitable thoughts about his former betrothed. Annabel had ended their engagement after finding him kissing her kitchen maid in the stables. A clap of thunder might have struck with less force than the clarity that now overwhelmed him: his behavior had been reprehensible.

Trembling, he leaned back against the wall, his knees weak and unsteady. He could not bring himself to move.

The girls on the balcony rounded the corner, finishing their conversation. The taller one—razor-tongued Sophia—stepped into the light spilling from the ballroom doorway. Richard recognized her instantly as his earlier dance partner.

Her companion followed, a diminutive girl with rich brown hair, but Richard barely noticed her. His eyes were fixed on Sophia, the so-called empty-headed miss, who had revealed her wit and depth with devastating precision.

How could he have been so wrong about her? This was no shallow debutante. She was a sharp-witted termagant who had laid bare the truth of his careless existence. Her cutting remarks had pierced him to the soul.

Shrinking deeper into the shadows, Richard prayed to remain unseen. The girls looked straight ahead, their gazes focused on the ballroom as they exited the terrace.

Alone now, Richard scanned the garden for a route to the mews where his coach awaited. He could not rejoin the ball, not in this state. His mind reeled as memories of his father's downfall surfaced—a man undone by indulgence and excess. Had he become the same?

A maelstrom of regret churned within him. If his mother were alive, he would not have been able to meet her gaze. She would have been ashamed—nay, wounded—by the man he had become.

CHAPTER ONE

"The influence of women in forming the manners of men is universally acknowledged."

Dr. John Gregory, A Father's Legacy to His Daughters

Sophia was enjoying an early respite in the Moreland breakfast room. She liked to begin her mornings before her aunt and uncle appeared at their fashionably late hour. Occasionally, her cousin Lily joined her, unless they had been up late at a ball the night before.

It had been two days since the Astley ball, but Lily had not yet recovered from the late hours and the frantic schedule of preparations her mother had put her through. Aunt Christiana was determined to see both her daughter and Sophia married off without delay, this being Lily's second Season and Sophia's fourth.

Sophia appreciated her early starts, relishing the cheerful, well-lit room in peace with a cup of tea, a book, and a full plate of eggs, ham, and fruit.

She inhaled the fragrant aroma of the Indian leaves, looking up from her book to sip her tea and take in the surroundings that always lifted her spirits.

The walls were covered in azure damask silk above white wainscoting. Over the white marble fireplace, a gilt mirror reflected the morning light from the tall sash windows into every corner of the room. It was a delightful setting, made all the more so by the stillness of the hour. These quiet moments before the household stirred were her favorite part of the day.

Later, her brother, Cecil, might make an appearance, though it was unlikely. The Morelands were hosting a ball that evening, and Cecil avoided polite events as much as possible, preferring to spend his time gambling and carousing with questionable friends.

It saddened Sophia to see her older brother following in their father's footsteps. Cecil seemed to have learned little from their father's untimely passing years earlier—a tragedy brought about by the strain of high-stakes wagers and excessive indulgences. Her mother had been devastated by the loss, her health and spirit failing rapidly in the weeks that followed, culminating in a fatal overdose of laudanum.

Sophia's uncle, now her guardian, was always vague about the details surrounding her mother's death, which had occurred so soon after her father's. This lack of clarity often left Sophia wondering whether her mother's passing had been due to overwhelming grief rather than an unfortunate accident.

It was because of her parents' deaths, more than ten years earlier, that she and her brother had come to live with

Lord Hugh Abbott, her mother's brother, and his wife, Lady Christiana Abbott, along with their two children. Her uncle had been generous, taking Cecil in along with Sophia despite the lack of a direct relationship between them. Cecil, being the child of her father's first marriage, had still been a boy at school when tragedy struck.

As a young girl, Sophia had vowed never to become her mother. On her first night at the Abbott home, she had solemnly promised Lily that she would never marry a man who gambled. Husbands could fritter away a woman's wealth and happiness while she had little or no recourse.

Sophia had no desire to fall in love with a man who could not walk away from a wager. Indeed, she did not wish to fall in love with any man at all. Love, in her experience, led to heartbreak and abandonment, leaving children reliant on the kindness of relatives for protection from life's harsh realities.

Only three more Seasons to endure, and then she would inherit the money from her trust directly—without the need for a husband. With her dowry under her control, she could finally begin her real life.

This was why she was spending her morning refreshing herself on Shakespeare's works in preparation for the Morelands' ball that evening. She liked to quote obscure verses to discourage the more ardent bucks who might otherwise be tempted by the allure of her dowry. Turning a page, she licked a finger and took a sip of tea, savoring the quiet moment.

Her peace was short-lived. Without warning, her aunt strode into the room, her purposeful steps breaking the morning stillness. Sophia's heart promptly sank. She had hoped to avoid her single-minded Aunt Christiana, who no doubt had courtship and marriage foremost on her mind.

"She is in here, Lord Moreland!"

Sophia's heart sank further. Cornered, she would now be forced to discuss marriage plans, outnumbered two to one.

Lord Moreland hurried in, his tall frame filling the doorway. He brushed a hand through his thick, graying hair. "Good morning, Sophia. Enjoying your breakfast?"

Sophia offered a resigned smile as her aunt and uncle joined her at the table. The white tablecloth gleamed beneath the morning light, adorned with silverware and cheerful blossoms in tiny vases.

Two footmen stepped forward with precise movements, serving the viscount and his wife tea in delicate china cups. The warm scent of freshly brewed leaves drifted through the air, mingling with the quiet clink of porcelain.

Sophia dearly loved her adopted family, but they were frightfully conventional. Lord Moreland, ever the protective patriarch, believed the best way to secure her future was to marry her off to a safe and proper gentleman. Lady Moreland, by contrast, was singularly focused on ensuring that both her niece and daughter secured matches with impeccable connections.

Being cornered alone with the two of them meant there was no escaping *The Conversation*. It was a ritual at the start of every Season, growing lengthier and more urgent each year as Aunt Christiana's desperation mounted.

Sophia sighed inwardly. She should have finished her meal and retreated to another room before they arrived.

Thoughtless move, Sophia—not predicting your aunt would choose the morning of the Moreland grand ball to confront you!

Her aunt sipped her tea, arching an elegant brow in her husband's direction—a silent command.

Uncle Hugh cleared his throat. It seemed he had been chosen to lead the charge.

Stay calm, Sophia. Do not show any reaction. Take your time responding to guide the conversation to your desired outcome.

With that reminder firmly in mind, she closed her leather-bound tome with deliberate care and set it aside. Then, she turned her gaze to her uncle, her expression expectant.

"Now, see here, Sophia. It is high time we saw you settled in marriage, with a household of your own to manage."

The words had a rehearsed quality, and Sophia suppressed a smile. No doubt her aunt had made him practice precisely what to say.

She parried with practiced ease. "Why, Uncle ... am I no longer welcome in the Abbott household?" She widened her eyes in mock dismay, letting her lower lip quiver ever so slightly.

Hugh Abbott's square, kind face immediately softened, his brow creasing in distress. "Never—no, never, my dear niece. You are always welcome here. We love you as though you were our own ..."

Uncle Hugh fell silent, his hand coming up to rub his jaw as he groped for words to repair the unintended slight. A panicked expression crossed his face as he glanced helplessly at his wife.

Sophia watched the exchange, careful to keep any trace of smugness from her expression. The first point might belong to her aunt for cornering her so early in the day, but the second point was hers alone for deftly turning the tables.

Her uncle was thoroughly floundering now, leaving

Aunt Christiana to take the reins. His guilt over possibly hurting his beloved niece's feelings had effectively removed him as a useful ally for his wife.

Such sentiment, however, was not a weakness Aunt Christiana shared. An elegant woman in her forties, she was a formidable opponent despite her lack of intellectual inclinations. Sophia had long since learned not to underestimate her aunt's tenacity.

Politely, Sophia turned her gaze to her aunt, who was now scowling in displeasure at her husband. No doubt she was lamenting his easy manipulation. Squaring her jaw and visibly regrouping, Aunt Christiana turned back to face her niece with renewed determination.

"Sophia, at the Astleys' the other night, Lord Saunton asked you to dance but then promptly returned you to me. I know he is searching for a wife, and he admires intelligent women like yourself. He is ever so wealthy. I hear his estates are thriving, and he never gambles. You must make an effort—"

"No!"

Sophia and her aunt both turned, startled by her uncle's unexpected interjection. His face was a thundercloud of undisguised ire. "The earl is a scoundrel, and he will not lay a finger on anyone under my protection. How could you allow them to be introduced, Christiana?"

It was clear her aunt and uncle had not sufficiently prepared for *The Conversation*. While Lady Moreland hissed a sharp response to her husband's accusations, Sophia seized the opportunity. Grabbing her toast and book, she pushed her chair back and slipped away before they could redirect their attention to her.

The handsome young footman, Thomas, stationed near the door, pressed his lips together to suppress a smile as she passed. Throwing him a quick, saucy wink was instinctive, and his quiet snort of laughter betrayed his amusement.

He raised a hand to his mouth, feigning a sneeze, as Sophia disappeared into the corridor, a flurry of embroidered white skirts marking her brisk exit. Her aunt would have to pursue her plans another day.

∽

RICHARD HAD CONCLUDED it was finally time for him to become a real man.

Nay, a gentleman.

The morning after the Astley ball, he had come to accept that he was at a crossroads. He could either embark on the path to becoming a better man or resign himself to becoming a grotesque caricature of the late earl. The realization that he was well on his way to emulating his father —a man whose selfishness and irresponsibility had led Richard's mother to an untimely death—was the prod he needed to reevaluate his life. Who did he want to be? What legacy did he wish to leave behind?

In the past two days, he had finally acknowledged the pain he had caused his longtime friend and former betrothed, Annabel. His cavalier treatment of her feelings and his rakish pursuits had wounded her deeply. Despite the shame of his actions, Richard now felt a sense of gratitude that his cousin, Philip, had stepped in to marry Annabel in his stead.

At the time, Richard had railed against Philip, but now he saw the truth: his cousin had been a true gentleman, doing what was best for Annabel. She deserved a real marriage—a partnership built on respect and honor.

Richard knew he would not have changed his ways to be worthy of her, and he was grateful she had found the life she deserved.

He resolved to make changes in his life and become a man worthy of the title gentleman—a man his mother would be proud of. With this newfound determination, he had already begun making adjustments, though he knew there was much careless behavior to atone for. He could only hope it was not too late to change his course and become a better man.

He also hoped it was not too late to earn the regard of a woman of substance.

Miss Sophia Hayward, with her cutting remarks and sharp wit, was never far from his thoughts. Her forthrightness, when unobserved by society, reminded him of the easy honesty he had once shared with Annabel—before he had ruined their friendship. No one had ever delivered such an unvarnished dose of truth to him. Of course, Miss Hayward was unaware of the impact her words had made, but her determined spirit and intelligence had left an indelible mark on him.

If he could convince her to trust him enough to reveal her true self, perhaps there might be a chance for something more. The thought of seeing the intriguing young lady again that evening lingered in his mind, though hours still stretched before him.

In the meantime, he had work to do. He would meet with his man of business to put certain inquiries into motion. It was time to ensure there were no lingering consequences of his past choices—choices he had once thought harmless but now viewed with remorse. Though he had always been careful to avoid fathering a child, the mere possibility gnawed at him.

Regardless of what his inquiries revealed, he owed apologies—and in some cases, financial recompense—to those he had wronged along the way. It was a daunting task, but one he was determined to face, step by step.

Before his meeting, Richard rang for his butler in his study. When Radcliffe arrived, Richard handed him a list of two housemaids with whom he had behaved improperly—a fact he acknowledged with deep regret. Both young women had been flirtatious at the time, and he, succumbing to his own weaknesses, had not acted as a gentleman should.

He informed Radcliffe that each would receive a handsome sum to ensure their financial comfort and instructed the butler to locate suitable new positions for them, if they so wished. The hawkish butler would bring the girls to him one at a time so he could meet with them to that end. His conscience demanded he take responsibility, and he knew he must clean house if he was to embark on a new way of life.

Though Richard managed not to wince during the discussion, Radcliffe betrayed no reaction—the impeccable English butler that he was.

Or perhaps he already knows about the girls.

For Richard, however, this was not merely about rectifying wrongs—it was about setting his life on a better course. His resolve to embrace a more honorable way of life required a fresh start. Though he maintained a calm exterior, discussing the matter brought an unmistakable sting of shame.

He reminded himself that facing these truths was necessary if he was to become the man he aspired to be. He intended to go courting in an honorable manner, and it would not do to have his past temptations dusting the banisters, reminding him he did not deserve this second chance he sought.

Once he had met with the two maids and made arrangements, his man of business arrived for their meeting. This marked the fourth uncomfortable discussion of the day.

Richard sat at his desk, pensive, as he stared at the bottle-green wallpaper while waiting for Johnson to absorb his instructions.

Johnson, visibly disconcerted, stared at the list in his slender hand. A competent man integral to Richard's financial success, Johnson looked inordinately like a banker, with his bulbous forehead, meticulous black hair, and close-shaven beard lining his narrow jaw.

They had worked together for years, yet Richard suddenly realized he knew nothing about Johnson's personal life. Did the man have a wife? Dependents? Richard had never inquired, assuming that women and men alike were eager to please him. Johnson was more than willing to work long hours for a generous salary, but had Richard unwittingly stolen time from his family?

"My lord, respectfully, I will repeat my understanding of your instructions to ensure I am perfectly clear," Johnson said.

Richard cleared his throat. "Go ahead," he replied hoarsely, fidgeting with his cravat. Oddly, the cravat had felt perfectly tied earlier, but now it was a hangman's noose squeezing his throat shut.

Johnson continued in a strained voice. "I am to seek, with the help of runners if necessary, four housemaids with whom you—ahem—indulged over the past several years. Two of these you do not recall by name, only by their descriptions and respective households. I am to establish their current circumstances and report back to you. We will then arrange meetings so that you may ... apologize ..."

Richard interjected smoothly. "I will meet with them discreetly to apologize for my past behavior and offer financial settlements to recompense them for my disrespectful advances. If any of them are in untenable circumstances, we will ascertain what improvements they desire and assist in securing them."

Johnson looked aghast but managed to respond, "Then once these housemaids—"

Richard interjected, "I do feel that if I ruined them, they would be the most immediately in need of assistance due to their lack of financial resources and connections."

Johnson cleared his throat. "Indeed. Then I am to continue the investigation and locate a further eight widows in order to determine their current situations, along with any consequences from your past ... acquaintanceships."

"That is correct. I did not include courtesans or women whose paths were already set in a direction similar to my own when we ... interacted, as I determined I was not the cause of their circumstances. That responsibility lay elsewhere. After all, the list must have a finite endpoint, don't you think?" Richard gave a hollow laugh, the sound devoid of true mirth.

Johnson echoed him with his own lifeless chuckle. "Yes, my lord. After all, an infinite list of amends would require infinite access to funds."

Richard and Johnson both looked away, suddenly finding the furnishings in the room far more fascinating than the endless parade of women in Richard's past. Redemption, it seemed, was proving to be as mortifying as

Richard had anticipated when he first contemplated this restorative rite.

Earlier that morning, he had sought advice from his cousin, the Duke of Halmesbury. Fortunately, he had not encountered Annabel during the visit. Halmesbury had been visibly appalled by the scrawled list of paramours, though Richard had refrained from revealing any names. The list had merely served as a prop to facilitate their discussion about taking responsibility for his actions. Sharing the actual list, he thought wryly, would surely be the height of poor taste.

Richard shifted uncomfortably in his chair, his face warming as he recalled the meeting. His cravat, which had felt perfectly fine earlier, now seemed unbearably tight. Thankfully, the duke had given his wholehearted support and provided practical guidance on how to make amends in various situations.

The stilted silence in the room stretched on, threatening to deepen into something truly excruciating.

Taking a steadying breath, Richard broke the quiet. "I need regular reports, and, of course, you will let me know when there is a meeting I must attend."

Johnson nodded, tucking the lists safely into his portfolio.

A sudden thought struck Richard. "Johnson, instead of taking my lists with you, copy them out for yourself and leave me the originals. I would not want something to happen to them and then be forced to make them again." Clearing his throat, he added, with a faint attempt at a smile, "Please."

Johnson's eyes widened, momentarily startled. "Please?" he echoed, as though the word were foreign to his ears.

A fresh wave of shame swept over Richard. "Please," he confirmed firmly.

Egads, how pompous must he have been in the past for Johnson to be astonished by such a rudimentary display of manners? This restoration of honor business was proving to have endless ramifications for his peace of mind. He could not decide whether he welcomed or resented his new awareness of how others perceived his behavior.

But it was imperative that his quest began in earnest before he attended Viscount Moreland's ball that evening.

He wanted to see Miss Hayward again, but he needed to be armed with some semblance of self-respect when he next encountered the young lady.

Sophia stood at the edge of the ballroom, watching the colorfully attired dancers twirl in time to the music. She had never held high hopes for her first Season. At the time, she had vaguely wished to meet a gentleman, marry for love, and experience the newfound freedoms one attained as a married woman. However, as her brother's poor choices over the past few years began to mirror those of their late father, Sophia's vague hopes had transformed into a firm resolve to avoid marriage at all costs.

Not that she could let her uncle and aunt know of her decision; the endless and trying conversations that would follow were best avoided. Instead, she had developed her two strategies for gently repelling would-be suitors.

Now in her fourth Season, it promised yet again to be an endless string of dreary small talk, mindless conversations, and carefully crafted performances on her part. Parliament, in its infinite wisdom, had decreed that the 1820 session would run longer than usual, stranding the peerage in London during the odorous summer—a prospect Sophia found deeply disheartening. Adding to the discomfort were the murmurings of the king's plans for an ill-advised trial of Queen Caroline.

Fluttering her dance card, she reflected that the novelty of the little booklet, introduced by Lady Astley upon her return from Vienna, had proven useful for cooling herself in the crowded ballroom. Now that word had spread of these *Programmes du Bal*, no doubt they would become ubiquitous as hostesses scrambled to outshine one another.

Her musings were interrupted by the realization that someone stood beside her. Sighing, she pasted on a polite smile and turned to face her new companion. To her dismay, it was none other than Lord Saunton: undeniably handsome, unquestionably morally bankrupt. Her heart—and her smile—sank as he greeted her and reached for her card. *Had she not already discouraged the man at the Astleys' ball?*

"I see your next dance is available," he said in his smooth baritone. "May I have this waltz?"

Belatedly, she curtsied. "Of course, my lord."

Lord Saunton led her to the center of the ballroom. As he positioned himself and took her hand in his much larger one, he spoke unexpectedly. "I have been thinking of you."

Sophia's head whipped up in surprise. She stared at him, too startled to contain her thoughts. "Why?"

Lord Saunton chuckled sheepishly. "You are more direct than I remember from our last dance."

Sophia inwardly cringed. "La, my lord, I am flattered you remembered our one dance together." She hastily fluttered her lashes in an exaggerated display of flirtation.

He grinned, shaking his head. "Now, now, Miss

Hayward, I preferred it when you were direct. It was not the dance that was unforgettable, but your candid thoughts about my character, which you shared with your friend on the balcony."

Sophia blanched, frantically trying to recall what she had said to Lily about Lord Saunton that evening.

"Do not be concerned; you gave me pause for thought. Consequently, I have made a decision. Several decisions. And, as a result, I was thinking I would like to call on you tomorrow."

Sophia's mind screamed, *No, no, no!* This was a horrible turn of events. Her aunt would quite literally skin her alive if she refused such an invitation—from an earl, no less. But she could not involve herself with an incorrigible rogue. She could not involve herself with anyone!

During their first dance, she had made a point of boring the earl in order to avoid his attentions. And now she was memorable?

This would not do.

This would not do at all!

"Sophia?" His intimate use of her name made her wince. He continued, lowering his voice, "Sophia, please say yes. I will not embarrass you or tell your aunt if you decline." *Wait! Was he reading her thoughts?* "I would very much appreciate the opportunity to call on you, and I would like it to be with your permission."

She stared at him as they spun past another couple. "I dislike cads," she whispered.

Lord Saunton sighed. "That is fair. You are a beautiful, intelligent woman—"

Sophia's jaw dropped as she gaped at him. She was?

"—and I promise to treat you with the utmost respect if you allow me to call on you. Please grant me the honor of a little time in your company, as I would like to get to know you better."

"Why should I believe that? About respecting me, I mean?" She strove to sound confident but feared she merely sounded breathless.

He looked down into her eyes, his expression earnest. "After learning your candid opinion of my character, I have decided to grant generous assistance to the housemaids you referenced, and I am working to be a better man. I was wondering if you could help me."

Sophia was so astonished by his words that she stumbled. His strong hand steadied her, ensuring no one noticed her misstep.

In befuddled shock, she heard herself say, "That is splendid news, but given your promise not to inform my aunt..." She paused, waiting for his confirmation. He gave a slight nod. "No, I would not like to be courted by you."

Disappointment flickered across his face before determination took its place.

"I understand, and I have no wish to coerce you. I did not expect this to be easy. However, I am resolved to learn more about you—the intriguing young woman who caused me to see the error of my ways. Tell me, Miss Hayward, do you believe it is possible for a man to change?"

Sophia pondered his question as he guided her gracefully across the floor. "He can get sick; he can get well. He can make poor decisions; he can make astute ones. I have seen men change for the worse, so logic dictates that if a man can worsen, he must also be able to improve."

Saunton regarded her with newfound respect. "I am glad to hear you say that. I am a young man who has just awakened to his own selfishness. I have to believe that it is never too late for a man to change, or I will go mad. My cousin, Halmesbury, assures me that amends can be made, and a new future built. Do you believe in second chances, Miss Hayward?"

"I would never deny a man's right to try to correct his path."

Her heart raced as their conversation veered into unexpectedly meaningful territory. No man had ever spoken to her so openly.

"Then know your words had a profound effect on me. Please, may I have another dance at the Yardley ball? I would like one more chance to persuade you."

Sophia's breath hitched as their eyes met. His gaze held so much hope that she found herself whispering, "I promise."

A genuine smile lit his face, and Sophia could not help but notice how compelling he was when he smiled with such warmth.

What harm could another waltz possibly do?

Feeling the increased beating in her chest, she worried that a single dance could do far more damage to her vow to stay unaffected than she could possibly conceive. Yet she could not bring herself to regret her decision to see him again.

CHAPTER TWO

"The domestic economy of a family is entirely a woman's province."

Dr. John Gregory, A Father's Legacy to His Daughters

After her waltz with Lord Saunton, he returned her to her aunt's side, who watched him walk away with a calculating gleam in her chocolate-brown eyes. Aunt Christiana was not a bad person. She was, however, ruthless in pursuing her goals, and her current goal was to see Sophia married to a well-connected gentleman. To be fair, Sophia's parents and their tragic end might have been to blame for inspiring her aunt's single-minded focus.

Standing in the crowded ballroom, with people continuously brushing past, stirred Sophia's customary anxiety within large gatherings, mounting to an uncomfortable level. Oddly, during her dance with Lord Saunton, she had not even noticed the other dancing couples despite their proximity. He had profoundly distracted her with his intimate conversation.

As her anxiety rose, she looked around for her cousin, thinking to escape to the terrace.

"Lily's dance card is filled for the entire night."

Sophia started. The uncanny announcement from Lady Moreland made her wonder if she had spoken her thoughts out loud moments earlier.

"It would behoove you to make an effort, Sophia. You could be married before the end of this Season," her aunt continued.

Sophia breathed a sigh of relief. She had not spoken out loud; her aunt was simply continuing *The Conversation*.

"Indeed, Aunty. I need to visit the necessary, and then I shall return."

Her aunt nodded, her eyes fixed on her daughter, who was dancing with Lord Baxton—a man with an obnoxious laugh whose love of snuff was nauseating. She hoped her cousin was holding her breath.

Sophia quickly walked off toward the necessary, but when she was sure her aunt's attention was still focused on the dancers, she veered down the corridor toward the library, her favorite room in their London home. She needed a moment alone to clear her thoughts and settle her nerves.

There are too many people in the Moreland townhouse tonight.

Once she reached the library, Sophia made her way to the annex at the back. Finding one of the library steps—polished mahogany, about the size and shape of a large armchair—she sank to the parquet floor and leaned against the back of the solid furnishing, which would hide her from any guests entering the room.

Drawing a deep, calming breath, she closed her eyes and savored a moment of quiet. The orchestra's music was dampened by the thick walls, leaving her alone with her thoughts.

Her encounter with Lord Saunton came vividly to mind. His confessions lingered in her thoughts: reparations to former paramours and an earnest effort to change his character. A monumental undertaking for such a man, all spurred by overhearing her mockery on the balcony. It seemed incredible.

Why would her words affect him to such a degree? Would this change of heart last, or was it merely a passing whim that would vanish by the end of the week? He was reputed to make sound financial decisions and, according to rumor, had tripled his family's fortune since inheriting the title as a young man at Oxford. That implied he possessed the intelligence and fortitude to follow through on difficult resolutions. But to claim *she* had inspired such a transformation?

Barely anyone knew of her existence beyond her immediate family, and no one had ever accused her of being inspirational. Yet, he seemed sincere. Could her words truly have such power? The thought was heady, if not a little overwhelming. Shielding herself from society had always been her first instinct, but the idea that her opinion might matter—even to a dissolute lord—was undeniably gratifying.

Suddenly, Sophia heard approaching footsteps. Quickly, she tucked her skirts behind the enormous steps. It would not do to be caught alone in the library; such a discovery could incite scandal depending on who entered the room.

Luckily, the annex was poorly lit, offering her some concealment.

"Hayward, why the hell did you insist I come tonight? I am not even on the cursed guest list, and when Lord Moreland saw me, he glared as though he wanted to throw me out on my ear!"

Sophia frowned in confusion. Her brother was in attendance?

"Leech, I beg your indulgence. I have news that will benefit both of us greatly. Did you happen to see my sister?"

Lord Leech? Sophia's eyebrows shot up in surprise. She encountered the man infrequently at social events. A scrawny, sallow figure with unkempt brown hair and a thick mustache, he flaunted a wicked reputation. Over the past few years, he had married two heiresses, both of whom had coincidentally died within months of their nuptials under suspicious circumstances. He was either an exceptionally unlucky man or, more likely, a despicable villain who had rid himself of his wives to claim their fortunes, all while leaving no evidence of his foul deeds. Though none openly accused him of murder, whispers of speculation followed wherever he went.

Unfortunately, Leech had powerful allies, which allowed him to remain within society despite his gruesome reputation as a possible wife-killer. However, fathers no longer offered their daughters to the fortune hunter in exchange for a title.

"The tall girl with the reddish-blonde hair and unbecoming white gown standing with your aunt? She looks worth a turn in the gardens. What about her?"

Sophia's lip curled in disgust at the thought of accompanying such a reprobate to the gardens.

"That is her. Miss Sophia Hayward. A right spoilt little

princess. It happens I was in my uncle's study and stumbled on some interesting documents."

"Stumbled? More like you searched his office. Are your gambling debts getting a little too deep to manage, Hayward?"

"Nothing I cannot deal with. Now let me tell you what I uncovered. The late Viscount Moreland—Sophia's grandfather—apparently did not trust my father. When the marriage contracts for Sophia's mother were negotiated, he took the rather unusual step of establishing a trust for the new Mrs. Hayward and any children resulting from the union. Since it was a separate trust, neither my father nor any of his creditors could make a claim on it. The old man ensured that his daughter and grandchildren would be taken care of, irrespective of my father's financial management skills—which were very poor because he was a degenerate gambler."

Sophia threw a hand up to cover her mouth, fearing she might chuckle. Her brother had the temerity to call their father a degenerate gambler? That was rich, considering his strong-arm tactics to seize her pin money for his own gambling habits.

"The point is, Sophia is the only grandchild from the union, and the old viscount must have been overly focused on preventing my father from controlling the funds because the trust does not provide specific protections for his grandchildren beyond that. It seems his solicitors failed to think past the immediate issue they were addressing. From what I understand, the entire trust will go to her husband if she marries—which, so far, has not been a risk. The silly chit cannot attract a man."

Sophia narrowed her eyes at her brother's nasty words. *That is deliberate on my part, thank you very much!*

Leech responded, "How much are we talking about?"

"Fifty thousand pounds."

Sophia clamped both hands over her mouth to stifle the exclamation of astonishment struggling to escape. The two men fell silent.

Finally, Leech whistled through his teeth. "That is incredible. The Abbott family must be plump in the pocket. Why has no one snatched her up, then?"

"The Abbotts are very protective, and they have kept the size of her dowry a secret. Uncle Hugh must have developed an abhorrence of fortune hunters after my father ran through the marriage settlement and gambled away all his income and assets before dropping dead during a high-stakes card game."

"And Moreland's only sister died of an accidental laudanum overdose because of her weak nerves after that incident." Leech's sarcastic emphasis left little doubt he believed it was anything but accidental.

Sophia winced.

"Pity the mother passed after birthing a brat, or you might have had grounds to argue that the blunt should drop on you as the heir of your father's estate."

Sophia shivered, icy tendrils of fear threading through her veins. They were speaking of her as if she had never been born, and she suspected the idea of her nonexistence was a key part of their plan. She had always known there was little love lost between her and her brother, but hearing the cold disregard in his tone still cut deeply.

"If I were to help you marry her, I would want a guarantee that you would split the dowry with me."

"What sort of help?"

"I can introduce you. And, when the time is right, I can let you into the house so you can take the little baggage to

Gretna Green. I have read the terms of the trust, and there is nothing the viscount can do once she is legally married. The trust will be paid out because she is the only remaining beneficiary."

That her brother would ally with this man to see her wed—likely with the possibility of her premature death factored into their calculations—was a chilling reminder of how little Cecil cared for his younger sister. Sophia struggled to calm her breathing as terror twisted in her stomach. There were few things that frightened her, but her brother's gambling obsession and the lengths he would go to for money left no doubt he was capable of following through with the plan he had just outlined to Lord Leech.

She listened carefully as they reached an agreement on how to exploit her, and there was no doubt in her mind that both her freedom and her life were at risk. Years earlier, she had learned that her older brother, who bore a marked physical resemblance to their father but lacked his charm or pleasant manner, was ruthless in taking advantage of her. Any hope she had once held that they might repair their relationship was well and truly laid to rest.

When she first came out into society and began receiving a larger allowance, Cecil had confronted her in her room. Grabbing her arm in a tight grip that brought tears to her eyes, he had demanded she hand over her coin. Trembling from the pain, she had finally surrendered the reticule she had hidden in her dressing table.

He had taken it without hesitation, along with the silver-backed brush and mirror that had belonged to their mother. As he walked out the door, she had called after him, warning that Uncle Hugh would not be pleased.

Cecil had stopped in his tracks and returned, his expression dark. Gripping her arm even tighter, he had hissed, "If

Uncle Hugh hears about this, you will regret it, little sister—more than you have ever regretted anything before this day."

Sophia had struggled to free herself from his iron hold, but the determination in his eyes had been equally matched by the threat in his words.

She had believed him. A direct confrontation with Cecil would never have worked. He was too large, too ruthless, and utterly without conscience. His drinking had already mottled his skin at a young age, and his eyes showed no signs of life in their reddened, watery depths. Her brother was a man trapped in liquor and sinful pursuits, living only for himself. He was on his best behavior around Uncle Hugh, who paid him a quarterly allowance, which prevented the viscount and the rest of the Abbott family from noticing how far he had fallen.

The Abbotts' heir, Aidan, might have observed Cecil's decline, but the two men spent little time together. Cecil had been at Harrow during their father's death before moving on to Cambridge, while Aidan had attended Eton and later Oxford. For reasons beyond Sophia's understanding, this difference in their schooling seemed to prevent them from having much in common.

Unwilling to be a victim, Sophia had quickly learned to hide any items she refused to lose to her brother's vices, hoarding the majority of her pin money in carefully chosen hiding places. The next time he came for her, she handed over her reticule without complaint. When he questioned the value of the coins contained within, she blamed their aunt, claiming she had insisted Sophia purchase gloves and accessories for her wardrobe.

Fortunately, her brother had not credited that his little sister could be lying, nor did he possess a firm grasp on what ladies paid for their trifles. He accepted her explanation after tossing her room for any items of value. Sophia had learned to outwit her nasty brother without him becoming wise to her tricks. Eventually, he left her alone, as the amount of blunt he could gain from her became too little to bother with.

Now, however, the promise of half of fifty thousand pounds was enough to renew his interest. There was no possibility that anything would distract or dissuade him from pursuing such a prize.

Sophia knew she was in grave danger. As she listened to the men leave, she debated how long she should wait before risking her departure from the hiding place. Her future was in imminent peril, and she would need to devise a plan. But first, she had to return to that infernal ball.

"What does your brother think he is doing?" hissed Lady Moreland.

Sophia looked at her aunt in puzzlement, then followed the direction of her gaze. Cecil, with Lord Leech in tow, was weaving through the bystanders on the edge of the ballroom toward them.

"It looks like Cecil is going to introduce Lord Leech to you. You must either dance with him or make an excuse to sit out the rest of the evening. Let me see your dance card, Sophia."

Her aunt sounded desperate as she took up the card tied to Sophia's wrist. Fanning it out, she groaned audibly at the sight of the empty slots.

"Listen here, girl—you injured your ankle and are sitting out the rest of the evening!" Lady Moreland whispered urgently, her tone intense as she searched Sophia's eyes for agreement, squeezing her arm in desperation. "Yes?"

Sophia breathed a sigh of relief. There would be no support from her family for Cecil's attempts to bring her and Lord Leech together. "Yes."

A lively country dance was in full swing when the two men reached them. Cecil introduced the unsavory gentleman, and Lady Moreland performed her best rendition of a polite but disapproving mama, which both men ignored.

Once pleasantries were exchanged, Lord Leech turned his malevolent eyes to Sophia. They were amber—nearly yellow—and reminded her of a snake. His strange gaze flicked over her face and bosom in a way that made her skin crawl before returning to meet her eyes. The icy depths revealed no hint of humanity as he reached for the dance card tied to her wrist.

"Miss Hayward, your brother's description of your beauty does you no justice. Shall we take a turn around the ballroom?"

Sophia pulled her arm away, unwilling to feel his touch. "La, my lord! I am so flattered by your esteemed attention. Alas, I just turned my ankle a few minutes ago, and I can feel it swelling as we speak. I am afraid there will be no more dancing for me this evening."

A muscle ticked along Lord Leech's jaw as he clenched his teeth. "How unfortunate. Perhaps I could have the honor of a dance with you at the Yardley ball, then?"

"We shall see," interjected Lady Moreland. "We will not know more about the injury until the physician is called. Best not to make any plans."

Leech's gaze flicked back to her chaperon.

"Of course, my lady."

Bowing deeply, Leech and Cecil made their departure. Both Sophia and her aunt exhaled in relief as they walked away.

Lady Moreland shook her head. "I am deeply concerned about Cecil if he is spending time with someone such as Lord Leech. What could they possibly share in common?"

"Nothing worthwhile," Sophia replied tightly, her stomach knotted with fear. "Nothing worthwhile."

CHAPTER
THREE

"Prudence is an essential virtue in a woman's character."

Dr. John Gregory, A Father's Legacy to His Daughters

Richard watched from his study window while Caroline Brown descended from the carriage he had sent for her. He guessed this was her first time visiting London, at his request, and based on her expression, she found the city daunting. She had probably never seen so many people, buildings, horses, heard so much sound, smelled so much humanity. London was more ... everything. She appeared quite out of sorts as she stared up at the four towering stories of Balfour Terrace, stretching five bays wide. Visibly gulping, she headed toward the servants' staircase.

"Mrs. Brown?" Although the window muffled the words, he could just hear them. His man, Long, called her by her courtesy title, a privilege of being a housekeeper in a respectable household, but to Richard's knowledge she was not a true Mrs.

Long assisted his man of business with Richard's vast holdings, and he had sent his loyal agent to find the former maid at the home of her employer days earlier. His man would have invited her to London for an audience with Richard, who had been expecting their arrival for some hours.

Out in the street, Caroline looked back at Mr. Long in question.

"Lord Saunton has invited you as an honored guest." Mr. Long held up his hand to indicate the way up the steps toward the front door. Richard could just make out her eyes widening in surprise as she stood undecided. "Please, come this way, Mrs. Brown."

Fidgeting nervously, the young woman most likely pondered her low status while she considered the front door. A common servant who had worked hard and raised her station to that of housekeeper in a doctor's household after Richard had nearly destroyed her future two years earlier. She was fortunate that after betraying Miss Annabel Ridley, her mistress had seen fit to find her a new position. Annabel would have been well within her rights to dismiss the kitchen maid without a second thought.

Richard could only assume the young woman to be confused by his invitation, but he had sent Long because the man could be most persuasive. He wondered how she had organized her affairs to accompany Mr. Long to the great city of London. Truly, she would have no idea why she was here, and she must believe that she had no business walking in the front door of a fine home such as Balfour Terrace in the famous Mayfair district.

"Mrs. Brown, the earl insisted you are to be treated as a

guest. He will be most displeased with me if he learns you entered through the servants' entrance."

The young woman reluctantly rejoined him and ascended the steps out of Richard's view. Long reappeared shortly, descending the steps toward the carriage.

"Mr. Long?" Richard heard Caroline call out in an alarmed tone.

Her companion was halfway down the front steps. He stopped to look back.

"Are you not joining me?"

"Nay, Mrs. Brown. I will return to escort you back to Filminster, but I have errands to run. The earl and his staff will take good care of you in my absence."

Richard assumed the woman must have looked anxious from the cajoling that followed that statement. "Don't worry, Mrs. Brown. I think you will be pleased to hear what his lordship has to say." Long gave an encouraging smile. Evidently, he succeeded in allaying her fears because he nodded a goodbye and continued his descent.

Richard turned back to his desk, anxiously checking his cravat and coat. He could not deny he was nervous about this meeting.

A few moments later, there was a knock at the door. "Come in."

Radcliffe entered. Behind the butler, Richard could see Caroline peering into his study with an expression that mirrored his own internal ferment. "Mrs. Brown is here to see you."

The young woman grimaced behind the manservant before being shown into the study. She came to a halt in the middle of the lavish room, looking around in bewilderment.

Richard pasted a smile on his lips and stepped around his desk to give a short bow. In that unorthodox moment, he thought about Caroline's perspective—what she might be thinking as her eyes flittered over the bottle-green wallpaper, the white trim, the polished mahogany desk and matching shelves. Her gaze rested for a moment on the set of plump wingback armchairs, upholstered in a cheerful ivory fabric patterned with rich greens, reds, and golds, before skittering to fall to the rug, which she stared at pensively.

"Mrs. Brown?"

Caroline whipped her head back to him. Richard was careful not to smile the characteristic glib smile he used to charm women, but schooled his face to display concern.

"Mrs. Brown, are you all right?"

"What am I doing here?" she whispered.

Richard looked over her shoulder. "Radcliffe, please bring tea and refreshments. Mrs. Brown must be exhausted after days on the road. Mrs. Brown, please take a seat?"

Carefully, he took her by the arm and steered her to the seating area, urging her to sit. She plopped down in a daze. After a moment, she untied her bonnet, placed it on the end of the table between them, and smoothed her hair with a trembling hand.

"I am sorry for the suspense, Mrs. Brown. When you hear what I have to say, it will be worth it, I assure you." With that, he took the seat opposite, his fingers drumming on the arm of his chair while he collected his thoughts.

"I summoned you to London because I wanted to make my ... apologies ..."

Caroline frowned in confusion.

"First, please, tell me how you have been since I last saw you?"

Caroline cleared her throat. "I am ... fine, I suppose. Miss Ridley—I mean, the Duchess of Halmesbury—and

Mrs. Harris assisted me to find a new position as a maid with the local doctor after she ... caught us kissing in the stables." She mirrored his own state of agitation with her awkward mumbling. They both well knew the disreputable circumstances of their last encounter. "Since that time, the doctor's housekeeper retired, so I was promoted to running his household. So I guess everything has worked out for the best."

"I am so glad to hear that." Richard did not reveal that he had gathered this information on her before the meeting. She was clearly distressed. "I wanted to apologize to you ... for my seduction ... or perhaps a better word would be my interruption of your life."

Caroline looked at the earl, aghast. "Apologize, my lord?"

He cleared his throat uncomfortably, tugging at his cravat. "It was not well done of me, engaging with you under your mistress's nose. And, after she found us, I did not step in to take any responsibility for you. If Miss Ridley had not decided to find you the new position, you would have been destitute, and I am profoundly embarrassed regarding my behavior with you."

"I ... see. I cannot blame you for the decisions I made, my lord." Caroline dropped her head, shame reflected on her face. What he had done to this young woman, it was her secret burden to bear that she was a fallen woman. Fortunately, those who knew about her indiscretions with him had elected to keep the affair private.

"That is generous, but I do blame myself. I had considerable experience that I brought to bear when I pursued you. Not to sound conceited, but few women would have resisted."

"I see. While it is very kind of you to apologize, is that

why I am here in London? It seems to me you could have sent me a letter to state your apology and spared yourself a great deal of trouble bringing me here."

"No … I wanted to apologize in person and to make an attempt at amends. I wish to make reparations … in the form of funds. Funds you could use to change your current circumstances or could be a means to your retirement in the future. I was thinking of putting two hundred pounds in your name."

Caroline gasped. Richard knew that two hundred pounds was a fortune for a woman in her position. His earlier meetings with similar women from his past had proved quite—

"No!"

No? What on earth?

"No?"

"No! It would make me feel like a kept woman. I did not engage with you for funds."

Richard's chest tightened in dismay. Would she not allow him to make amends? This was unexpected. He needed to assist her in some way to free his soul, but— "But Mrs. Brown, I want to do this. To take responsibility for my actions as I should have done—"

"No. I accept your apology, but I need something else … not a payoff."

Oh, thank heavens! She had a request of some sort. She was not merely refusing a small fortune.

Richard leaned forward eagerly. "There is something I can assist you with?"

"I do not wish to sound presumptive, but Miss Ridley and I were friends. Did you know that?"

He frowned. "I did not."

"I came to work in her household as a girl. Miss Ridley

gifted me a book, and when she discovered I could not read, she taught me. She also taught me numbers and showed me how to manage an accounting book. She purchased me fabrics, and she prepared me ... to follow my dreams."

"Dreams?"

"Yes, milord. Miss Ridley promised me that once she was married to you, she would help me with an investment using her pin money. She was to assist me in purchasing a dressmaking shop. We discussed finding one in a market town. I could not ... I could not believe I betrayed her in the manner that I did. It was ... so utterly foolish. I have worked hard since to prove to myself that I was ever worthy of her support. Now you say you want to make amends. *That* is the path you interrupted."

Richard sat back in his armchair, stunned. Not only had he betrayed Annabel and ruined a vulnerable young woman in the process, he'd also permanently severed the close friendship shared by the two women and laid waste to all of their hopes and plans. He really was a blackguard of the worst sort. In light of the new information, he was truly humbled by Annabel's integrity in doing right by her former friend after the incident and respected Caroline's current bravado.

"You wish to own a dress shop?"

"I do, my lord."

"Well played, Mrs. Brown."

She gave a nervous smile in response.

He thought about it for several moments. "I will task my man of business to work with Mr. Long to locate an appropriate shop, and I will loan you the funds to purchase it. The loan will be interest-free, and you can repay me from your profits. Will that do?"

Sheer joy blossomed, a smile spreading across her face

while tears welled in her eyes. "That will do," she croaked out.

Richard cleared his throat, his eyes prickling in response, which he furtively blinked away. "I am so happy to hear that. Thank you for the opportunity to remedy this, Mrs. Brown. And for agreeing to come to London to see me. I am ... quite heartened to have this chance to talk with you."

Caroline appeared too overcome to speak. She nodded in acknowledgment and looked relieved to hear Radcliffe return with the tea tray. Richard realized she needed time to compose herself after making her impudent demand. He was infinitely grateful she had agreed to come, and even more grateful that she was allowing him to assist her in her dreams after the damage he had wrought on her young life. Women were so vulnerable within their society, and since his rude awakening, he had been battling with self-loathing for his past behavior. With each of these meetings, his conscience was eased, and he looked forward to the day he no longer had to squirm in discomfort for his callous past.

Speaking with Radcliffe to give her the time she needed, Richard felt well pleased with her audacious negotiation in response to his proposal to rectify his past mistakes with her. Caroline was going to own a dressmaking shop, and he was responsible for improving a young woman's circumstances instead of worsening them. Richard observed from the corner of his eye when she did a happy bounce on her chair at the unexpected turn of events and smiled in secret pleasure to have done something so momentous for a woman he had wronged.

Malevolent yellow eyes bored into hers as she struggled to draw breath, the crushing weight on her chest leaving her paralyzed with fear. She tried to scream, but her voice failed her, caught in the tightening grip of panic.

"You are all mine now, Sophia," whispered Lord Leech, his tone as cold as ice. "Soon, we will reach Gretna Green..."

Sophia sat up abruptly, her heart racing and her nightgown damp with sweat. It was the fourth time tonight she had woken this way—not to mention the restless, sweat-soaked nights that had preceded it.

Gasping for breath, her hand instinctively reached beneath the pillow on the other side of the bed. When her fingers brushed the cold steel of the knife she had begun keeping there since the night of the Moreland ball, she exhaled a shaky sigh of relief. Gripping the hilt, she slipped quietly from her bed to check her room once more.

First, she padded to the door to confirm it was securely locked and that the chest she had dragged in front of it was still in place. Next, she moved carefully through the darkness, her fingers grazing the three china figurines she had balanced along the edge. They were still set as she had left them—ready to fall and shatter if anyone attempted to force the door.

Once she was certain the entrance was barred, Sophia made her way carefully to the windows across the room. She checked each one, ensuring they were securely locked. On each windowsill, a figurine had been placed to fall and sound the alarm if Cecil or Lord Leech attempted to climb through.

This had become her nightly routine. She stayed awake until the early hours, securing her room and then rechecking it again and again. Exhaustion weighed heavily on her—deeper than anything she had ever experienced before—but she refused to let her guard down. She was determined not to wake up as a captive, carried off in Lord Leech's carriage to the Scottish border.

Sophia climbed back into bed, her eyes wide with fear and her thoughts racing.

The problem she faced now was that Cecil's plan could be enacted at any time—tomorrow, six months from now, or even next year—and it would still work to his advantage. It was not a matter of whether she could hold out and defend herself forever. Eventually, she would let her guard down, and Cecil would only need a single opportunity to carry out his scheme.

With a willing conspirator aiding him, the stakes were even higher. Her freedom—and perhaps even her life—could be in jeopardy.

As long as she remained unmarried, she remained a target for such a plot. The weight of that realization pressed down on her, but she vowed to stay vigilant and seek a way to protect herself before it was too late.

If she approached her uncle to reveal Cecil's plans, the viscount would likely insist she marry immediately to ensure her safety. While his intentions would be protective, such a decision would further curtail her freedom.

Even if she did not marry, there was little to stop Cecil from continuing to plot her abduction to Gretna Green. Her dowry would still be paid out in the event of her marriage, and there was nothing her uncle could do to prevent that. Cecil had calculated his scheme well—she feared he had discovered that her consent might not even be required for his plan to succeed. Though Sophia was unclear on the legal intricacies, she understood enough to know that a wedding in Scotland, officiated by someone willing to ignore any hesitation from the bride, could make Cecil's scheme a reality.

None of these possible outcomes were appealing. The common thread running through them all was her lack of control—her inability to choose her own course in life.

For the first time, Sophia allowed herself to admit what she had never dared to before. She wished ... she wished ... With a deep, trembling breath, she faced the truth: she wished she had a protector.

A husband—not one drawn to her for her dowry, but someone who truly cared for her. Someone who did not imbibe to excess, like her father or brother. A man who possessed his own wealth and strength, someone who did not need her fortune but wanted *her*. Someone who could make her feel safe.

Most importantly, she wished for someone of her own choosing. Someone who could stand between her and her brother's schemes, shielding her from the danger he posed.

Her thoughts drifted to a certain devilish earl. Did Saunton drink to excess? Would he be willing to stop drinking altogether if she asked it of him? Surely he had no interest in her dowry? From all accounts, he had walked away from the wealthiest debutantes of last Season after a single dance, apparently not having found what—who—he was looking for.

And now, he was expressing interest in her. The exact amount of her dowry remained a closely guarded secret, which gave her some hope that his attention might be genuine. Perhaps she should hear him out, as he had requested.

Sophia's nerves were worn thin after enduring the last few days. Four nights and three days of unrelenting strain had left her feeling utterly depleted. She did not know how much longer she could endure this pressure, especially with no clear plan to counter her brother's relentless scheming.

For now, she needed to keep her wits about her and consider every option carefully.

RICHARD WAS anxious to see Miss Sophia Hayward again. He had thought of her many times since their last dance—the young woman with a sharp mind and a sharper tongue, so different from anyone he had ever known. There was a quality about her that intrigued him, an intuition that life with her would never be dull.

Standing at the top of the steps leading into the Yardley ballroom, he scanned the crowd of dandies, debutantes, and watchful mamas, seeking her fair, oval face and distinctive red-blonde hair.

He could not quite name what it was about her that stirred his senses, but since that night on the balcony, she had occupied his thoughts. He found himself wanting to know her better, to uncover the layers of her sharp wit and spirited nature.

Finally, his gaze landed on her. She stood across the ballroom near the terrace doors, her aunt at her side. For a moment, he allowed himself to take in the sight of her, noting how poised she seemed amidst the chatter and chaos of the gathering.

Drawing a steadying breath, he descended the steps, intent on making his way to her. Perhaps tonight, she would be more receptive to his suit.

Sophia scanned the ballroom, searching for Lord Saunton. Would he be here as he had promised? After another sleepless night, she felt an almost desperate need to see him. She needed to know if his interest in her was genuine—her very safety might depend on it.

As her gaze swept over the crowd, her heart sank. There, moving through the throng, was her brother. And beside him, Lord Leech. They were headed directly toward her.

Sophia's pulse quickened. If she wished to dance with Saunton tonight, she could not afford to refuse a dance with Lord Leech, as doing so would require her to sit out the subsequent dances for propriety's sake.

Thinking quickly, she stepped behind Aunt Christiana, who was speaking to another lady, and hastily penciled Lord Saunton onto her dance card. Then, before doubt could creep in, she added his name for the next dance as well.

Now, all she had to do was find him—quickly—before Lord Leech reached her.

"Aunt?"

Lady Moreland turned to her. Sophia gave a quick nod of her head, and Lady Moreland looked in the direction she gestured and hissed. "Leech is headed toward us! Go to the necessary." Sophia looked at her in surprise. "Now, go now! They have nearly reached us."

Without another word, Sophia briskly walked away, weaving through the crowd toward the necessary. She resolved to stay there all night if need be—but then she would miss Lord Saunton.

Her steps faltered as she considered an alternative. Perhaps it would be better to keep walking the room until she found him? Determined, she began a circuit of the ballroom, her eyes scanning for Saunton while keeping an anxious watch on Cecil and Leech behind her.

Her heart sank as she glanced back and saw them closer than expected. Panicked, she quickened her pace, but Cecil stepped in front of her, blocking her path.

His bloated face was red from exertion, and his reddish-blond hair clung to his forehead, damp with perspiration. He pulled a handkerchief from his pocket and dabbed at his brow, his expression both smug and triumphant.

"There you are, Sophia dear! Lord Leech is quite adamant that he must have a dance with you."

Sophia paled but kept her face composed as she glanced over to Leech. She curtsied, noticing that Leech's yellow eyes were as sinister in real life as they appeared to her in her dreams. He gave a cursory bow. "Miss Hayward, I have not stopped thinking of you since we met. May we take a turn around the room while we await the next dance?"

"I would love to, but I need to refresh myself and then my next dance is already promised, my lord."

Leech looked skeptical. He reached out and grasped her wrist before she could prevent him. Looking down at her dance card, he looked up at her and sneered. *Sneered!*

"Lord Saunton? I do not believe he is even here tonight, and you are certainly not his sort. Are you sure you did not write in his name yourself?"

"Quite sure, Leech."

Saunton's deep, velvety voice interrupted the tense moment, cutting through the din of the ballroom like a trumpet announcing the arrival of the cavalry.

Sophia's breath caught, and she nearly wept with relief when his handsome face appeared just beyond Leech's shoulder.

With an air of quiet authority, Saunton brushed past

the bristling gentleman and came to stand at her side. Offering her a polite, graceful bow, he turned his attention fully to her, his presence a reassuring shield against the unwelcome company.

"Are you ready, Miss Hayward?"

She gave a nod. More ready than she had ever been.

Leech was not so easily dissuaded. "I will see you for the next dance, Miss Hayward."

Saunton flicked his gaze over Leech, his expression cool and dismissive. "I do not think so, old chap. The next dance is mine as well. Miss Hayward is quite captivating, and I have concluded that I am ... well, captivated, I suppose. And then, I believe, it will be time for supper."

Leech gasped, his indignation barely contained, while Sophia's heart quickened at Saunton's declaration. Two dances—it was a bold statement, practically an announcement to the assembled guests that he was serious in his pursuit of her. A third dance would be tantamount to declaring their engagement.

Had she been prescient to pencil him in twice?

Inhaling deeply to steady herself, Sophia placed her hand on the arm Saunton offered her and allowed him to lead her farther into the ballroom. The firm assurance of his presence beside her banished the lingering fear from moments before, leaving her with a flutter of hope.

"You said the chit had no earnest suitors, Hayward!" Leech's low hiss made it to her ears, causing Sophia to smile widely as Saunton took hold of her hand and placed his gloved fingers on her waist. She had never been so happy to see any man before.

As the waltz began, Saunton looked down in her face. "If Leech is attempting to court you, there must be a sizable dowry involved?"

Sophia bit her lip, unsure of what to say.

"You wrote my name in? Was it because you promised me or to avoid Leech?"

"Both. I have been waiting for you, but you never appeared."

Saunton's eyes flickered away. "I ... was getting up my nerve. I was trying to think how to persuade you to allow me to call on you tomorrow. Now we are engaged for two dances, which will cause society tongues to wag in speculation."

"I already decided to accept your request if you made it again."

He looked incredulous, but pleased. "You did?"

"I want to learn more about this crusade to redeem yourself. Does it include drink?"

"You mean spirits?"

Sophia nodded.

"I only drink spirits occasionally. When my betrothed married the Duke of Halmesbury, I enjoyed a last hurrah and then mostly lost interest. I was never that fond of the consequences of drinking, and I find I like to keep my mind clear."

"Truly?"

"Truly. Does that make me a more desirable suitor?"

"It does."

Saunton's distinctive green eyes blazed. "So, I am to call on you tomorrow? And we will talk? I mean ... talk openly?"

Sophia inclined her head. "We are well beyond propriety, are we not?"

The earl's face lit with the same warm expression she remembered from the night of their last dance. His delight was evident as he gracefully guided her through the steps of the waltz.

Sophia's heart skipped a beat as her gaze lingered on his sculpted lips. She found herself wondering—what would it feel like to kiss such a handsome rogue?

As if reading her thoughts, Saunton's gaze grew more intense, dropping briefly to her lips. Nervous, she flicked the tip of her tongue to moisten them, only to catch the subtle tightening of his jaw and a shift in his expression.

It was clear that the earl saw her as more than just a dance partner. The realization sent a flutter of awareness through her, leaving her both flustered and intrigued.

Sophia found herself growing accustomed to the idea of this man taking on the role of her protector. It was a surprising thought, but one she was beginning to accept as a credible escape from her current predicament. Saunton was a bit too tarnished to be considered a conventional hero, to be sure, but she had always prided herself on her ability to set things to rights.

CHAPTER
FOUR

"Modesty is the citadel of female virtue."

Dr. John Gregory, A Father's Legacy to His Daughters

∽

The following morning, Sophia walked into the drawing room with Nancy in tow. Saunton's eyes flicked toward the elderly maid as he bowed to greet her. "Miss Hayward, I was thinking we might take a drive through the park."

As Sophia curtsied, she smiled and shook her head. "Nay, Lord Saunton, I arranged for us to talk in private, as you indicated we had intimate matters to discuss today."

Lord Saunton narrowed his eyes in confusion as he stared pointedly at the old woman beside her.

"Nancy is hard of hearing, aren't you, Nancy?" Sophia directed her question to the short maid with the full head of gray hair pinned under her mob cap in disarray.

"Too fancy? I don't think so, miss. I think you look like a

perfect young lady!" Nancy responded with a perplexed expression.

"Nancy was my uncle's nursemaid when he was a boy, and he is very attached to her. Fortunately for us, she does not wish to retire, so the household accommodates her limited communication abilities," Sophia explained before raising her voice. "NANCY, WHY NOT SIT HERE AND WORK ON YOUR MENDING?"

"Bending? I don't really do much bending anymore, miss."

Sophia blinked, her head beginning to ache at the strain of talking to the beloved but exasperating maid she had sought out thirty minutes earlier to attempt to explain that she would chaperon a visit.

Nancy blinked back, and several seconds of silence ensued before she said, "I think I shall sit here in this chair by the door and do some mending."

Sophia beamed her approval, nodding enthusiastically before any further conversation was encouraged. Turning back to Saunton, she saw his handsome countenance relax into a relieved expression. He stepped forward to hand her a bouquet of hothouse flowers with a bow. She smiled in pleasure at the gesture, thanking him warmly. He gestured to the seating area. "Shall we, Miss Hayward?"

Accepting his invitation, she strode forward to take a seat on the hard, silk-covered sofa and primly folded her hands into her lap—the picture of maidenly modesty. She had no intention of being proper this morning, but if Nancy looked up, she would not find any cause for alarm.

As Saunton flicked the tails of his wine-colored coat to take his seat, Sophia could not help but notice that the infamous earl boasted a masculine form that was near perfect, with a flat stomach and powerful thighs encased in buckskin breeches. His black and brown Hessians were polished, his shoulders broad, and his silky, curling hair brushed his white stock. She had heard him compared to Lord Byron, but she personally thought Saunton had a friendlier and more approachable demeanor than the arrogant poet she had heard tales about.

"Tell me about your crusade of amends, my lord."

"I have been meeting with the women of my past to apologize and make reparations. It has been unexpectedly uplifting to do so." Sophia was uncertain what else to ask on this subject, so she moved on.

"Are there any children from these past encounters?"

Saunton grimaced. "So far, I have been fortunate. The precautions I took were effective."

Sophia wondered what precautions one could take to prevent children, but she refrained from asking, not wanting to reveal her ignorance.

"And you are seeking to court me with a view to marry?"

Saunton's eyes glowed in affirmation. "I am."

"Are you sure ... I mean, about me? You barely know me. How do I know you will not lose interest next week when you meet another woman?"

He frowned at this. "Never. I have only been interested in marrying one woman before you, and I have been seeking a wife for some years now. You are unlike anyone I have ever met, and now that I have started on this road, I have no intention of turning back. Once I make up my mind about something, I am steadfast in my resolve. And you ... you fascinate me."

Sophia's cheeks warmed at his words, her heart quickening. To be the focus of such determined attention from a man of his stature and charm was both thrilling and humbling. She straightened her posture, meeting his steady gaze. "We do not have much time, my lord. So tell me—why should I accept your offer?"

Saunton leaned forward in his seat, his face earnest. "I will allow you your freedom. As my countess, you may do anything you want and I will support you, as long as you are at my side."

"Anything? What if I do not wish to host balls?"

"Then we shall forgo balls. Is that what you want?"

"I am not fond of crowds, so I would prefer to hold dinner parties and small events. What if I wanted to write a book?"

"Then you shall write a book. Do you have one in mind?"

"I do not. What if I wanted to hold salons and invite intellectuals to our home?"

"Then I shall greet our guests and take part in your discussions. Whatever your heart desires. My only requests are that our marriage be a true partnership and that you provide me with an heir."

"Why should I believe you?"

Saunton chuckled, leaning back in his seat, his gaze warm as it settled on her face. "I am famously unconventional, am I not?"

Sophia nodded, a small smile tugging at her lips.

"I need an interesting woman to keep me grounded. And for the first time in my life, I want—truly desire—to find that balance. This requires trust, and I am taking the same leap of faith by trusting you. I trust you to be your genuine self, to speak your mind freely, and to help create a future that we can share—a future built together."

Sophia regarded him thoughtfully, his sincerity shining through every word. Memories of her sleepless nights, grappling with uncertainty and fear, flickered through her mind. Yet, as she considered the possibility of taking a chance on the earl, a quiet realization emerged. She was not a conventional woman, and she would need a partner who could embrace her unorthodox nature.

And here sat the Earl of Saunton, candid and uniquely himself—unlike any man she had ever conversed with.

Today she stood at a crossroads—she could spend another night terrified in her room, or she could take a leap and hope that he was strong enough to catch her. There were no guarantees that their relationship would work, but it sounded so awfully appealing to try. To help the gentleman forge a fresh path. It sounded infinitely more appealing than evading the murderous Lord Leech over the coming weeks or months.

"How do we proceed?"

"I will return tomorrow, and we will take a ride through the park?"

"Hmm ... it sounds wonderful, but my uncle will never agree to you courting me."

"I see. I shall contrive a plan to persuade him, then."

Sophia stood up, prompting the earl to rise. She could hear Uncle Hugh's heavy footfalls in the hall. By now, one of the servants had informed him that a notorious rogue was in his drawing room, paying addresses to his niece. Stepping around the table, she stood directly in front of the earl.

"I already have a plan. Are you certain you wish to see this courtship through to the end? This is your last chance to walk away."

Saunton's eyebrows drew together in confusion. "Yes ... I am certain."

Sophia stepped closer, noting his pupils dilated as she approached him. Out of the corner of her eye, she saw the tall form of her uncle stepping into the drawing room. With a deep breath, she leapt into the earl's arms, springing up on her toes to throw her arms over his wide shoulders, and kissed him full on the lips.

As Sophia stumbled into his arms, Richard staggered back, startled by the unexpected impact. Her soft weight pressed against him, and before he could steady his thoughts, her lips met his in an impulsive kiss. The gesture was unpracticed and fleeting, but it carried a sincerity that left him momentarily undone. For the first time in years, Richard felt completely unguarded, his usual polished exterior giving way to raw, genuine emotion.

Sophia's innocence and earnestness broke through his defenses, leaving him captivated. The connection between them felt undeniable, as though she were the earth and he a helpless moon drawn into her orbit. His heart raced, and for one fleeting moment, he allowed himself to respond, pressing his lips gently to hers in return, savoring the sweetness of the encounter.

"WHAT IS THE MEANING OF THIS?"

The furious voice shattered the fragile moment, and Richard blinked, his thoughts scrambling to catch up. Releasing Sophia's slim waist, he turned slowly to face the source of the interruption—a middle-aged lord whose face was red with indignation.

As Richard pieced together the events leading to this moment, Sophia's cleverness became clear. Her words, her timing, and now this—she had orchestrated the scene with precision. Yet, far from feeling manipulated, Richard found himself strangely relieved. Sophia had not forced him into anything; she had simply ensured he recognized what he truly wanted.

And now, standing before the furious lord and the young woman who had changed everything, Richard knew what he must do.

He rubbed a hand over his jaw and then dropped a respectful bow. "Lord Moreland, I wish to marry your niece."

Lord Moreland ignored his declaration. "Sophia, where is your chaperon?"

A bleating snore echoed throughout the drawing room. Lord Moreland swung around to find Nancy sleeping in the chair by the door. He spun back.

"*Nancy* is your chaperon?" he growled at his niece.

Sophia looked unrepentant.

"Well, there is no foul. I am the only one who saw—"

"Lord Moreland!" The viscount's face fell.

"Now see here, dear—" Turning to the doorway, he attempted to placate his wife. He failed.

"Lord Moreland, an *earl* wants to marry your niece. I suggest you hear him out!" The viscountess was magnificent in her demands as she swept into the room. Richard mused that this was becoming a glorious muddle, but it was acceptable to him if he wound up betrothed.

"Christiana, he is a disgraceful rake!" The viscount was not yet defeated, it would seem.

"Lord Moreland, I suggest you hear what the earl has to say." The lady's voice was steely.

The viscount turned to Richard and demanded in a surly tone, "Are you not a rogue? Why should I even consider allowing my niece to marry you?"

"A reformed rogue, my lord." Although Richard outranked the man, he decided discretion was the better part of valor in this instance, so he acted as the man's inferior. "Your niece has captivated me from the start, and I have been putting my affairs in order."

"Affairs!" The man responded with something between a snort and a sound of disgust. Richard could not blame him.

"Perhaps affairs is a poor choice of words. I stand before you, a reformed man, seeking your niece's hand in marriage."

"What kind of reformation results in a man taking advantage of a woman under her guardian's roof?"

Richard was stuck for words. He could not very well reveal Sophia had flung herself into his arms. "I ... I was ... overcome."

"Lord Saunton was overcome when I accepted his proposal, Uncle Hugh."

Lord Moreland looked slightly mollified by Sophia's announcement. "Is this true?"

Richard inclined his head in agreement.

"Is this about her dowry?"

"No, my lord. Whatever funds Miss Hayward brings to the marriage can be settled on her and our future children. I would be more than happy to settle additional funds in the marriage contracts for her future and to provide her with pin money out of my estates."

Moreland relaxed further. The subject of funds appeared to be a sore point. Richard vaguely recollected that Sophia's father had been an unwise gambler, which was rumored to have led to the premature death of Moreland's younger sister.

"Lord Saunton should arrange a special license while the two of you negotiate the contracts," Sophia advised. Richard shot a look at her. She shrugged at him with an innocent look on her face. "There is no choice but to see this through as soon as possible. Now that his lordship has engaged in such scandalous behavior!"

Lord Moreland humphed.

"You have no choice, husband. It is what Sophia wants," a pleased Lady Moreland piped in. It appeared she supported the union wholeheartedly, which was fortunate because Lord Moreland was seriously considering ejecting Richard from his home, if his expression was anything to go by.

"Niece, is this what you want? There is no need to worry about a scandal, and I will not require you to marry this reprobate just to avoid gossip."

"I am certain, Uncle Hugh. I wish to marry Lord Saunton," Sophia reassured her uncle before muttering something under her breath. It sounded like she said, 'forthwith,' which gave Richard pause. He wondered why she was so eager to tie the knot after trying her best to get rid of him on earlier occasions.

"Then Saunton and I best go to my study to discuss terms."

Richard's heart hammered in fearful excitement. He had not expected matters to proceed so rapidly, but it appeared he would be married to the lovely Sophia before the week was out. Doing his best to look repentant, he followed Lord Moreland from the room, but not before winking at Sophia to express his agreement with her manipulation of events and enjoying the answering smile that spread across her face in acknowledgment.

By the time Richard returned home to meet with his man of business, he was trembling with a mix of excitement and anticipation. He was about to marry a vibrant, intelligent young woman whose sharp wit and keen sense of right and wrong would challenge and inspire him. The way her presence quickened his pulse and brightened his days was an unexpected delight, dispelling any lingering uncertainty about the path he was choosing. For the first time in years, the prospect of a shared future filled him with hope and joy.

He poured himself a drink from the crystal decanter. "I have been most fortunate thus far, Johnson." He raised his glass in a toast. "Here is to good fortune holding out." He turned around.

Trepidation assailed him when he saw the nervous expression in Johnson's darting eyes.

"What is it?" he groaned. "Do not tell me good fortune has not prevailed?"

"Her name was Kitty. Kitty Smith," Johnson croaked.

"Was?"

"My lord," Johnson began, and then paused as he wrung his hands. "*Ahem.* Do you recall 'blonde housemaid, five foot, about three and twenty years of age, worked at Duke of Rosbury's castle in Kent in 1815'?"

Richard blanched and gave a curt nod.

"Kitty Smith died in childbirth in March 1816. She refused to name the father. Her son, Ethan, lives with Kitty's aunt and her family in Derby. He—*ahem*—has dark brown hair and green eyes ..." Johnson's ramble ended. "My lord," he remembered to interject.

Johnson shifted uncomfortably from foot to foot, his demeanor most unhappy.

"The boy is four years old?" Richard whispered. Johnson gave a quick nod.

"Any chance he is not mine?"

Johnson looked away and coughed discreetly. "The house staff in Kent knew of no liaisons, despite being offered a reward for information. They did indicate that Kitty handed in her resignation about two months after the summer house party, which comprised mostly gentlemen from London. From what they said, Kitty was enamored with the peerage and they suspected she had fallen for the glib lines of one of those guests. They considered she was a good girl, properly raised."

Richard could hear his heart thudding loudly in the ensuing silence.

"And what of the aunt's circumstances?" Richard finally asked.

"She is married to a tenant farmer and has six children of her own besides Ethan. They appear to be a relatively successful and upstanding household. The aunt and her husband would be willing to hand him over to the father's care if promises were made to maintain their family connection. She wants to know about family visits before she will acknowledge parentage."

Richard had not thought that a man could experience two earth-shattering life revelations within the span of less than a week. He had been wrong.

"Green eyes are not common," he choked out.

"No, my lord."

Looking at his reflection in the glass cradled in his hand, Richard recognized, more than a little nonplussed, that he, in fact, knew of no other men in his acquaintance with green eyes other than his own brother and the late earl.

Drawing a deep breath, silently he prayed that Sophia would not call off the wedding at this news. He would not blame her if she did. She certainly deserved better than him. However, his duty to the boy was clear. He was ashamed that strangers brought up his son, while he did not even know of his existence. There was only one honorable move to make, and that was to claim his child and take responsibility for his upbringing and future.

"Return to the aunt and offer them one of my smaller unentailed properties in gratitude for all they have done to take care of my ... my ... son," he croaked. He fought to compose himself before he continued.

"The estate is to be held while the steward apprentices them in the managing of the estate. We will arrange visits over the summer so that the boy may join them. He is to come stay with me, and I would like to interview prospective nursemaids to look after him. I will inform Radcliffe to prepare the nursery, and perhaps we have someone suitable on our staff to promote to that position. My boy must receive the best—a loving hand to take care of him as we become acquainted." It gratified him to hear the decisive ring in his voice as he spoke. He sounded more confident than he felt.

Staring at the tumbler in his hand, he recalled that Sophia would prefer it if he did not drink. He was to be married and answer to another person, which was startling enough. Now he must think about a son—a living, breathing four-year-old boy who would enter his household with needs and expectations.

"*Drat!*" He roared and threw his cut glass across the room, where it shattered in the fireplace. Johnson jumped.

"How do I tell Sophia?" Richard muttered to himself, pacing the room with his hands clenched at his sides. "Will she still want to marry me after this? What lady of the *ton* would willingly join a family with a child born outside of marriage?" He ran a hand through his hair, his shoulders heavy with shame. "What a mess I have made of things! How can I possibly make amends for the harm I have caused? If only I had shown more restraint, but instead, my selfishness and lack of foresight have hurt so many—my son, his mother, and now Sophia. They all bear the weight of my mistakes."

He spun toward Johnson. "Tell me that no one knows of this disaster except for the boy's family?" Before Johnson could answer, Richard threw his hands up in despair.

"Never mind. All of polite society will notice that I have a natural born son living in my household before the Season is over," Richard muttered, his voice tight with frustration. "They will call him that dreadful word—illegitimate—through no fault of his own!" He resumed pacing, his mind racing with the complications ahead. "This is unbearable. I have let so many people down."

He stopped abruptly, dragging a hand through his hair as guilt washed over him. "Leave me, Johnson. I need time to collect my thoughts before I throw myself on Sophia's mercy." His voice broke slightly as he turned away. "Richard, you fool," he muttered bitterly, the weight of his emotions threatening to overwhelm him.

Johnson took his cue to scurry out the door, his relief palpable. Richard sank into a chair, dropping his face into his hands. He had been so careful not to sire any children, but his indulgences had caught up with him and now he learned he had a son living without a father all these years. He was so ... so ... mortified by his selfish carryings-on.

CHAPTER
FIVE

"There is a native delicacy in women which guards them against many dangers."

Dr. John Gregory, A Father's Legacy to His Daughters

~

Peregrine Balfour strolled into Richard's study, his demeanor as nonchalant as ever, while Richard sat with his head in his hands, weighed down by the burdens of his past. Richard raised his head, his expression darkening as he caught sight of his younger brother pouring a glass of French brandy at the sideboard.

"Where have you been, little brother?" Richard growled, his tone edged with frustration.

"A vivacious widow held me hostage," Perry replied with a mischievous grin.

"For more than a week?" Richard's eyebrows rose in disbelief.

"She kept me thoroughly occupied," Perry quipped. "It took all my cunning to escape her clutches.

Richard groaned, dropping his head back into his hands.

"What is eating you? It's too early in the day to be soused, surely?"

"I have not been drinking. You have missed a great deal in the past week," Richard complained. "I needed you, but I had to make do. Fortunately, Halmesbury was available."

"The duke? Whatever plagues you must be serious if you braved his front door with your Annabel in residence. He did not throw you out?"

Richard ignored Perry's attempts at humor. "She is not my Annabel—she is all his. I am making changes. I made a list of women I have wronged, and I am setting matters to right."

Peregrine turned to stare at him, his mouth agape. "You cannot be serious, old chap?"

"Deadly serious. Halmesbury assisted me in your absence with ideas of how to make reparations."

His brother looked him over with mild disgust. "What brought this on? Have you fallen in love or something just as daft?"

"I do not know about love, but I did find a young lady I wish to wed. That I *will* wed. On Monday morning. She gave me cause to rethink my life, but mostly she forced me to confront that I was becoming ... our father."

Perry's eyes flared in shock before he walked over to slump into an ivory armchair. His face was haunted as he stared into the distance. His sibling could have been his twin, they looked so much alike. Unfortunately for his younger brother, Richard knew his father had been particularly cruel toward Perry, although he was hazy about the details because he had been attending Oxford while Perry remained at home with tutors. His brother never discussed what it had been like to live in proximity to the mad earl in his final years. Their father had refused to send him to Eton, as was tradition, preferring to keep his spare within his household to torture in some manner that Richard could only guess at. Even a mere mention of the old man made Perry morose and bitter.

"I ... see." Perry shook his head as if to clear his thoughts before he looked over at Richard. "If making amends to the women of your past is proving so painful, why are you doing it?"

"It is not painful. It has been a wonderful experience, very uplifting. I am reclaiming my life ... stitching my soul back together one apology at a time. Until today ... I just received dreadful news. It must be faced, but I do not know how it will affect my wedding. I want to marry Sophia, but I do not know if she will reject me when she learns that ... that ... that I have ... a son."

Perry shot up to sit on the edge of his chair. "What? I thought you took precautions?"

"Apparently precautions do not always work out the way one might hope. I will be fortunate if this turns out to be my only child."

"What are you doing about it?"

"He is being collected and brought to London. What the deuce do I do about Sophia?"

"Does she know? About your past and the possibility of a child?"

"She does ... but she knows nothing of ... Ethan." Richard felt a flutter in his chest as he spoke the name of his son for the first time.

I am a father!

It could not be comprehended. How could he be a father? What if he was as terrible a parent as his own father? Richard dismissed that concern. No one could be as terrible a parent as the earl. The correct question was, could he do better at it than the aunt's family who had taken in Kitty and Ethan?

"Well," Perry said with a lazy smirk, "I, for one, cannot fathom why anyone would willingly get leg-shackled. But if she is truly prepared to tie herself to your sorry hide ... I say tell her about the boy after the wedding."

"Perry! This is not how I wish to begin my new life."

His brother shrugged. "Then tell her and take your consequences."

Richard groaned and dropped his head back into his hands. "Please do not talk of consequences. I am dealing with consequences from every direction. What was I thinking, indulging in such reckless behavior? Why could I not have followed Halmesbury's example and shown some restraint?"

Perry pulled a face. "Halmesbury had the good fortune of not growing up under the influence of our father. It is a marvel you have any restraint at all. I seem to recall ... no, never mind. Dwelling on Father's excesses is enough to turn my stomach."

"Truly? You think I have shown restraint?"

"Oh, brother, I *know* you have shown restraint. Now, are you going to show me this list and tell me what you have done thus far? It sounds like quite the lark."

Sophia brushed out Lily's hair in front of her cousin's dressing-table mirror. She had convinced her cousin the day of Richard's visit that, because she would depart the Abbott household soon, she should sleep with Lily in her gigantic bed so they might spend as much time together as possible.

She hated lying to her best friend. Perhaps she would tell Lily the truth once the wedding was done and the entire matter was a *fait accompli*. Until then, she did not wish to burden her cousin with the knowledge that Sophia was terrified of her desperate brother assisting Leech to steal her from her bed on the eve of her wedding. She was sure she was being excessively cautious, but it was so refreshing to sleep without fear the past few nights and she enjoyed the extra time with Lily.

The Abbotts were good people, and they deserved to be free of the worry that her situation with her depraved brother would cause them. She had taken care of the problem, and she could not deny a thrill of excitement that she would marry the earl in the morning. Once she had decided on her new course, she had become quite taken with her future, married to the handsome lord and, perhaps, assisting him in his project to restore his honor. It sounded far more entertaining than being society's oldest debutante or a ward in another family's home.

Lily giggled. "You are tickling me!"

"You are too ticklish. What will you do when you receive your first kiss? Twist about and lose your breath?"

Lily's enormous eyes widened in trepidation. "You think? That would be a disaster!"

Sophia chuckled at her younger cousin. "You are such an innocent! Please never change. And, no, you will figure it out with the right beau." She leaned down and gave the girl a swift hug. "I love you, Lily. I will miss you."

"That is good, for if Mama does not relent on pushing

me into the path of every well-connected man in London, I may have to come knocking on your door."

Sophia smiled at her in the mirror. "Just promise me you will not settle for someone unsuitable? I want you to be happy, cousin."

Lily shrugged. "It will all work out."

She smiled at the girl's optimistic outlook. Lily always found the silver lining. It was one of her most endearing qualities and helped balance Sophia's more jaded point of view. It was why they were such good friends.

She plaited Lily's hair. They had dismissed their lady's maid hours earlier and were up late, talking the night away. It was the last time they could spend this sort of time together. Tomorrow Sophia would be a married woman, and their relationship would shift to something new.

In the distance, she heard the tall case clock down the hall toll twice.

"Two in the morning! We need to get some sleep, or I shall marry with dark circles under my eyes!"

She tied Lily's plait in a ribbon and hustled her cousin to the bed. Sophia made her way around the room to extinguish the lamps while Lily used the steps to crawl into the bed. Sophia had no need of the steps, being several inches taller than her petite cousin. She strode over and pulled the sheets back.

"WHAT'S THE MEANING OF THIS?" The shouting, along with scuffling sounds, was coming from the hall.

She glanced at Lily in confusion, who stared back at her in consternation.

"That sounded like Papa."

Sophia nodded in response as dread crept over her. She had thought she was being overly cautious when she bribed the footman, Thomas, to sleep in her room with coin and the promise of a position in the Saunton household if his current became forfeit because of his cooperation. Now, with the commotion out in the hall, she was alarmed that her caution had been warranted. She ran over to the door and opened it a bit, noticing Lily join her while she peered into the dark corridor.

"Where is Sophia?" Lord Moreland cried out.

Sophia swung the door wide and stepped out into the hall, where she found Thomas holding on to a squirming Lord Leech whose eye was swelling shut.

Uncle Hugh appeared fearful but exclaimed when he caught sight of her, clutching his chest as he inhaled in relief. "Oh, thank the Lord! Niece, where have you been?" He was dressed in his nightclothes and barefoot, evidently running out of his bedchamber after the initial scuffle between Leech and the footman.

"I was sleeping in Lily's room."

"What? Why? And what was Thomas doing in your room?"

"I asked him to sleep there ... in case."

Uncle Hugh scowled. "In case of what, exactly? Were you aware that this ... this scoundrel intended to intrude upon your room?"

Sophia bit her lip, ashamed that she had not informed her uncle what had been happening under his roof. She had not wanted to burden him with the worry, and she wanted to take care of her own problems to maintain some tenuous control over her choices, but the concern etched on his face ... Perhaps she should have told him what Cecil had planned. Her fingers tugged nervously at the cotton of her night rail. She felt awkward in her half-dressed state, but she doubted anyone was noticing her attire given the situation at hand.

"Sophia! Tell me, what is this about? Why is this disgraceful blackguard in my home?" Uncle Hugh gestured with disgust toward the squirming Lord Leech, who was muttering in indignant outrage at the servant holding him fast.

Aunt Christiana hovered down the hall in the doorway to her chamber, tying her dressing gown nervously, but she moved toward the gathering. "Sophia, what is this?"

Lily took hold of her hand and squeezed it. "Did you expect Lord Leech, Sophia?"

Sophia shook her head in disbelief. She could not believe Cecil had tried to go through with his plot. She was utterly grateful she had taken the threat seriously, or even now she could be tied up in Leech's carriage, racing out of London with no one the wiser that she was absent until the morning.

"Unhand me or you will regret this!" The despicable Leech chose that moment to interrupt.

Her uncle turned to glare at the man. "Charges can be brought for breaking into a peer's home, and even you cannot sweep such a matter under the rug. I, too, have powerful friends, Leech."

Leech fell silent at the threat. Turning back, her unexpectedly fierce relative gestured for Sophia to talk.

"Cecil ..." she began, then stopped.

Uncle Hugh walked forward to grasp her gently by the shoulder. "Tell me! What has happened?"

She took a deep breath. "Cecil learned about the terms of my dowry and plotted with Leech to exploit them." She waved a hand toward the outraged lord, still detained by the much larger footman whose powerful arm wrapped around Leech's trapped arms and waist. "They planned to kidnap me to Gretna Green to force the trust funds to be released."

Uncle Hugh grunted in dismay. "Oh, mercy!"

He rubbed his jaw with a hand as he paced back and forth for several moments. Finally, he came to a stop and glared at her. "Is this why you were so willing to marry Saunton?"

Sophia nodded. "But ... I still wish to marry him. I realized I will not be safe without a husband. Cecil could strike an agreement with any fortune hunter. Saunton does not care about my funds, he only cares about me—for some inexplicable reason he has settled on *me*, but I know it is not for the want of funds."

Silence followed this pronouncement for several moments.

"What do we do now?" Uncle Hugh walked over to Leech to flick his eyes up and down over the heaving, struggling form. "You, sir, are utterly repulsive. Absolute dregs!"

Leech glared at him, his yellow eyes glowing eerily in the dimly lit corridor. "You will regret treating me this way, Moreland!" he spat.

"My only regret, Leech, is that I did not have my servants throw you out when I saw you sneaking into my ball the other night! Can you believe it was to prevent a scene? Had I any idea of the threat you are to my niece—"

"Uncle Hugh, we will have to let him go. It will only cause a scandal to ..." What did one even do in a situation like this? Calling for a runner or taking the lord to a magistrate would be more ruinous to her own reputation than to his once word got out.

Her uncle took a deep breath and spoke to Thomas. "See Lord Leech out and do not be gentle about it. If he happens to hurt himself on the banisters on the way out ... well, that is what happens when you steal into another man's household. Do not hesitate, Thomas. Leech cannot complain to the authorities"—Moreland gave the lord a speaking glance—"because he will have to explain how he came to be at the tender mercies of a footman in my household at two in the morning."

Thomas grinned in delight. He dragged the struggling man away, his voice carrying back to where the Abbott family stood with Sophia in a huddle. "Oops, did your head hit that wall? So sorry, milord."

Lord Moreland turned back to find his family staring at him in consternation. "Burn my buttons, I wish that Aidan was back from Paris to assist me with this disturbance."

"I think you are doing a fine job, Papa!" Uncle Hugh's face relaxed in response to Lily's encouragement.

"You will all go to bed. I will take charge of securing our home and discover Cecil's whereabouts, but there is a wedding in the morning, so you must rest." He raised an eyebrow in question. Sophia nodded to reassure him that this remained her desire. He nodded in acknowledgment and took his wife's hand to settle it on his arm. "Come, my dear. We have a wedding to attend in a few hours. I shall take care of this situation, but now it is time for you to return to your chamber to get some sleep."

Sophia realized her pulse was racing as she and Lily returned to the bedroom, her breathing rough with shock at what could have happened while Lily led her to sit on the bed.

"Why did you not tell me about Cecil?"

Sophia looked up into her cousin's innocent eyes. "Mostly, I was ... embarrassed. You have a wonderful brother who would kill any man who tried to harm you, and I ... I ..." To her horror, she burst into tears. Lily leaned forward to embrace her.

"Oh, Sophia, I am so sorry. You can share my brother! If Aidan were here in London right now, he would give Leech a sound beating!"

Sophia laughed through her tears. "Thomas looked more than happy to mete out some justice on the way out. And he had already gotten a few punches in by the looks of it."

Lily grinned in response as she continued to hug her. "Good, that vile man will think twice before involving himself in any more plots. As it is, I am sure he will be forced to stay out of sight for a number of days with that face of his marred by bruises."

Sophia nodded with a wan smile. Returning to a more serious frame of mind, she dried her eyes. "I know our grandfather was doing his best to look after his family, but the trust he set up ... it did not take into account reprobate brothers and villainous lords who might take advantage of the terms."

Lily sighed. "It is most fortuitous that you attracted Lord Saunton, I think."

"I hate that as a woman with few legal rights, I must rely on someone else to protect me, but I could not think of another way. Cecil could attempt this again at any time. Marrying a man of my choosing seems the only way to ... to be sure that I maintain control of my own future."

Lily gazed at her. "I think you are able to protect yourself, cousin. You found a way to deal with this situation, and I think no matter the circumstances, you are resourceful and would always find a method to survive any situation. Not like me. I have never needed to fend for myself. But you, you are a heroine!"

Sophia raised her arms to hug her cousin back. "You silly girl, you have been reading too many novels. I am just doing my best to be my own person."

"Your best is admirable, Sophia. I could never be so brave on my own. You took steps to protect yourself *and* you found a handsome husband who admires you. You are most clever and courageous, cousin! Are you going to tell me how you learned of Cecil's plot?"

Sophia grimaced. "Can you believe he is involved with Lord Leech? The man is despicable."

"He is a villain right out of a gothic novel. I could not believe it when I followed you into the hall and learned he snuck into our home. But tell me what happened. How did you know?"

They climbed back into the bed, and Sophia put out the oil lamp while she told her cousin about the conversation in the library. Lily gasped in horror. "I had no idea Cecil was so ... so ..."

"Evil?"

"Yes. I wonder what Papa will do about him. He takes family responsibility seriously, and I think Cecil is in for a world of trouble. Why is he so greedy? I thought Papa was quite generous in taking him in and providing him with an allowance. He treated him like his own family!"

"I think Cecil has been gambling away his funds ... more funds than he actually possesses. He is determined to follow in our father's footsteps, it would seem, and has been on a downward path since our father died. Maybe before, for I do not know what he and my father might have gotten up to together."

Lily was silent for several seconds before responding. "I am very glad the men in my family eschew gambling. And I am glad you came to live with us. And I am even more glad that Lord Saunton took an interest in you. You already solved the problem, you clever woman!"

Sophia smiled into the darkness. She, too, was grateful for Lord Saunton's interest. She reached up to touch her fingers to her lips, remembering the feel of his mouth on hers when she took that irrevocable step to compromise herself. This may have been a shocking evening—a shocking week—but tomorrow she would wed the devilish lord and she would begin a new life far, far, far from her brother's influence. In fact, she would probably never need to see Cecil again.

CHAPTER SIX

"Marriage can only be happy where there is a perfect conformity in principles and taste."

Dr. John Gregory, A Father's Legacy to His Daughters

~

It disgruntled Sophia to see Cecil waiting in the vestibule. It was time to leave for Balfour Terrace and, apparently, Uncle Hugh had decided Cecil would still be attending the wedding for the sake of appearances.

Her brother looked pale and glared at her malevolently before casting his eyes back to stare at the floor in resentment. It appeared Uncle Hugh had already spoken with him about the prior evening's incursion. She wondered if Cecil had spent the night in his room because there had been no sign of him when Leech was caught. The whiff of hard liquor seeping from her brother meant he must have gotten soused after letting Leech into their home. Perhaps a sign that he had some conscience, then? Not that Cecil ever needed an excuse to drink.

His presence that morning suggested that he was doing his best to hold on to his allowance and connection to the viscount, who was taking full advantage of his desperation to keep up appearances.

Thinking of the evildoer, Leech, being bruised and battered this morning brought a small smile of relish to her lips. The man had been hoisted with his own petard, for which she harbored no regrets. It could have been her, bruised and battered, if she had not taken measures to protect herself.

Uncle Hugh entered the entrance hall, swinging his head around as if he was counting up family members. "Everyone ready to leave, then?"

Aunt Christiana sighed. "After the events of last night, I am more than ready to see our girl safely wed. And the sooner we are done, the sooner I can return home to take a lie-down. I missed much sleep."

The older woman appeared peaked. It made Sophia ever more certain she was making the right decision to wed Lord Saunton. Her adopted family did not deserve to be exposed to such villainy of the kind Cecil had visited on them. With Sophia wed, the risk would be terminated.

It was a sad state of affairs that once a woman wed, she lost all rights to her own income and possessions, but she felt she had found an excellent resolution to the problem that her dowry in trust presented. And if Lord Saunton thought he could change his mind and return to his philandering ways, he would discover that she did not tolerate such behavior. But the earl seemed sincere about his efforts to alter his course, and she was certain she could assist him to find his way. His issues were far easier to solve than drinking and gambling, especially when taken into account with the fact that he was taking calculated steps to correct his past mistakes, which demonstrated his commitment to his crusade of redemption.

Uncle Hugh frowned in concern at his wife. "Are you all right, dear?"

Her aunt smiled. "I am happy to marry Sophia off to such a well-connected peer. It will be quite the relief to know she will be taken care of. Losing a little sleep is a small price to pay for such a prestigious event."

Her uncle broke into a smile. "I had my reservations about allowing this marriage, but I had time in the past few days to get a report on Saunton. He is considered quite moderate in how he spends his money and, from all accounts, has expanded the wealth of the Saunton estates and investments considerably since inheriting the title. He assured me he has every intention of seeing our niece happy and healthy. I think this is a good match, wife. My apologies for doubting you."

The entire family was evidently relieved to marry Sophia off today in order to end the threat of a scheming brother and any future fortune hunters he may ally with. Except for Cecil himself, of course. Sophia was quite looking forward to the security that marriage to Saunton would bring.

Aunt Christiana beamed in response while Uncle Hugh took up her gloved hand to press a kiss to her fingers. The two of them stood staring at each other with loving gazes, causing Sophia and Lily to fidget. The cousins looked at each other, and Lily quirked an eyebrow at Sophia in silent remark. Sophia shook her head and exhaled a brief chuckle of discomfort.

"I think the carriage is waiting for us, Papa. I trust *Cecil* is not traveling with us?" Lily pointedly interrupted the moment between her parents.

Uncle Hugh looked over at Cecil with distaste. "No. He is making his own way to Balfour Terrace. *But he will be on time.*" The menacing tone made Cecil straighten in agitation.

"Yes, my lord."

With that, Lord Moreland ushered the women out the door to the carriage awaiting them.

RICHARD FIDDLED with his pristine cravat while Peregrine stood grumbling under his breath across the library. His brother was still coming to terms with his hasty wedding and complaining about having a woman underfoot in their family home. He even mentioned finding rooms, but Richard interjected that they were family and Perry's place was in this ridiculously large family home. His brother relented but asserted he would stay at his clubs frequently in order to pursue his pleasures.

Richard shrugged in nonchalance, but secretly he hoped that his path back to honor would, mayhap, inspire his brother to rethink his own course. Richard was very much afraid that his own questionable history had infected his younger brother immeasurably, or, at least, done nothing to mitigate the damage their father had done to him.

Richard paced, switching his thoughts to Sophia. He needed to pull her aside before their vows and inform her about Ethan. She deserved to have an opportunity to cancel the wedding if she wished. Richard had conducted his negotiations with Lord Moreland without seeing her for the past few days. He wanted to do the right thing and inform her about his son, but at the same time, he was strangely reluctant to impart the news. He grew more and more certain that any sane woman would immediately screech and run from him. The terrible scandal would affect her life in ways he could not imagine. Many would turn away from him and his family due to his recognition of his son, openly residing at Balfour Terrace.

He would adroitly explain his presence, perhaps claiming Ethan was his ward, because that was the way of polite society. But everyone would still know Ethan was his natural born son, especially if the boy turned out to resemble him as much as Johnson had intimated.

Richard felt light-headed, nauseous even, with the stress of confronting Sophia with the news. Mayhap his brother was correct and he should inform her after the wedding? Sophia knew something like this might come to light. *But you assured her no progeny had been uncovered just a few days ago in the Moreland drawing room.* Then the delightful hellion had kissed him, the sensation of which was ever present on his lips and his mind since that astonishing moment.

No, he must inform her. She must have the right to choose if she wanted to become the *de facto* mother to his four-year-old illegitimate son.

Grrr!

Perry called out from the other end, "If the idea of being wed is making you growl, it is not too late to find a way to break the contract."

"Ha ha. I think it would be easy to reach a mutual agreement to have the contracts canceled. I simply tell her about Ethan, and Lord Moreland slaps me across the face as they all storm out with much shouting and weeping."

Perry raised his eyebrows. "A reactive bunch, are they? Then it sounds best to get the cancelation moving ahead."

Richard shook his head. "Perry, I want this. I want to marry Sophia. She is an interesting young woman, and I am certain you will grow to like her."

His brother huffed in disgust and turned to stare out the French doors into the garden, his arms folded to show his ire at the nuptials.

Richard stared at his brother, not knowing what to say to reassure him they would still be brothers, that their relationship would not be altered. Then he recollected he needed to speak with Sophia and started pacing in agitation once more.

"The wedding party has arrived, my lord," Radcliffe intoned from the doorway.

"Right. I will come greet them, then." Richard followed the butler out, his stomach twisting in nervous excitement.

Lord and Lady Moreland stood in his front vestibule, looking very proper. The cousin, a Miss Lily Abbott if he recollected correctly, was a diminutive fairy staring up at the artistry of his Italian frescos with open-mouthed delight, while a thickset man with the same reddish-blond hair as his betrothed stood detached from the family, appearing quite belligerent. He briefly wondered if the gentleman protested the union before his eyes found Sophia, and he was robbed of thought. She was beautiful. Exquisite. Dressed in an indigo pelisse which brought out the red highlights in her blonde hair, the blue glints in her eyes, and the warm tones in her silky skin. He was speechless with wonder. This intelligent, vivacious young woman had consented to marry him, and he was awed.

Reminding himself to draw breath, he hurried forward to greet the party.

After brief pleasantries, he bade his butler to show them to the library and to collect the vicar from the drawing room. As the family passed him, he shot out a hand to gently grasp Sophia by the arm. "I would like to speak to you for a few moments, Miss Hayward."

She hesitated and then stepped aside as her family continued down the hall.

"Miss Hayward, you are ... well?" Richard asked, finding himself rather ill-prepared to talk with her. For some reason, her appearance was causing his tongue to tie up, and he felt intimidated. What on earth? She was not the most beautiful woman he had ever encountered, although she was striking. It was her unbridled and spirited nature. He dearly wanted to earn her good opinion, more than he had ever desired it from anyone. It was ... disconcerting.

Sophia looked up at him with her large blue eyes and gave a nod. "Yes, my lord."

"Please, call me Richard. We are moments away from being wed." *Maybe. If she does not run screaming into the street.*

She smiled, the corners of her eyes creasing slightly. "Richard." The way she said his name sent a warm shiver through him, filling him with both joy and trepidation. *Richard, you must tell her what weighs on your heart,* he reminded himself.

He sighed deeply in resignation at the intruding thought. Sophia's face would twist into anger, she would yell for her family and depart his home, never to give him a second thought other than to gossip about 'that awful Lord Saunton and his vile ways.'

He opened his mouth to speak, but choked on the words. He tried again. "I ... I ... do you have any doubts?"

Sophia tilted her head, her eyes filled with concern. "No. Do you?"

"NO!" Richard shook his head violently. Calming himself, he spoke with more composure. "No. I have looked forward to this all week."

"As have I."

He paused in consternation. "You have? But ... what about my past?"

Sophia nibbled on her lip. "This has been a strange alliance we have forged, has it not?"

Richard nodded numbly. There was no denying that the progress of their relationship was odd.

She continued. "I find you interesting ... and unique. Your crusade intrigues me. I did not think I would ever marry, but I have changed my mind and I am ready to embark on an adventure with you."

She gazed at him with such earnest admiration that it caused his heart to squeeze painfully. It was so ... sincere. It made him want to be worthy of her regard, to have her look at him with that expression for ... well ... forever.

Screwing up his courage, he asked the question burning through his mind. "And what if I make mistakes ... or it turns out there are consequences to my past? What then?"

"We shall deal with it."

His jaw fell open. He was stunned. This girl was so unlike the people he was accustomed to associating with. She reminded him of Annabel Ridley, or rather the Duchess of Halmesbury now, but this relationship with Sophia was different. Perhaps he could have found this with Annabel if he had stripped the veneer of his charm off to reveal himself as a flawed man. With Sophia, he revealed himself and, instead of flinching or shying away, she seemed to be attracted to his honesty. Closing his mouth, which was still hanging open, he leaned down to press his lips against hers. She mumbled in surprise, but, to his delight, kissed him back.

He should be honest, explain the consequences of which he spoke, but then ... then he would have to stop kissing her and take the risk that she would reach her breaking point of allowable consequences. She sealed her fate with her sweet esteem, and he could not let her go. She was vital to the healing of his soul. He should tell her, but he could not bring himself to do it. He *would* tell her ... he would *tell* her ... *tomorrow*.

Instead, he leaned in and kissed her gently, his lips brushing hers with quiet reverence. She fit so perfectly in his arms, her warmth and presence filling the space between them as he drew her close in an embrace. When her arms lifted to encircle his neck, he felt a surge of tenderness, her fingers threading through his hair as the moment deepened into something both beautiful and profound.

AS THEIR KISS DEEPENED, Sophia sensed that Lord Saun—nay, Richard—wanted to tell her something. But the truth was, if that something would potentially affect their wedding, she did not want to hear it. Perhaps she was a gambler, just like her father and her brother. Perhaps even her mother had been a gambler at heart, wagering her future on a marriage to such a man. Regardless, Sophia's impulse was to throw caution to the wind and embark on a new life with Lor—Richard, whose heavenly kisses and caresses in that moment were greatly encouraging her impulse. Still, whatever consequences he feared, they would confront together. Her decision was made, and she was ready to proceed.

Then an alarming thought went through her mind. She leaned back to look up at him. "You do not have some ... unmentionable disease?"

He stared at her in dazed confusion, apparently struggling to make sense of her words as their kiss ended abruptly. Sophia tried again. "The consequences ... is it a ... dread disease?"

He burst out laughing. "Young ladies should not know or speak about dread diseases. But, no, I am healthy."

She blew an unladylike puff. "Oh my, that is a relief! And if you wanted a proper young miss, you should not have pursued me. I did my best to dissuade you."

Richard smiled down at her while letting her go. "You are very sweet."

"I am not being sweet. I am being quite selfish, I assure you. I do not wish to contract ... an unmentionable illness!"

Richard chuckled again. "Neither do I, Sophia, neither do I. Shall we?"

He offered her an arm, and she took it so that he may lead her to the site of their nuptials.

What a very strange week it had been. And now she would wed, hopefully for the only time in this life, which made a strange week even stranger. She could not help but think that life would never be dull with Lord Richard Balfour, the illustrious but sullied Earl of Saunton, and she hoped fervently that she was correct as he escorted her through his grand London townhouse. He was unlike any other man of her acquaintance, and it fascinated her to discover where their path together would lead.

~

Their vows took place in the library overlooking the gardens. Sunlight streamed in through a wall of French doors edging the length of the room. Everyone was in good spirits. Everyone, that was, except for the aloof Mr. Peregrine Balfour who barely said a word, and, of course, her own seething brother who stood apart from the wedding party, glowering near one of the French doors. When not scowling at her directly, Cecil spent most of the ceremony with his back turned to glare into the gardens. Sophia ignored him. He had created the situation with his greed, and she was unwilling to assume any guilt.

Aunt Christiana sniffed into a handkerchief that Uncle Hugh had handed to her during the vows. She and her aunt might not see eye to eye about a woman's role, but Sophia appreciated the older woman stepping in to mother her, always doing what she thought was best for Sophia's future.

Lily was particularly fey, taking in the vows with an expression of sheer joy. Her large brown eyes that dominated her dainty face were lustrous, and she glowed with the light of a thousand candles. There was no doubt that her cousin was happy for the fortuitous turn of events, especially now that she knew about the grave danger facing Sophia.

Lord Saun—Richard—*I need to become accustomed to his name ... we are marrying, after all!*—Richard stared down into her face with reverence, looking not at all like a shameless scoundrel but an enthralled youth, never taking his eyes off her. She did not quite know what to make of it; his green eyes glowed with admiration in the well-lit room. She could drown in his soulful gaze, but she was mildly uncomfortable. She wanted to assist him with his crusade, but she was not a savior, and she hoped his ideal of her would measure up to his expectations.

The ceremony ended and the wedding breakfast began, with the unlikely gathering of personalities sitting around the breakfast table. Her aunt and uncle talked with the vicar, while Lily chattered to Sophia. Perry, as Richard called him, picked at his eggs and ham while swallowing down endless cups of coffee and speaking little unless Richard addressed him directly. Perhaps his brother was recovering from a night of drinking?

Cecil was in the foulest mood, stabbing at his plate aggressively to make loud clinking noises with the cutlery. It was quite ill-behaved, but a minor offense compared to his other transgressions. That her brother had not said a word, even to greet the earl, did not bother Sophia. He was no longer her problem, and Uncle Hugh would address the matter.

She reserved no doubts that Lord Moreland was dealing with her sibling because the Moreland title was synonymous with family. Both her uncle and her grandfather before him were dedicated to safeguarding their household, which had proved very fortunate for both Sophia and Cecil when their parents died within weeks of each other. She still could not believe that Cecil had thrown away such a loyal family connection for the sake of high wagers and spirits.

Shaking her head, she decided she would not waste any further thoughts on the scapegrace, so she turned to Richard only to find him once again staring at her. She shifted uncomfortably.

"You look ravishing today," he murmured in her ear, his words thrilling against her skin.

"Um ... thank you?" Sophia could not claim to be

familiar with compliments from handsome men. She had spent much of her time dissuading them of any interest.

"I hope you like the ring? We can get another if you wish?"

Sophia looked down at the gold band on her finger in a floral design of diamonds and sapphires. "I love the ring!"

"It belonged to my mother."

Sophia felt her cheeks warm with pleasure. It seemed a high compliment to bestow his mother's ring on her.

"It would seem neither of our brothers are happy to attend our vows this morning." Richard tipped his head toward where Perry and Cecil sat side by side in silence across the table.

"Peregrine did not desire our match?"

"Perry did not desire any match. He is not ... inclined to form attachments. He is having difficulty understanding why I set my current course, but I am hoping in due time he will realize the advantages of clean living and healthy kinship. We never experienced a proper family because my mother passed away when he was just a few years old and my father ... was ... um ... not a family man. Even I hardly remembered my mother until you said ... what you said on the terrace. I hope between the two of us we might influence him over the coming months."

Sophia perked up at the thought of a second challenge. The truth was, she was rather bored living with the Abbott family. They were all so even-tempered and moderate. No one ever needed her help. Growing up with her parents, she had been needed, especially by her mother, who would grow quite despondent during her father's long, unexplained absences. Sophia had made it her mission to cheer her sorrowful mama by bringing her gifts, such as hand-picked flowers, and reading to her novels or poetry. Sophia missed the sense of purpose she had experienced as a child to lift everyone's spirits and bring the family together.

The Balfour family needed her, and she could not deny the rush of resolve and intention that filled her at the thought of assisting her new family. To be sure, the idle life of a viscount's ward and heiress had bored her since she had completed her schooling and found herself with nothing to do but prepare for social events. And read, of course.

Now Richard was offering her not just a chance to manage her own household, but to bring his family together. What a delightful challenge to fill her days with a sense of responsibility once more.

"I would like that."

Richard looked surprised for a moment, then grinned. "You are an exceptional woman, Sophia Balfour."

He grabbed the hand resting beside her plate and brought it up to his lips to press a soft kiss to her fingers, the contact sending a fissure of warmth up her arm. "I am glad to hear that because I insisted Perry continue to reside at Balfour Terrace. He should not feel displaced by our marriage. I did not know if you would object to his presence."

Sophia shook her head. "I look forward to learning about Perry ... and ... you."

"Then you shall. But today you will only learn about me. Once this breakfast is over, I plan to spend the day alone with you. I have a surprise for the moment your family departs."

Sophia felt a rush of warmth at his words. Richard was taking their marriage seriously, and it was deeply validating to be the focus of such a handsome and intriguing man. Her thoughts turned to the day ahead, and she found herself eager to finish breakfast so they could share a moment in private—just the two of them. She caught herself as a slight blush crept up her cheeks at the thought. It would be the first time she would be alone with a man who was not a family member. What would it feel like, this new chapter of her life? Whatever awaited her, she trusted Richard to lead them forward with care.

CHAPTER
SEVEN

"Meekness is a virtue that adorns the female character."

Dr. John Gregory, A Father's Legacy to His Daughters

∼

Two hours later, Richard ushered her out of his—*their*—townhouse to a waiting curricle with a matching pair of chestnut bays swishing their tails in the crisp spring air.

"What is this?" she queried in a breathy voice. She smoothed her pelisse and the ribbons of her bonnet, nervous about her first time in an open-air vehicle. She had never gone driving with a beau, having avoided courtship for so many years, and a thrill of excitement ran through her that she was to do so now with her handsome husband by her side. Although, anyone who saw them together in the curricle would likely assume he was merely courting her with this traditional method, for a drive in an open-air carriage did not require a chaperon. To her knowledge, the gossips were not yet aware of their unexpected union.

Richard turned to her. "I never had a chance to woo you. With how events transpired, I feel I owe you a courtship, which will be even better now that we are wed and do not require a companion. Shall we get to know each other?"

Sophia was dumbstruck. It was so ... so thoughtful. A shy smile spread across her face, and she nodded. Richard lifted her into the carriage while the tiger in his knee-length coat stood politely looking away while holding the team. Once Richard walked to the other side and embarked to take hold of the reins, the servant moved to the back and mounted the rumble, causing the curricle to shift into a new position. She gasped slightly at the shift of balance, shooting a hand out to grab the edge of her seat. The light-weight curricle was a very different experience from the large family coach she was accustomed to.

Richard shot her an encouraging grin, then deftly guided the horses into motion. Soon they were driving through the light traffic in Mayfair. When they entered a congested street into Berkeley Square, she realized where they were heading. Although she had never desired a courtship before this strange turn of events, suddenly she felt giddy with delight.

"You are taking me to Gunter's?" she exclaimed.

Richard smiled as he continued to drive the horses patiently through the square, heading for a line of trees and railings where several curricles and phaetons were parked. Ladies perched in their shaded seats, while a number of foppish lords leaned idly against the railings and observed the square.

"I have never been!"

Richard turned his head in surprise, before straightening to look back at the street he was navigating. "Never?"

"Lady Moreland receives visits, and she pays calls on her friends, but she rarely goes out in public. Mostly we go to the modiste, the haberdashery, and occasionally the theatre or opera. My cousin and I are sometimes allowed out with servants in accompaniment, but we always use the opportunity to go straight to the bookshops. Which is to say, I have passed by this square, but I have never stopped here."

Richard appeared pleased at this news. "I have chosen well, then. Every lady should visit Gunter's before she weds, but at least we got you here before—" He stopped, then lifted a hand to rub his neck in slight embarrassment. *Before our wedding night,* she supposed was the end of that sentence.

Richard brought the curricle to a stop by the trees. The tiger descended from the rumble and came forward to help place the carriage under a large tree, the branches of which extended out to provide welcome shade from the midafternoon sun. Then the servant moved a respectful distance away to lean against a tree far apart from the patrons of Gunter's.

To her surprise, Richard remained seated and did not disembark to go stand with the other lords, who were staring at them with curiosity. She recalled, from the various gossip between her aunt and her friends, that he had not openly courted any woman before, although he had been hunting for a wife for several Seasons. There had been a rumor that he had been jilted by the daughter of a baron in Somerset, but that must have been two Seasons earlier, if recollection served, and no other woman was rumored to have caught his eye. She wondered briefly about the broken betrothal. It was likely that his indiscretions might be the cause of the rift, considering that his crusade to redeem his honor had just begun, according to him, the night of the Astley ball when he overheard her criticism. The woman in question had purportedly wedded Richard's cousin, the Duke of Halmesbury, in his stead. *Should I ask him about it?* No, she decided. This was a day of courtship, not the time to discuss difficult topics.

"You are the first woman I have brought to Gunter's." Richard leaned in to inform her. "We may raise some eyebrows, and gossip that I am courting you will run rife throughout the day until news of our wedding gets out. As far as these gentlemen know, this is merely an outing with an eligible young woman."

Sophia giggled. The gossips would get their conjecture wrong today.

"How does this work, then?"

"A server will come out to take our order for ices, then bring them out to us. We will eat them, return the dishes, and when you are ready, I have another destination in mind."

"And you will not join the lords over by the railings?"

Richard shook his head. "I am not here to visit with the fashionable set. They come here to be seen, but today is for learning about my bride so that we may begin our life together. Have you had an ice before?"

"I have not. What do you recommend?"

"I despise the Gruyère cheese, so do not order that. Perhaps ..." He thought for a moment. "... the chocolate cream ice?"

Her mouth watered. Feeling like a naïve young debutante rather than a woman who had navigated three

Seasons and wed that morning, she nodded enthusiastically. "That sounds lovely."

Richard turned away upon the waiter's arrival and ordered a chocolate and a maple cream ice. When he settled back on his seat, he commented to her, "You may try my maple ice, if you like. It will cause quite the rumpus." He gestured toward the other carriages and lords. She looked around and realized that the ladies and gentlemen were openly gawking in their direction and talking amongst themselves. Apparently the very eligible Earl of Saunton was the subject of much speculation, especially since his companion was a self-designated wallflower whom barely anyone had paid attention to since her come-out four years earlier.

"Pay no mind. Nothing useful is ever said." Sophia looked back to find Richard gazing at her with slight concern in his vivid green eyes.

She shook her head. "It is a little daunting to be so closely scrutinized, but I do not usually concern myself with gossip. People should live their lives based on what they feel is right. I do not care what others' thoughts might be about my decisions."

His face relaxed. "I am glad to hear that. Your connection to me … it may expose you to a great deal of gossip."

She put out a hand to cover his gloved one. "Do not concern yourself. I was well aware of your reputation when I first encountered you. Which reminds me, I must apologize."

He frowned slightly, perplexed. "For what?"

"You overheard me mocking you about rumors that I paid attention to."

His gaze shifted away, clearly troubled. "Your words

were warranted. I am fortunate to have overheard them, or I would not have elected to change."

"Richard?" She waited for him to look back at her. "I cannot have worked such a miracle. On some level, you must have been ready to shift your course. The reparations you are making ... they were your decision. *You* are the one doing the work."

Richard stared at her for several moments. Eventually, he nodded in agreement, but Sophia perceived he was still directing criticism at himself. Her husband was going to require patience so that he might heal and rediscover his self-respect. She felt honored that he was involving her in his transformation. He was an important man who influenced thousands through his estates and leadership. It was a terrifying responsibility to aid him in his endeavor.

Their ices arrived, and their discussion moved to their family histories while they spooned delicious, melting ice. As promised, Richard took up a portion of maple cream ice and brought it to her lips to sample. The chatter spiked as their observers witnessed the inappropriate sharing, but Sophia smiled up at him and accepted the offering with relish. Damn the gossips! She was sharing a wondrous afternoon with her new husband, and they could go to the devil.

Soon they left Berkeley Square, and he drove the curricle to Hyde Park. Once there, he disembarked and then reached up to lift her from the curricle and settle her onto her feet. They walked along the Serpentine, passing couples and families on the banks of the river as he showed her some of his favorite spots. The entire day was magical, and she regretted its end when they returned to the townhouse and he sent her up to her new chambers to prepare for dinner.

THE DAY HAD BEEN a great success. Richard's bride was relaxed in his presence, and they had spent the day learning about each other. The ennui that had plagued him for years had been steadily dissipating since his initial encounter with her. With each apology he made, with each step he took toward Sophia, a little more life and energy loosened within him. His soul had been frozen in darkness, but now he was thawing out to feel more alive with each passing day.

He laughed to himself as he climbed the stairs after dinner. The flashes of discomfort and shame about his past still hit him unexpectedly, but they were lessening, and he was astounded to find he was optimistic about the future for the first time in many years.

Soon he would join Sophia in her bedchamber to enjoy a tender wedding night with his bride.

He reached the hall leading to his bedroom, whistling while he walked the long path. Hard work was still ahead of him, but every step he took brought him closer to a peace of mind he had never expected to find. He was learning that true joy was only possible with a clear conscience, and he was eager to continue clearing his.

Opening the door to his bedchamber, he was hit by an overwhelming wave of cloying perfume. He stopped abruptly, bewildered by the overpowering scent. The usually clean, refined air of his rooms was gone, replaced by something heavy and garish, utterly out of place.

"Milord, we have been waiting for you," said an unfamiliar, syrupy voice. Richard whirled toward the bed, his breath catching in alarm. To his utter dismay, he saw three women draped across the bed, their attire and exaggerated makeup leaving no doubt as to their occupations.

"What is the meaning of this? Who are you, and what are you doing in my rooms?" His voice was firm, tinged with urgency, as his thoughts turned to Sophia preparing for bed in the adjoining room. Panic gripped him as he stormed across the chamber, carefully but resolutely urging one of the women off the bed. The stench of heavy perfume and spirits mixed with stale sweat made him recoil slightly, but he stood his ground. "You must leave at once! My bride is in the next room!"

"But we were hired to take care of you, and we know how to do it," the woman said, her voice suggestive as she trailed her fingers down his arm. Richard recoiled inwardly, trying to clear his thoughts. He had always disliked those who frequented disreputable establishments. The memory of his father's corrupting behavior when he was a boy came rushing back—how his father had once hired two such women when Richard turned fourteen, deeming him a man. Richard had spent the night hiding in a guest room, desperate to avoid them. It was a humiliating experience that had left a mark on him. He wondered, with a sinking feeling, if Perry had suffered something similar while Richard was away at Oxford. His brother had always refused to step foot in places where such women could be found.

Choking back his frustration, Richard gently grasped one of the women by the arm and guided her from the bed, hoping the others would follow suit. Forcing a polite but firm smile, he attempted to reason with them. "Ladies, I fear there has been some misunderstanding about my need for your ... presence. It is time for you to leave. Immediately!"

The woman shuffled along reluctantly, her hands still lingering uncomfortably on his sleeve. Richard stiffened, a vivid memory of his father's reckless indulgence flashing through his mind. He could not allow Sophia to be exposed to such a scene. He had to get them out of his chambers—at once.

Where was his valet?

Faith! Sophia could arrive any—

He froze, squeezing his eyes shut as he heard the sound of the adjoining door creak open. Slowly, he turned, dread pooling in his stomach, to find Sophia standing in the doorway. Her expression was grim as her gaze swept over the women still lounging on his bed, their attire disheveled and their poses anything but modest. Then her eyes settled on the woman beside him, who was trailing her hands over him like the tentacles of an octopus.

"Sophia, this is not what it appears!" Her blue eyes met his to stare directly into his soul for what felt like an eternity. She tilted her head as if to ask a question.

"The young lady can join us if she wishes, but it will cost extra, milord." The slurred voice cut through the silence, followed by a coarse, mocking laugh. Richard's jaw tightened as he forced himself to remain calm, his anger simmering beneath the surface. The audacity of the remark was appalling, and his stomach churned at the thought of Sophia witnessing such an indecent display. He struggled to contain his rising frustration, determined to shield her from further humiliation.

A hand slid toward his thigh, and Richard swiftly caught it with his own before the woman's actions could escalate any further—especially not in front of his new wife.

A clear voice cut into the drama of the moment.

"Richard, pay these ladies their coin so they may be on their way."

Had he heard her correctly? Perhaps his thoughts were befuddled.

Pay these women? Pay *these* women to leave. *Pay* these women to *leave*!

She was brilliant. His bride was nothing short of a genius! In hindsight, he felt like a fool for not thinking to simply offer the women coin to leave. Exhaling in relief, he released the lightskirt he had been holding and quickly reached for his purse. Clutching it firmly, he strode toward the bed with newfound determination.

"Time to go, ladies! I shall give you two—no, three guineas each if you follow me downstairs immediately!" he declared, his tone brisk but polite. The women blinked at him with bleary, unfocused eyes before the offer began to register. Slowly, they rose from the bed, the promise of such a fortune cutting through their gin-induced haze.

He would pay them more if they would move quicker. He handed coin into their hands, their fingernails chipped with grime underneath. What friend would think this humorous? Who would play such an ill-conceived prank on him? Had they known it was his wedding night—*would Perry do this as a lark?* He immediately brushed that thought aside. Perry would rather pull out his own teeth than come within speaking distance of these women. His brother abhorred Birds of Paradise and favored spending his time in the company of widows.

Do I need to talk to Perry about what happened while I was away at university? What did Father do in my absence?

The welcome sight of Richard's valet appeared at the door.

"Shaw, we need to show these young ladies out."

Richard wanted to personally escort them out of his townhouse to ensure that they left. And to question them downstairs. He swung his head in Sophia's direction. She gave him a nod; it appeared she understood his need without him voicing it.

"You shall find me in my chambers when you are done, my lord."

Richard was relieved, but also concerned. Why was she 'my lording' him? *Faugh!* This day had been so promising, but now it was going to be a very long, very disappointing evening.

Courage, Richard.

He must deal with this. Only then could he return to explain the situation to his bride.

One step at a time. *One* step at a time.

He drew a deep breath. *Take them downstairs, Richard. Then find out how they gained access.*

Only then could the depth of his bride's disdain be established.

One step at a time.

CHAPTER
EIGHT

"The education of women should be particularly directed to improve the heart."

Dr. John Gregory, A Father's Legacy to His Daughters

~

Once he had established very little—other than a cloaked, hooded figure had ushered the women through the mews and into one of the garden-facing doors before leading them to his rooms—Richard returned to his bedchamber. Which reeked.

The overpowering scent of cheap perfume filled the room, making it difficult to ignore the disarray. It was what he imagined an unsavory establishment might smell like, though he had never set foot in one. Richard had always avoided such places, unwilling to risk the dangers or indignities they entailed. Over the years, his easygoing charm and status as a handsome, successful peer had ensured no shortage of attention from more refined women.

Not that he felt successful or easygoing at the moment.

His valet arrived with a swarm of footmen to hurriedly provide a tub of bathing water and whisk away bedding to be cleaned. Richard had already thrown open the windows despite the chill of the evening in order to air the room out.

Once the bath was prepared, he quickly took advantage of the steaming hot water to bathe the stench off his skin and hair. In his imagination, the odor lingered still, but Shaw assured him that he currently smelt delightful. He was uncertain if the man was funning him with his droll words, but the servant stated it with no trace of humor.

Clothed in loose cotton trousers and a shirt, he pulled on a dressing gown and approached the adjoining door to Sophia's chambers. For several moments, he stood there in silence, his forehead resting against the cool wood. What could he possibly say to her? He could not explain what had happened, as he barely understood it himself. Surely, his bride now thought him the worst sort of rake—perhaps even worse than his own father. The thought filled him with a deep, gnawing regret.

All his hard work forming a connection with her, destroyed by some unknown figure ... presumably a so-called friend who was utterly lacking in taste. Mayhap he had done too many terrible deeds in his past, and this was his penance. Perhaps his cousin was wrong, and it was far too late for him to amend his ways. Perhaps he should go sleep in a guest room and leave his bride alone. He dreaded entering the room to find her embittered toward him after their enchanting day together.

Inhaling deeply, he accepted he was well on his way to relying on her esteem, and he felt angry desolation at how their day was ending. Nonetheless, the problem would not evaporate on its own. He must confront it now before it worsened so he knocked on her door.

IT HAD TAKEN Sophia only a moment to register her groom's distress when she entered his rooms. She quickly ascertained from his expression, and his general demeanor, that he was not involved in inviting the women into his chambers.

Had he done such a thing in the past?

Hearing the quiet knock on the adjoining door, she sprang up from the bed to race across the room on her bare feet and open the door. She found her husband on the other side, looking worn out. And well-scrubbed, his hair damp.

"I am so sorry. This was not planned." His voice was gruff, and Sophia took pity. Claiming his hand with her own, she drew him into the room and over to the seating area.

"I know."

He frowned in confusion.

"It only took a moment to realize you did not possess the look of a man with an agenda. You looked like a man in a blind panic."

He chuckled dryly. "That would be an accurate description of how I was feeling."

"Did they come on the wrong night?"

Richard's head bobbed up in surprise. "What do you mean?"

"I thought perhaps ... this was an old meeting you forgot to cancel. Or a standing arrangement had not been ... well ... called off? From before. When you ... I mean, you only recently decided to change your ways ... Perhaps this is how you spent your evenings ..." She trailed off, feeling silly.

"No! I never paid coin for ... that. I would never risk my health on ..." He took a deep breath to continue. "Apparently, some acquaintance of mine thought it would be amusing to play a lark on me and showed them to my rooms. If I find out who exposed you to this, I will kill them with my bare hands. Radcliffe is downstairs questioning the servants to find out if any of them assisted with this ... this ... invasion of our home."

Sophia stared at him for an eternity, not sure what came next.

"Sophia, I do not think this is the night to celebrate our wedding." Richard turned away to glare at the wall.

She could see his point. He still appeared disturbed, and the wonderful rapport they had built earlier in the day was missing. They sat together in their dejected silence while Sophia pondered what to do. She wanted to assist him, to play a part in his restoration of honor. This seemed like a moment that she should show her mettle in some way, to somehow mitigate this disastrous night. Show some kindness to alleviate his mood.

"Perhaps ..."

His eyes found hers. "Perhaps?"

"Perhaps you would care to lie in my bed with me? Just to sleep?" she asked softly.

The regret in his eyes softened, and he exhaled deeply, his posture relaxing. "I ... I would like that very much."

Sophia rose and took his hand, leading him to the large canopied bed. Releasing his hand, she slipped off her dressing gown and quickly climbed under the coverlet, pulling it snugly around her. She glanced over as he removed his own robe, hesitating briefly before joining her. She turned onto her side, her back to him, as he extinguished the lamp.

In the quiet darkness, she felt him shift closer, his hand settling gently on her hip. The simple touch carried a tentative reassurance, and she pressed back slightly, offering comfort in return. His tension seemed to ebb away, replaced by a steady warmth that eased them both.

Closing her eyes, she let the exhaustion of the long day wash over her. There would be time to address their troubles in the morning. For now, she allowed herself to savor the quiet closeness of his presence, the warmth of his nearness lulling her into rest.

SLEEPING near his bride without acting on his feelings had been a true test of his resolve. His body ached with longing, but his conscience held firm, reminding him of the trust she had placed in him. It was not simply a matter of physical desire—he had never wanted anyone as much as he wanted Sophia, and that made his restraint all the more difficult.

When the tension became too much to bear, he shifted slightly, putting a small distance between them to compose himself. Only then, after what felt like hours of inner turmoil, did he finally drift into an exhausted sleep, her presence still a comforting balm to his restless heart.

Slowly, he awakened and opened his eyes to discover it was morning. He blinked in surprise when he found clear blue eyes staring into his. His bride was awake and watching him closely.

Tentatively, she leaned forward and pressed a soft kiss

to his lips. He shifted slightly, a wave of emotion surging through him at the unexpected gesture. Her free hand emerged from the covers and reached up to smooth back his hair, her touch gentle and reassuring.

Her fingers lingered, tracing softly along his temple and down his neck, her attention tender and curious. She rested her hand lightly on his chest, her fingertips brushing over his torso as though memorizing the shape of him. Each touch sent a shiver through him, and he clenched his hands to keep himself still, letting her explore without interruption.

When he could no longer contain his feelings, he rose onto one elbow, gazing down at her with an intensity born of affection and longing. Lowering his head, he met her lips in a kiss full of warmth and sincerity, a reflection of the connection blossoming between them.

This seemed a perfect moment to—

A discreet knock interrupted his intentions. "My lord, there is an urgent matter to attend to."

Richard lowered his head onto her shoulder to scowl at his butler's intrusion.

What could be important enough to interrupt me in my bride's chambers?

Belatedly, he recalled the events of the night before.

On second thought, perhaps his butler had cause. Sighing in resignation, he leaned forward to press a kiss against Sophia's forehead and then withdrew from the bed. He donned his robe over his night clothes and went to the door, stepping out into the passage to talk with Radcliffe while shutting the door behind him.

Radcliffe looked a little worse for wear, dark shadows under his eyes, but otherwise his usual tidy self. Richard wondered if his faithful servant had been to bed or if he had been questioning the servants all night.

"A certain guest has arrived early, my lord."

Richard frowned. He was not expecting any guests ... other than ... other than ... *Stuff!*

"My son has arrived?" he asked below his breath.

"Yes, milord."

Richard raised a hand to swipe over his face. He had planned to inform Sophia today about his natural born son and his imminent arrival. He had thought Ethan would not arrive for another day or two. This was too darn early. How could he spring this on her after the terrible night she had endured? How much could one woman be expected to forgive?

He ordered his butler to send his valet up to his rooms to help him dress. He refused to meet his son for the first time in his nightclothes.

One step at a time, Richard.

Swiftly, he walked down the hall to the entrance of his room. Shaw arrived moments later and quickly dressed Richard. Before he had much time to think, he ran downstairs to look for his man of business who had collected his son from the Davis family.

RICHARD WALKED into his study to find Johnson missing and Radcliffe standing beside a small boy of about four years old. The little chap possessed soft brown locks, and when he raised his face to look at Richard, he revealed the distinctive green eyes of the Balfour family. He could not deny that the boy must be related to him.

Richard shifted uncomfortably from foot to foot, trying

to decide how to greet his son. Did the boy know who he was, or must he explain their relationship? He was still pondering how to begin when the door behind him swung open.

"Who is this, Richard?"

Richard spun around to stare blankly at Sophia, words escaping him while several moments passed. How had she dressed so quickly?

"Richard, who is this?" Her voice rose to a shrill level, piercing his fog.

Richard opened his mouth. Then closed it when he still found no words to say. She stared at him expectantly, but he was speechless.

For pity's sake! What is this?

He always knew what to say, but this past day was unprecedented. He had no experience to draw on, and he felt exposed emotionally.

Emotionally? What does that mean? When did I begin to wield emotions?

"Richard, I need to know, who is this boy?" Sophia asserted, maintaining a cheery tone likely intended to prevent the child's alarm, but her smile was tense.

All Richard could think about was that redemption was difficult. Telling the truth was difficult. It was difficult to know what was the right thing to do. Life was complicated. He knew he needed to explain the truth but, though he opened his mouth to speak, still no words would form.

Sophia brushed past him to kneel before the little lad. "Hello. What's your name?"

"Ethan," said the boy. He gave an adorable little bow. "Pleased to meet you."

Sophia stood to give him a solemn curtsy in response.

"Sophia," she replied. "I am Lord Saunton's wife. And, who, may I ask, are you to Lord Saunton?"

"Is that Lord Saunton?" asked the boy, pointing to Richard where he stood in pained silence. Sophia nodded. "Emma says he is my papa, and I must listen to what he says. But he has not said anything yet."

"I see. While we wait for your ... papa ... to speak, perhaps you would like to eat? I am sure Cook could find some milk and perhaps cake to go with it."

Ethan's eyes rounded in delight, and he nodded vigorously in response.

Sophia turned to Radcliffe, who was politely standing by and stoically studying the wall. "Radcliffe, can you see that Ethan finds his way to the kitchens and is well fed?" The butler inclined his head and took the boy by his tiny hand to exit the room.

Sophia waved her fingers to Ethan, smiling. As she turned back to Richard, her smile fell away and she glared at him. "Perhaps you should explain why Ethan thinks you are his father?"

Richard winced as he made his way to the drinks cabinet across the room. Then he recollected his promise to avoid spirits. He brought such chaos into the life of his bride; he owed it to her to attempt to keep at least one promise.

"When you asked me if I had any natural born children, I did not know about Ethan. Later that day, I came home to meet with my man of business, which is when ... I was told about his birth." He stared down at the decanter of French brandy with yearning.

Sophia was silent. So silent he was afraid that the silence would stretch out, wrap around the world, and all speech would be canceled for eternity. His own breathing sounded like a cacophony of sound in the deafening silence that—

"So, the people whom I do not like will no longer wish to associate with us," she finally blurted out so loud it made him jump.

"I do not understand ... what?" He turned to face her.

"So, we are to be a scandal. The members of the peerage whom I dislike the most will be the first to avoid us. I may never be required to speak to them again. No soul-draining small talk with my aunt's friends; no chitchat with that obnoxious Lady Jersey or her husband. I can live with that. And our family just grew larger," she finished in a pragmatic tone.

Richard shook his head in disbelief.

"However, I would have appreciated being *forewarned* ..." She scowled at him, hands fisted on her hips, then brought a finger up to tap her lips pensively before pointing it at him. "On the other hand, I think I may have dissuaded you from telling me something before the wedding. Was this what you pulled me aside to discuss?"

He nodded ruefully.

Sophia appeared thoughtful until excitement crossed her face. "*Oooh!* I shall spend my evenings with thinkers and literary geniuses instead. I shall be an irregular bluestocking who holds salons."

Richard tried to make sense of what was unfolding before him. Was his wife somehow pleased with the recent turn of events? Her mind zigzagged, not unlike the military maneuver, and he realized his bride was an enigma that he might never fully comprehend, but she would keep him endlessly entertained in the years to come.

He stepped forward and wrapped his arms around her.

"You are a wonderful woman. You accept that my son will live with us?"

"Where else would he live? He is your son."

Richard had suspected when he had eavesdropped on Sophia and Miss Abbott less than a fortnight ago that he had met a compelling woman. Now that he held her against his chest and breathed in the scent of roses, he was certain that Sophia was his perfect woman. He could think of no other lady of the *ton* who would have accepted his son into her home.

"And will you be his mother?"

"If he has no mother, I will fill the role in any way that Ethan requires."

Richard let her go and walked over to drop into one of his plush ivory armchairs. He leaned his elbows on his knees in relief. His wife was a revelation, and he felt like he, yet again, had been granted a reprieve. It did not surprise him when she came to stand over him.

"Are you all right, Richard?"

He nodded, clearing his throat in embarrassment at the display of emotion. He reached out to grab her slender hand. "Thank you."

"I know you have a troubling past. But from here on out, can we work together?"

"Yes."

"Are there any more surprises?"

"No."

"Well then, shall we go meet your son properly?"

"Yes."

Richard stood and held out his arm to his remarkable bride.

In the kitchens, Sophia met the housekeeper and kitchen staff while Ethan demolished a large ham sandwich that barely fit in his small hands. Once he was done, they brought him back to the study to talk. The child proved to be bright and well-spoken, chattering away about his journey from Derby and all that he had seen and experienced.

Sophia had been remarkable, talking to his son with directness while giving him her full attention, which the boy responded well to. It soon came to light that Ethan could read when he commented on the books on the shelves, and Sophia promised they would visit the library together to select books appropriate for him or, if they could not find any, would visit Hatchards for new stories.

Ethan was exploring the study when Sophia lowered her voice to speak with Richard. "I do not think a nursemaid will be sufficient. I will cultivate the boy's love of learning, but he may require a tutor to keep him occupied. Whoever this Emma is, whom he keeps referring to, she has clearly taught him beyond his years. Perhaps the boy is a genius? Reading at his age?"

"Johnson will bring us candidates for tutors, then. But I do not want my boy to be educated by the kind of men my father hired when I was a child. We must find someone who will foster his enthusiasm rather than squash it."

"Agreed."

Sophia strode across the room when Ethan called her over. Richard watched her crouching to talk with him. He was overjoyed to witness her acceptance of Ethan, not to mention the salve of having her support while he grew to know his son. Although usually a decisive man, he was uncertain of what to do with a young child, but fortunately Sophia was taking the lead.

Richard crossed the study to join them at the shelves when Sophia beckoned him. He dropped to one knee to join their chat.

"Sophia said that you and I could play chess tonight, Papa!" Ethan looked up at him with an excited, wide-eyed glance and pointed to the chess set that lay forgotten on the shelf. Richard followed his finger to look at the set and perceived for the first time that, as Sophia had pointed out, the four-year-old boy was learned beyond his years if he was interested in a game of chess.

"You play chess?"

Ethan chortled. "Of course. Emma said it would teach me to think and to plan a *strat ... e ... gy*." He drew out the word carefully.

"Do you know what it means to plan a strategy?" Richard asked him.

"It means to play smarter than your *op ... po ... nent*." The boy sounded out cautiously.

Richard smiled down at the boy, an errant rush of warmth causing him to raise his hand to affectionately ruffle the silky locks of his ... *child*. "That it does, Ethan. That it does. Who is Emma?"

The boy looked at him oddly. "Emma is ... Emma." Ethan frowned slightly, then elaborated. "She is my *cuz-zin*. And my friend."

Richard winced, but quickly cleared his face to smile at the boy. Might he have been too hasty ripping the boy from his family? Should he have collected the child himself? Perhaps spent a few days with the boy's family and come to know them, and this Emma, and the life that Ethan had led? Had he been arrogant to send his man of business to collect the boy and make the arrangements?

He was not accustomed to knowing how to treat family

matters such as this and feared he may have been ruthless in his single-minded focus to claim his son.

He raised his head to stare at Sophia. She raised her eyebrows in question, but he could not talk about it in front of the boy.

Radcliffe entered the room accompanied by a short, young maid with a wide, pleasant face and dark brown hair scraped back in a bun. Richard thought she might be new.

"Milord, this is Daisy. She has come to work with us from one of your Somerset estates, and she has several younger brothers and sisters. I arranged for her to act as a nursemaid until permanent arrangements can be made."

Richard was relieved as he stood up. He needed to accustom himself to his changed circumstances, so a temporary reprieve was in order.

"Perhaps we can walk with Ethan up to the nursery to see him settled, Richard?"

Accepting Sophia's guidance in the matter, he gave a nod. Taking Ethan by his small hand, he smiled down. "You want to see your rooms, son?"

Ethan grinned and nodded. The boy was sociable and inquisitive. He chattered about the books Sophia would show him later as he tugged Richard into a walk.

Sophia followed them while they walked up the stairs to find the nursery. She looked around with keen interest, and Richard sensed she was noting the rooms and their contents in order to make improvements. Once Ethan started yawning, no doubt the effect of his long journey and hearty meal, she encouraged him to sleep. The boy nodded, swiftly dozing off on his small bed while Sophia quietly instructed Daisy about his belongings, meals, and recreations, along with arranging a time for his promised game of chess with his papa.

Finally, they left the nursery to walk back downstairs.

"Do you mind if I made arrangements to remodel the nursery? I will want to make purchases."

Richard shook his head. "Of course not. I did not expect you to be involved, but I would appreciate your input."

"I think we will need to ensure we spend quite a bit of time with Ethan. It sounds like he has come from a large family and will not be occupied with only a nursemaid to keep him company. I think we should find a nursemaid who is educated and can discuss his books with him. Or even a governess who might continue his studies until he is a little older?"

"I bow to your insights, wife. We will find my man of business so he may begin searching for someone appropriate. You mentioned a tutor might be needed sooner rather than later, so we will discuss our needs with Johnson, but perhaps a governess would be a good start, considering he keeps mentioning this Emma. It is not the done thing, but as you pointed out, we no longer need to concern ourselves with that."

Sophia smiled up at him, her arm woven around his while they walked down together. "This is quite a turn of events. Last week I was a mere ward in my uncle's house, and this week I am a bride and I guess I am standing in as a mother. Who would have predicted such a change in circumstances?"

It was uncanny to hear his earlier thoughts mirrored in her words, but her pleased expression brought a smile to his face. His gaze lingered on her lips, and he found himself longing for the moment they could fully begin their life together as husband and wife. Today, however, seemed unlikely to allow for such closeness.

Still, the memory of her gentle touch lingered in his

mind, a quiet reminder of the bond they were building. Her kindness toward his son and the quiet grace with which she embraced her new role only deepened his admiration for her. The strength of his feelings took him by surprise, leaving him eager for the day when they could be alone and fully share the bond growing between them.

CHAPTER NINE

"The best way for a woman to acquire knowledge is from conversation with a father, a brother, or a friend."

Dr. John Gregory, A Father's Legacy to His Daughters

~

Richard led Sophia down to his study, closing the door once they entered. He guided her to an armchair where, to her surprise, he took a seat. She stood by hesitantly, unsure what to do. Suddenly, she felt his hands at her waist as he picked her up and settled her down on his lap.

Squeaking, she looked at him in surprise, noting the rather pleasant experience of being in his arms. He buried his face in her neck and breathed in deeply.

"You smell so sweet," he murmured softly against her skin, his breath warm near her ear. The gentle closeness sent a shiver through her, and she instinctively tilted her head to the side, allowing him to linger near. Her hand rested lightly on his chest, the steady beat of his heart grounding her as his lips brushed her cheek in a tender caress.

When their lips finally met, the kiss was hesitant at first, a sweet exchange that deepened as she leaned closer. The warmth of his embrace surrounded her, and she lost herself in the moment, the quiet stillness broken only by the soft whisper of their breaths.

Slowly, he pulled back, giving her sweet kisses before withdrawing to look at her. She opened her eyes and found herself enthralled by his gaze.

"Why did you marry me?"

She shook her head to clear her thoughts. "You intrigued me."

"Yes, but that first time you dissuaded my interest with that vapid act of yours—it was very effective, by the way. When I danced with you the second time, you showed no interest. What changed?"

"I ... did not want to marry. But then my circumstances caused me to change my mind. Once I changed my mind, I realized that your crusade to reclaim your honor intrigued me."

"What circumstances?"

She flushed in shame. "It became clear that the terms of my dowry created an untenable situation in which I was exposed—vulnerable to fortune hunters. As the terms were set long before my birth, they could not be altered. I concluded that the most favorable solution was to seek security through marriage to a man of my own choosing, and I immediately thought of you. Your interest in me appeared genuine."

Richard looked troubled. "Is that the only reason?"

She bit her lip, her eyes focusing on the hand resting on

his shoulder. "I ... found you fascinating after our second conversation ... and ... attractive during our first dance," she blurted out, the last in embarrassment.

He grinned in delight, wrapping his arms around her to embrace her close to his body, which emanated heat. He lowered his head to rest on hers, and she gave in to the impulse to burrow against his chest and remain there.

"We should eat soon," she ventured after a while.

"Soon. Right now, I just want to hold my bride before any more excitement can find us."

She smiled at his words and nestled her head against his shoulder. Several quiet minutes passed as she listened to the steady rhythm of his heartbeat beneath her cheek. The comforting sound and the strength of his presence filled her with a quiet anticipation, her thoughts drifting to what their future together might hold.

He spoke in a low, soothing voice. "How is it you knew what to do with Ethan? I am at a loss, but you did not hesitate."

"I was a girl not that long ago. A motherless one. I simply thought what I would like in Ethan's place and acted accordingly."

"What about the mothering?" He gestured his head up toward the nursery.

"Lady Moreland is a capable woman. I was older than Ethan when we arrived at the Abbott household, but I thought he would need similar things. Time spent with family, including meals. Something to engage his curious mind. My aunt and uncle are very involved with their family, and I was fortunate to be included. I observed them for many years, so I developed some instincts, I suppose."

"I am impressed. You are quite composed for such a young woman."

Sophia raised her head to roll her eyes. "That does not serve as a compliment. Am I not composed for an older, more experienced woman?"

Richard chuckled, leaning his forehead on her shoulder. "I stand corrected. You are quite composed—period," he emphasized.

His hand rested gently against her midsection, the touch sending a flutter through her chest. Even with the fabric of her day gown and shift between them, the simple gesture carried an unexpected intimacy that made her breath catch.

"I am afraid there is something I failed to mention."

Sophia stopped breathing. She had been taking the events of the past evening and this morning in her stride, but she thought she might have reached her capacity for surprises.

"I accepted an invitation to a musicale for this evening. Before I knew I would marry yesterday."

Sophia exhaled in relief. This was a minor issue, then.

"I know you have not had an opportunity to order a new wardrobe befitting a married woman, but do you mind if we attend? The gentleman is a friend, and he has two daughters to marry off. He asked me to lend my support, and there has been no opportunity to speak with him about my getting wed."

Sophia smiled. "I think we can manage that if it is someone you consider a friend. Who is it?"

"Lord Lawson."

"Oh! I heard his daughters are quite talented musically. I think we could enjoy a most agreeable evening."

"I hope you are right. I would hate to sit through pitchy singing and missed notes on the pianoforte. Even worse, if they cannot properly play the harp, it could be a loud and painful evening."

Sophia giggled and swatted his shoulder. "Nay, husband. This is a perfect evening of entertainment. Shall we learn about each other once more? Yesterday the time spent together was enjoyable before ..." She did not wish to recall the awful night.

Richard grimaced in distaste. "Yes, before. I want to apologize for the chaos you have encountered since taking up residence at Balfour Terrace. I would have preferred our marriage to begin differently."

"You could not help that someone played that vicious prank on you. However, Ethan should probably not have been a surprise?"

"I assure you that I was as surprised as you the past few days. More so."

"Yes, but moving forward ... perhaps you could inform me of such things. I would very much like to be your helpmate in this marriage. My own parents were ... quite broken. Father always kept secrets about his gambling, and his drinking made him difficult to communicate with. And Mother wallowed in self-pity. Lord and Lady Moreland are much closer, and they work together. I would like our marriage to be more like that. A partnership and meeting of the minds."

Richard chuckled. "Quite the revolutionary I married."

"If it is revolutionary to know my mind and to speak my truth, then yes."

"I agree. We will try it your way. You may require patience because I do not come from a close-knit family and I have not had a feminine influence in my life to soften me since I was a very small lad. I will learn."

Sophia stuck out a hand. Richard stared down at it for a moment in surprise.

"Is it not what close friends do?"

"I suppose it is." He shook her hand.

"It is an agreement, then. No more secrets."

When Richard and Sophia entered the large room of Lord Lawson's musicale, there was a momentary lull in the background chatter. Faces across the crowded room swung to stare at the two of them before talking resumed. Clearly conversation was shifting to the subject of the Earl of Saunton's unexpected nuptials with that Hayward girl.

His bride held her head up high, her arm woven through his own, and they walked in together to greet Richard's acquaintances. They soon found the Morelands and her cousin Lily near a marble column, and they arranged to sit together. Richard bid them to go ahead so he could collect refreshments for Sophia and himself.

The musicale was very crowded. Having located a server amongst the thronging guests, he held two glasses of orgeat, which he loathed but was all to be had, when he was jostled. Stumbling forward, he managed to hold the drinks steady and quickly returned to Sophia.

Taking a seat at her side, with the Abbott family lined up in chairs to her right, he handed her the drink. She pulled a face. Leaning over to him, she whispered, "When we hold our dinner parties and salons, there will not be any orgeat in sight. Must it always be sweet and watered-down?"

"You have not tried it yet," he pointed out.

"You know I am right."

He lifted his glass to take a sip, grimacing. "Indeed, it tastes like watered-down almonds with an excess of sugar."

She grinned in response.

At that moment, Lord Lawson called for the audience's attention. He was a swarthy man with graying hair at his temples, dressed in a black tailcoat, silver waistcoat, and snowy white linen. He introduced his young daughter, Lady Jane, who hurried forward to take her seat at the pianoforte with a daunted expression. Richard could not blame her. This event was very well attended, with more than a hundred guests in the room.

The debutante played the opening bars of an Irish aria which Richard did not recognize, but when she began to sing in a clear, high voice, he breathed a sigh of relief. Sophia had not overstated the Lawsons' musical talent. He settled back in his hard-backed chair, easing into a position that was more comfortable. The seat was not designed for a man of his stature, and he was compelled to drop down to stretch his legs out under the row in front of him.

The music proved excellent, and he enjoyed observing the rapt expression on his bride's face as she leaned forward to listen, tapping her foot in time beneath her skirts while her cousin swayed her head until she received a cutting glance from her mother. Sophia looked beautiful with her red-blonde hair braided into a coronet and soft curls falling to frame her face, which was glowing with excitement.

Richard scanned the crowded room, his posture stiffening when his eyes landed on a familiar figure from his past. Lady Partridge, a striking blonde widow with an infamous reputation, was staring openly at him. Their paths had crossed once before, two years ago, under circumstances he had no desire to revisit. Her bold tastes and forward manner had left a lasting impression—one he was content to leave firmly in the past. Yet now, she was smiling at him with a knowing look, her intentions unmistakable.

He quickly averted his gaze in quiet refusal, only to spot another familiar face—Lady Wood, seated beside her imposing and brutish husband. Their paths had briefly intertwined the previous year, and though their acquaintance had been short, he had sensed an undercurrent of unhappiness in her demeanor. Tonight, her pale complexion and subdued expression only confirmed his suspicions. Lord Wood was known for his harsh temper, and Richard couldn't help but feel a pang of sympathy for the lady, wondering how much she endured in silence.

Clearing his thoughts, Richard shifted his gaze, careful not to let his lingering observations draw attention. A prickling sensation along the back of his neck made him aware of a guest seated just behind him, glaring intently in his direction. His nerve endings tingled with unease. Casting a subtle glance from the corner of his eye, he noted the dark-haired man but could not place him. A fleeting thought crossed his mind—it might be a husband with an understandable grievance.

Richard turned his gaze back to the songbird, Miss Lawson. With his storied past, it was not safe to let his eyes drift around the room. It was deuced uncomfortable to discover the musicale was littered with his indiscretions, and he would happily have stayed at home with his bride rather than be confronted by his mistakes.

As Richard thought about Sophia, his mind drifted to the quiet evening ahead, when they would leave for home. The day had unfolded pleasantly after the surprising arrival of his son was addressed. He had taken Sophia on a tour of Balfour Terrace, sharing the gallery with its treasured family portraits and recounting highlights of his family's history.

They had spent time with Ethan in the library, playing chess and enjoying the boy's eager enthusiasm for the game. Though still learning, Ethan's grasp of the rules impressed Richard, and he found satisfaction in teaching him new strategies after their initial match.

Throughout the day and during dinner, Richard and Sophia had gradually restored the easy *camaraderie* they had shared on their wedding day. The warmth and companionship between them felt natural, a promising foundation for the life they were building together.

Now that the day's tensions had eased, Richard allowed himself to imagine the quiet moments they would share later that evening. He looked forward to the intimacy of their new life together, the bond between them growing stronger as husband and wife. Sophia's warmth and trust throughout the day had only deepened his admiration for her, and he found himself eager to explore the closeness their marriage promised.

Mayhap they could leave a bit earlier than planned, allowing them time to enjoy each other's company away from the crowd. He briefly considered slipping out to ensure their carriage was first in line. Catching himself, he redirected his attention to the music, recognizing the need for patience. It had been too long since he had felt such anticipation, and the thought of sharing time alone with Sophia filled him with quiet excitement.

∽

Sophia noticed that Richard had left her side, but the popular music was riveting so she did not pay much mind.

Which was why she was so startled when he dropped back into the seat beside her.

Leaning closer, he whispered softly in her ear, "Tell your family you are feeling fatigued, so we can leave now." His warm breath brushed against her ear, sending a gentle shiver through her as her senses stirred in response.

"But I am quite alert and I am enjoying the music," she protested under her breath.

"The music is nearly over. I ordered the carriage because you and I have unfinished business." Richard said softly, his voice warm with meaning. He let his hand rest lightly on the edge of her seat, the subtle motion conveying a quiet intimacy.

Sophia's heartbeat quickened, a rush of warmth spreading through her as his words and nearness stirred her senses.

"Oh," was all she managed to say, her mind swirling with memories of the closeness they had shared—their kisses and the warmth of his embrace. She leaned toward Lily, speaking in a low voice to inform her cousin of her impending departure.

Lily, understanding at once, caught Lady Moreland's attention. The older woman turned toward Sophia with a questioning glance, prompting her to offer polite excuses and farewells. With everything settled, she prepared to leave, her heart beating faster with anticipation.

Richard rose, and she followed him out. As they walked down the corridor to the front door, he grabbed her hand. She was shocked, swiveling her head around to ensure no one could see them engaged in such impropriety, but there was only a lone footman standing next to the front door, his gaze politely averted to the opposite wall.

Soon, Richard was helping her step into the carriage. He

followed, swinging the door shut behind him and drawing the curtains for privacy. Sliding along the bench, he shifted to sit beside her, his movements deliberate and unhurried.

Sophia's breath quickened with anticipation as he reached up to caress her cheek, gently guiding her to face him. His gaze locked with hers, and he leaned closer, stopping just shy of her lips. The pause was electric, his eyes searching hers with an intensity that sent warmth flooding through her.

When he did not move further, her patience wavered. Gathering her courage, she leaned forward, pressing her lips to his in a tender kiss. A smile curved against her lips as he returned her kiss, the moment full of warmth and quiet joy.

He leaned closer, his clean-shaven cheek brushing gently against hers. "I love that you trust me," he murmured, his voice low and warm. "The way you held me this morning ... it meant more than I can say." His words, spoken so tenderly, sent a delightful shiver through her, wrapping her in a sense of closeness that left her breathless.

His hand came to rest lightly on her knee, the touch reassuring rather than bold. As his fingers brushed gently back and forth, a warmth blossomed in her chest. His lips lingered near her cheek, pressing a soft kiss before moving toward her ear. His nearness, the sound of his voice, and the gentleness of his touch overwhelmed her senses, filling her with a quiet anticipation.

Sophia let out a soft sigh, leaning into his touch as his hand settled lightly at her waist, a comforting presence that spoke of the trust and growing affection between them.

The carriage came to a sudden halt, jarring them both from the moment. Richard pulled back, his hand slipping from hers as he rested his head against the squabs with a deep, steadying breath. Sophia, flushed and unsure of what to do, watched as he closed his eyes for a moment, clearly gathering himself.

A discreet knock sounded, and the door swung open. Sophia slid to the door as the footman extended his hand to help her down. The soft glow of light spilled over the steps as Radcliffe waited calmly by the entrance to the house. She hesitated, glancing back toward the carriage, but Richard soon emerged, his expression composed as he stepped out to join her.

Together, they walked toward the house, the quiet night air a sharp contrast to the charged silence lingering between them.

"Radcliffe!"

"Yes, milord?"

"I need Shaw immediately. And send someone to assist her ladyship at once."

Sophia felt a flicker of satisfaction at the urgency in Richard's tone. It was comforting to see that his patience with the day's interruptions was as worn as her own. When he reached for her hand, pulling her gently but decisively through the front door toward the grand staircase, she couldn't help but smile. There was a certain thrill in his focused attention, and it gave her a sense of shared purpose as they ascended together.

RICHARD DIDN'T WAIT for his valet to arrive. Instead, he began wrenching off his tailcoat, tossing it across the chest of drawers. His waistcoat quickly followed, and he sat down to pull off his shoes, discarding them in haste before impatiently removing his stockings. When he started on his cravat, his fingers fumbled with the knot, his eagerness getting the better of him.

Just as his frustration peaked, he noticed Shaw's shadow cast across the floor a moment before the valet appeared in the open doorway.

"Milord! Allow me," Shaw said, hurrying forward. Richard dropped his hands, letting his manservant swiftly untangle him from the troublesome cravat.

He couldn't explain the sudden urgency coursing through him. In the past, he had always approached such moments with calm precision, but since the quiet intimacy shared in the carriage, his thoughts had been in a whirlwind. All he could focus on was the fact that his wife—his remarkable, kind-hearted wife—was in the next room.

Sophia, who had accepted his son with grace, cared little for society's approval, and valued substance over shallow connections. She was unlike anyone he had ever met, and the thought of her filled him with a mix of tenderness and longing.

The moment Shaw finished, Richard sprang to his feet, still in his trousers and linen shirt, and crossed the room in determined strides. Reaching the connecting door, he opened it with purpose, stepping into his bride's chamber with his heart pounding and a growing sense of anticipation.

CHAPTER
TEN

"The amusements and occupations of young women should be innocent, elegant, and improving."

Dr. John Gregory, A Father's Legacy to His Daughters

∼

Sophia flinched in surprise as the door to her chamber opened suddenly, the young maid attending her squealing in fright. She swung her head to find her husband standing in the doorway, his chest rising and falling as though he had hurried to reach her.

"Out," Richard commanded firmly, stepping into the room and closing the door behind him with a decisive motion.

The maid's eyes widened. "But ... her ladyship's hair?" she stammered, holding up a handful of pins as explanation.

"I will take care of her ladyship's hair," he said, his tone softening slightly as he gestured toward the dressing table. "Set the pins down and leave us."

The maid curtsied quickly, placing the pins on the table before hurrying from the room and closing the door behind her.

Sophia chuckled as she turned to Richard, her eyes glinting with amusement. "Satisfied? You frightened the poor girl."

"If she had stayed any longer, I might have frightened her more by ignoring her presence entirely," he responded with a crooked smile.

Her cheeks flushed, but she tilted her head, teasing, "Are you going to help me with my hair now, husband?"

Richard approached her with a gentleness that belied his earlier urgency, raising his hands hesitantly before beginning to remove the pins still nestled in her hair. His fingers worked carefully, and as he unraveled the braids and her hair fell loose to her waist, she couldn't help but feel a shiver of delight at his touch.

"So beautiful," he murmured, the words so soft she barely caught them. He leaned closer, breathing in the faint, familiar scent of her hair before stepping around to clasp her hand. "Come," he said, drawing her to her feet.

His gaze swept over her, his green eyes locking with hers, and she felt her heart flutter at the intensity she found there. "Are you ready? For this?" he asked quietly, his voice carrying a vulnerability she had not expected. "After everything that has happened, I would understand if ..." He gestured toward the bed, searching for the words.

Sophia rose onto her toes and pressed a soft kiss to his lips. "I do not wish to wait," she said simply.

Richard exhaled sharply, a smile curving his lips as he lifted her into his arms as though she weighed nothing at all. He carried her to the bed, his movements steady and purposeful, before lowering her gently onto the turned-down sheets.

Sophia gazed up at him, her heart racing with anticipation. "You are most impressive," she whispered, a playful glint in her eye.

He chuckled, shaking his head. "So I have been told," he replied, though his tone softened as he continued. "But with you, I am learning a new kind of admiration. You challenge me, Sophia. And I want to build a life with you, not just as my wife, but as my partner."

Her smile widened as she reached for his hand, feeling a warmth blossom in her chest. "And I with you," she said.

The moments that followed were filled with quiet laughter, whispered words, and an intimacy that deepened their bond as they began to truly share their lives. Sophia marveled at the strength of the man before her, not just in body but in heart, and as they lay together in the quiet stillness of the evening, she felt a certainty she had rarely known: life with Richard would be an adventure, and together, they could face whatever might come.

RICHARD AWOKE as dawn's soft light filtered into Sophia's room. Staring up at the fabric draped across the four-poster frame, he reflected on the wonder of the previous night. Somehow, Sophia made him forget his past missteps and filled him with hope that he could become a better, more honorable man. Her presence eased his worries and made him feel whole in a way he had never known.

He couldn't help but compare the peace he felt with her to the hollow distractions of his past. Had he been trying to bury his troubles in fleeting company? Sophia made him want to live fully, while others had merely helped him escape.

Rolling onto his side, he prepared to rise, only to startle at the sight of Ethan standing beside the bed, his wide green eyes watching him at almost eye level.

"Ethan?"

"Good morning, Papa. I've been waiting for you to wake up. Emma says it is polite to let people wake on their own instead of startling them."

Richard blinked, still groggy. "Uh ... good morning."

"I've been waiting a while," Ethan continued, unabashed. "We wake up early on the farm, but Emma says city people stay up late."

Richard let the boy's remarks pass, rubbing his eyes. "How did you find me?"

"I followed your *vah-let*," Ethan said, stumbling over the unfamiliar word. "But when you weren't in your room, I tried the other doors. Papa, what is a *vah-let*?"

"A valet is a servant who helps a gentleman dress and look his best," Richard explained, suppressing a yawn.

Ethan's round face scrunched as he considered this. "Am I a gentleman?"

Richard hesitated, considering the question carefully. Society would say no, given Ethan's parentage. But Richard knew a true gentleman had little to do with lineage and everything to do with character. "A gentleman is someone who is well-mannered and considerate of others," he said at last. "And by that definition, you are certainly a gentleman."

Ethan's grin was instant and wide. "Does that mean I'll get a *vah-let*?"

Richard chuckled, ruffling the boy's curly hair. "When

you are older, perhaps. But only if you promise not to wander off from your nursemaid."

Ethan's expression turned pensive. "She's supposed to stay with me all the time?"

"Yes. To keep you safe and make sure you eat," Richard replied.

"Mama said I could go anywhere in the house. Did I make a mistake finding you?"

Richard froze, the word *Mama* ringing in his ears. "Mama?"

Ethan nodded, pointing to the cascade of red-blonde hair spilling across the pillow. "I asked Sophia if she was my mama, and she said I could call her that if I wanted. I never had a mama before, and she seems nice. Do you think she'd mind?"

Richard's heart twisted, a surge of emotion leaving him momentarily speechless. "I cannot say for certain," he said softly. "But I think she would like it very much."

Ethan beamed at this reassurance. Richard marveled at how fortunate he was to have such a sweet-natured son. He wondered briefly about Emma, the woman Ethan had mentioned, and whether she had played a role in raising the boy so well.

Shaking himself from his thoughts, Richard realized he was trapped under the covers without clothing and could not rise until Ethan left. "Could you find your way back to the nursery, Ethan?"

The boy nodded, leaning in for a hug before trotting out of the room and closing the door behind him.

Richard rose quickly, pulling on his shirt and smoothing the covers. He laid Sophia's shift across the bed for her to find, a rush of warmth flooding him as he remembered the tenderness they had shared. Brushing those thoughts aside, he dressed swiftly and headed for his own chamber.

There, he found Shaw, who looked up with a disapproving sniff.

"Is there a problem, Shaw?"

The valet pursed his thin lips. "The coat, milord. I fear it may be irreparably damaged."

Richard sighed but managed a smile. "If anyone can fix it, it's you. You are the best valet in London, after all."

The praise mollified Shaw, who held out a folded piece of paper. "I found this in your coat last night."

Richard frowned as he took the note, wondering how it had ended up there. He unfolded it, his pulse quickening as he read the threatening words scrawled inside. His blood ran cold.

Confound it! What fresh trouble had landed in his lap? Just yesterday, Sophia had confessed that her marriage to him had been motivated by a need for security, and now this?

His mind raced. He needed counsel, someone wise and trustworthy. Perry, though usually dependable, was too preoccupied with his own affairs. No, he needed someone more measured. Someone like ... Halmesbury.

The decision made, Richard resolved to send for the duke, a man who had offered him guidance despite their complicated history. But first, he would take steps to ensure Sophia and Ethan were safe. Whatever this threat meant, he would face it head-on, determined to protect the family he was beginning to cherish.

~

Sophia awoke much later than usual, a soft glow of contentment wrapping around her as memories of the night before surfaced. Richard had been so tender, his care and patience leaving her both touched and awed. His devotion to her comfort and happiness had been unmistakable, and the memory of his loving attentions made her cheeks warm.

She smiled to herself, feeling a deep sense of gratitude for the man who had shown her such kindness.

Humming a popular tune from the musicale the night before, she entered the breakfast room. Several footmen were in attendance, so she assumed her maid had alerted them she was coming down to break her fast. She had met all of the servants over the past two days, yet she noticed a new man standing by the door.

She turned to him for an introduction but hesitated when she took in his appearance. The unknown manservant was several inches shorter than the others. Footmen were usually chosen for their height and handsome features because they were part of a household's display of wealth and status. This man was not only shorter, his livery was ill-fitting, as if tailored for one of the taller men. Sophia hated to be critical, but the man was not ... handsome. In fact, he was a bit rough-and-tumble, with his stocky build and a dark shadow across his clean-shaven cheeks. He looked like he might be quite hairy, bearing evidence of the overshadow of a beard this early in the day.

"Hello?"

"Um ... milady." He acknowledged her with a clumsy bow. It did not appear he was familiar with the movement. Sophia fought back a frown. Something was off. Also, had the man been inside the breakfast room when she arrived, or had he followed her into the room?

"Your name is ...?"

"I am ... John, milady." John appeared to forget his own name. Sophia grew ever more suspicious.

"Have you worked at Balfour Terrace long, John?"

The man dropped his eyes for a moment. "Not long, milady. I arrived from one of the country estates recently."

She hated to be rude, but a warning bell was sounding in her head. "Well ... pleased to meet you ... John." With that, she continued her path to the sideboard with covered dishes.

Sophia was an observer of people—needs must, to avoid betrothal for three Seasons—so she had learned how to read people, especially men, in order to dissuade their attentions. She definitely would seek Richard out after she ate to ask about this bizarre footman who had turned up.

CHAPTER
ELEVEN

"A woman of delicacy and sensibility seldom receives much happiness from the generality of mankind."

Dr. John Gregory, A Father's Legacy to His Daughters

~

Richard sat at his mahogany desk, reading his neglected correspondence of the past few days. He was to meet with Halmesbury that afternoon at one of their mutual clubs, White's. He could do nothing more about the note planted on his person at the musicale the night before. All he could do was attempt to address his mounting work before the meeting.

He heard Perry's distinctive gait enter his study, then loiter near his desk. Richard bit back his irritation and looked up to find his brother looking disconcerted. *Hades, has something else happened?* He did not think he could handle any more surprises this morning.

Perry fidgeted in discomfort before opening his mouth to speak, then shutting it.

"What is it?" Richard asked in the most patient tone he could manage, not quite daring to hear the answer.

"You know those print shops? The ones that display caricatures in their windows, like the ones Rowlandson and Cruikshank draw?"

Richard closed his eyes, a wave of unease washing over him. Despite his less-than-virtuous past, he had largely managed to avoid being the subject of scurrilous drawings—unlike the new king, whose reputation often suffered at the hands of satirical illustrators. Judging by his brother's lack of composure, however, Richard feared his luck might have taken a turn for the worse.

Perry continued. "I was walking past some of those shops this morning, and I saw a great quantity of these displayed." He tossed a paper on the desk as if he wished to be parted from it as quickly as possible, then swiftly stepped away.

Richard opened his eyes and reluctantly glanced down at the colored print in his hands. The illustration appeared to depict him, dressed in nightclothes and surrounded by a tangle of scandalously dressed women. Across from his likeness stood a figure unmistakably meant to be Sophia, her flowing red-blonde hair a clear identifier.

He exhaled sharply, a mix of agitation and disbelief rising in his chest, before lifting the image to read the caption beneath it.

Somerset earls and their scandalous habits. "I swear I did not invite these women to our wedding night."

Richard dropped the print like it was scalding hot. Exhaling heavily, he pushed his chair back to rise, running his hand through his hair in agitation.

Perry ventured a question. "Do you suppose one of the servants tattled about what happened?"

Richard paused, his thoughts turning to the threatening note he had found in his pocket. He shook his head, the pieces beginning to fall into place. "No, it must have been the man who let those women into the house. It must be him."

Perry tilted his head. "What do you mean? This is another prank?"

Richard scowled. "Not a prank. I believe whoever let those women in wished me ill. I received a threatening note, so it must be linked because it is too many situations converging at once to be a coincidence."

"But who?"

"I do not know. A jilted lover? A wronged husband? The possibilities are endless, given the foolish choices of my past." He raked a hand through his hair, exhaling sharply. "Why, oh why, could I not have exercised a shred of self-restraint?"

"May I read the note?"

Richard tugged it out of his coat and threw it at Perry, who caught it deftly. He resumed pacing, thinking about how he had decided not to tell Sophia about the note yet. He must alert her to the caricature, however. She might be a laughingstock, and it was only fair to warn her to expect trouble the next time she left their home.

Perry whistled after reading the page. "What will you do?"

"I am meeting with Halmesbury this afternoon to discuss it. This is beyond my experience, and I need an outside perspective. In the meantime, I increased security for Sophia and Ethan. My wife married me for safety, and all I have done is bring her chaos!"

His brother came over to hand the note back. "Halmesbury is a good idea because I find myself quite unprepared for this. But what can I do to help, brother?"

Perry's face reflected genuine concern. Richard sighed in relief. His brother's recalcitrance of the past few days appeared to have passed, for there was no evidence of it now. His help in dealing with the matter would be valuable.

"Perhaps you can attend your clubs and listen for gossip. Any clues to who is tormenting me would be helpful."

Perry nodded. "I can do that. What will you tell ... your wife?"

Richard dropped his gaze. "I will need to warn her about the gossip, but I do not want to scare her about the note. I must take care of it, but she will be safe. I made sure of it."

Drawing in a steadying breath, Richard moved to his desk and retrieved the dreadful print before leaving the room in search of Sophia. After checking a couple of rooms, he finally found her at breakfast, seated with a full plate and raising a strawberry to her lips. The sight brought back memories of the tender kisses they had shared the night before, a warmth blooming in his chest at the thought. "Richard!" she called out in delight, dropping the strawberry.

"Good morning, Sophia. Did you sleep well?" A pretty flush covered her cheeks, and he recognized that she was thinking similar thoughts to his own.

"Yes, my lord."

Richard grinned for a moment, suspecting he was being 'my lorded' because she was embarrassed and nervous.

"Can you clear the room?" He directed the command at the footmen, who quickly left and closed the door.

Sophia's features reflected worry when he walked over to pull out the chair next to her. "Is something wrong? With Ethan?"

"Ethan is fine. I have a bit of news this morning. Bad news. I wanted to share it with you before you became aware of it ... some other way." He offered her the print he was carrying. Perplexed, she accepted it and scanned the print.

"Oh my!" She made a snorting sound and her shoulders shook. Richard's heart sank. He was causing his bride to sob not three days in to their marriage.

Then the snort turned into ... laughter? Sophia howled, wiping tears of mirth from her eyes. Had she lost her mind? Had he driven her to hysteria with one too many problems? Thankfully, he had not informed her of the threatening note or—

"This is priceless!" Her exclamation marked the end of her laughter. Richard raised his eyebrows. Noting his expression, she raised her own. "Never say this concerns you?"

"Of course it does. I made you the object of gossip and—"

"Pish! Marrying you has made me interesting for a minute. But next week someone will draw yet another print of King George and that silly rumored trial of Queen Caroline. All will be forgotten of the Saunton household, and we will move on. Whatever we must contend with will be no worse than polite society's reaction to Ethan living in our household. If I can cope with that, then I can cope with this, too ... but I appreciate the warning," she finished in a cajoling tone, as if she was comforting him.

Richard hadn't realized he was holding his breath until

her words prompted him to exhale in relief. "What did I do to deserve you?" he asked softly.

Sophia coughed delicately into her hand, her eyes glinting with mischief. "Quite a few things I would rather not mention."

Richard chuckled, catching the playful reference. Her wit and warmth made his heart swell, reminding him once again of how fortunate he was.

Grabbing her hand, he raised it to his lips. "You are a marvelous woman! Beyond compare."

She blushed in response before waving him off so she could eat her meal. Richard was determined to prevent any more crises from arising before his wife ever discovered that he put the valued security she sought in jeopardy with his immoral past. He would finish his correspondence and then it would be time to meet Halmesbury to discuss the note burning a hole in his pocket.

Sophia held her skirts aloft while climbing the stairs to the nursery. She planned to take Ethan out to the gardens to enjoy some sunshine, and perhaps share some hothouse fruit with the boy. Reaching the landing, she turned in to the corridor leading to the nursery. Out of the corner of her eye, she noticed a flicker of movement and spun around in surprise to see that the new footman, John, was climbing the stairs behind her. He quickly stepped over to the banister, pulled out a dust cloth, and started wiping at the grooves.

Sophia frowned. She thought the chambermaids did the dusting. The man was behaving suspiciously, and she did not trust him. Perhaps she needed to talk to Richard about it when he returned home. News of the print had caused her to forget her desire to talk with him about the new footman earlier. Turning back, she made her way to the nursery, where she found yet another footman dusting picture frames hanging on the wall. Stopping near him, she looked him over, noting she had not met this servant either. He gave her a quick bow. "Milady."

"Are you new?"

"No, milady. I ... am recently arrived from ... one of Lord Saunton's country estates." The man spoke like he was remembering lines in a play. Sophia's suspicions mounted once more.

"And your name is?"

The man, who was very similar in appearance to the footman she had met at breakfast, looked uncertain for a second. He was slightly taller, but his livery was just as disheveled and his collar was crooked.

"John, milady."

"John?"

"Yes, milady."

"Like the other footman just arrived."

His expression was strained. "Yes, milady."

"Two Johns?"

He gave a nod.

"Both arrived from the Saunton country estates?"

He nodded again, appearing to be tongue-tied.

"Well. Good to meet you, John. I hope you enjoy London."

Sophia abruptly opened the door to the nursery before he could reply. If he offered her another lie, she was going to vent her frustration, so she strode away.

When she entered, she found Ethan drawing on a page with a graphite pencil while his nursemaid, Daisy, sat across from him. His sweet face lit up at the sight of her. "Mama!"

Sophia froze in surprise. His small face scrunched. "May I call you Mama? Papa said he thought you would like it."

Sophia's eyes prickled, a lump in her throat while she nodded with enthusiasm. "Of course! I was just surprised. If you want to call me ... that ... I would be most honored." She turned her face to dab at her eyes. When she turned back, Ethan was right before her, having crossed the room as silently as a cat.

"I have never had a mama before," he said earnestly, his small face angled up to look at her.

On the verge of weeping, Sophia swallowed the thick emotion and dropped to her haunches.

"Now you do." She reached out to hug him, and he ran up to embrace her with his small arms. Sophia rested her cheek on the crown of his head, his thick curling hair tickling her nose, and she did her best to fight back the tears welling up. Across the room, Daisy caught her eye and gave a wide smile in encouragement.

Sophia leaned back to look Ethan in the face. "Have you eaten?"

"Yes. Daisy and I had breakfast early. Not as early as the farm, but early enough."

"Good. Would you like to go with me to the gardens?"

He nodded vigorously. Sophia smiled, rising to her feet to take his little hand. Daisy rose to follow her out of the room.

Exiting into the hall, Sophia came to a stop when she found the two Johns both waiting outside the door. She frowned, mistrusting that the two men were, in fact, footmen when she noted how they were slouching against the wall, quickly straightening when she had opened the door and surprised them.

There was no doubt in her mind that they were up to something. She resolved to seek Richard out.

～

STILL WORRYING about the unexpected note, Richard strode into White's for his meeting with the Duke of Halmesbury. He soon found his cousin sitting at a table with two fresh drinks on it.

The duke always put Richard in mind of a Norse god, with his powerful frame, broad good looks, and full blond hair. Although Richard was no lightweight at six feet, his cousin topped him by several inches. But Halmesbury possessed a friendly manner, and he was a true gentleman, which acted as a counter-weight to his intimidating physical stature.

Richard collapsed into the chair next to his cousin, the stresses of the day weighing him down.

Arching an eyebrow, he indicated the drinks with a nod of his head. "I thought you did not drink."

"We are sitting at White's. It is easier to order a drink to avoid being constantly pestered by the servers. You can have mine, if you like. I have not touched it."

"My bride prefers if I do not drink. Something to do with her father, I think. It is the least I can do, given the chaos of the past few days."

"Indeed, it quite surprised me to read about your nuptials, considering you made no mention of courting the lady at our last meeting. When we discussed your list of paramours."

Richard flushed at the memory of that particular meeting. Thankfully, he had since made amends to several of the women on the list. "The union was unexpected. I had intended to court her properly, but during my first visit, she interviewed me for the position of husband and then threw herself into my arms just as her uncle entered the room."

Halmesbury's lips twitched, clearly suppressing a smile. "The countess compromised *you*?"

"Indeed," Richard replied, shaking his head with a mix of exasperation and admiration. "After confirming my intentions were sincere, she declared her uncle would never agree to the match and kissed me senseless."

Halmesbury snorted, trying not to laugh. "An apropos manner for such an accomplished rogue to be caught."

"Rogue no more. Laugh, if you will, but she is a unique and intriguing woman."

Halmesbury frowned. "And my Annabel was not?"

Richard grimaced. It was a fair question, one he had asked himself countless times since meeting Sophia. Why had he not changed his ways when he had asked Annabel for her hand in marriage? His cousin was his closest friend, apart from his brother, and the memory of that failure still lingered, even after nearly two years.

"I ... I was not ready to change then," he admitted, his voice low. "I was dishonest with myself and incapable of forming a true connection with her. You made the right choice when you stepped in. Annabel deserved better—she deserved you."

Halmesbury leaned back in his chair, astonished. Richard squirmed, unsure what to say next. "Well, it would seem quite a change has been wrought since I saw you last?"

"I have been meeting with the women I wronged and

setting matters to right with them. In fact ... I met with Caroline Brown and made matters right with her."

"The maid whom Annabel ... witnessed you with?" Richard gave a nod. "Annabel will be pleased. She has expressed worry about the girl from time to time. They were apparently close."

Richard stuck a finger behind his tight collar, attempting to ease the pressure restricting his breathing. This was so dashed awkward to discuss with the husband of the woman he had wronged so unjustly. He caught the moment Halmesbury took pity and changed the subject.

"Tell me about your wife?"

Richard blew out a breath in relief. "She is feisty and intelligent. And more direct than I expected. We have experienced an outrageous few days, but the countess has shown great composure and presence of mind. I have met few women so impressive ..." He stopped, not wishing to reference Annabel again. "But now I fear I may have put her in danger when I married her."

Looking round to ensure no one was within earshot, and appreciating the duke's foresight in ordering the drinks so that the servers did not hover close by, Richard quickly filled his cousin in on the events of the past few days. There was much to discuss, including the discovery that he had fathered a natural born son who had arrived in his home, and that someone had placed a threatening note in his pocket, most likely at the Lawson musicale. When he was done, he leaned back in his chair to hear what the duke would advise.

"So, you have found a woman you can love."

Richard straightened up, knocking against the table and nearly upsetting the untouched drinks. "I admire her. With her help, I believe I can remain on the path to regain my honor. I did not mention love."

Halmesbury stared at Richard without a word. After a deep silence, he spoke. "You admire the woman. It is my understanding from our last meeting that overhearing her at the Astley ball prompted you to begin this quest you are on. You are attracted to her, and you appear very concerned with her well-being. It is not love?"

Richard shook his head in denial. His family history proved that Balfours were incapable of love. The only one in his family who had possessed the capacity to love was his mother, but she had had no Balfour blood in her veins. Love had broken her heart and contributed to her death. Love was a foolish endeavor.

"Nevertheless, I brought you a wedding gift." The duke placed a small leather-bound volume on the table.

Richard picked it up. "Poems of Wedded Bliss?"

"The author is Lord John Pettigrew. Do you remember him from Oxford?" Richard nodded. "John's writing is the reason I met Annabel. The reason I was ready to risk marrying again after the death of my first wife. Since his own marriage two years ago, he has published his advice on marriage in the form of some very fine poetry. The poems contain exceptional advice about maintaining a happy marriage. The importance of honesty and such. I highly recommend reading it."

Richard's agitation grew with each mention of the duke's wife, the spirited yet sheltered noblewoman who had ended their engagement after discovering him in an indiscreet moment with her maid. Unwilling to linger on the painful memory, he quickly shifted the conversation, determined to mask his discomfort.

He was not ready to confront his past with Annabel—

not yet. The weight of shame over his behavior, both then and afterward, pressed heavily on him, making it difficult to breathe each time her name arose.

"Thank you." Richard put the small volume in one of his pockets and removed the note from another.

"The matter of the note, it is quite pressing. Sophia, and even Ethan, may be at risk. I have increased security, but I must take stronger action to protect them."

The duke nodded. "I understand. You feel the responsibility of your new family."

Family? He now had ... family? To protect and safeguard against the threats of the world around him. He shook his head in disbelief. He had not made that connection until the duke voiced it, but a wife and a son waited for him at home. His need to defend them from this fresh threat filled him with resolve.

"May I see the note?"

Richard unfolded it to stare down at the ominous words inked on the page. So few words, yet so much meaning contained within the simplicity of two sentences.

You enjoy stealing the loved ones of other men. Perhaps someone should steal yours?

The duke pulled a face. "The note implies that you interfered in loving relationships?"

Richard was indignant. "Never."

Halmesbury arched a questioning blond eyebrow, his gaze steady. Richard avoided meeting his cousin's eye, focusing instead on his hand resting near the untouched brandy on the table. The words he was about to speak felt heavy, leaving a sour taste in his mouth. "It is ... easier to pursue the attention of unhappy wives," he admitted reluctantly.

He glanced up and caught the flash of distaste that

crossed his cousin's face before the duke composed himself, but Richard could not blame him for the slight reaction. Even he was experiencing a reaction to the shallowness of his past pursuits. He had awoken from the bad dream to realize that he was the villain of the piece. Now he wished to reinvent himself as an honorable gentleman. There was still much work ahead. But first, he needed to ensure his ... *family* ... would be safe.

Halmesbury pushed the note back across the table. "You need to tell the countess."

"But she married me for security. If she thinks I cannot provide it to her, she may turn away from me. Or leave me, to return to the Morelands."

Halmesbury shrugged. "I do not think you described a woman who is so inclined. Your priority, now that you have provided additional security to protect her, is to keep your developing marriage strong. You cannot withhold a secret of this magnitude without consequences."

Richard grabbed the note to put it away, irritated. This meeting was turning out to be most unhelpful. He could not frighten his new wife with this problem, which was his fault to begin with. It was mortifying how much she had been forced to contend with since the day they said their vows, and he could not reveal that she had put herself in danger by joining his household.

He knew she was an exceptional woman, but this situation was beyond the pale. Nay. He needed to deal with this matter without alerting her to what another of his past mistakes had exposed them to. Sophia deserved the safety she sought in marrying him, and he would move heaven and earth to provide it.

Halmesbury sighed. "I see you will not."

"I cannot. Eventually, my past will be too much and her patience will reach its limit."

"I do not think you give the young woman enough credit. From what you described, she entered this marriage with her eyes open, willing to assist you on your quest. But I cannot make your decision for you. I can only encourage you to think on it. There was a time you encouraged me to talk to Annabel rather than run from my feelings. I now encourage you to do the same because it is liberating to have a life partner. Someone who is always at your side, no matter what you may have done. Or have to do. I urge you to reconsider your decision to conceal this matter."

Richard gave a curt nod. He would think about it, but he doubted he would change his mind.

"Do you have any idea who could have sent it?"

"Any number of men who might consider themselves wronged."

"I suggest you make a finite list and then task your runners to investigate. The goal would be to reduce it down to a manageable list of likely suspects while maintaining increased security. Just realize that your countess would be better equipped to avoid danger if she is aware that she needs to be cautious."

"I agreed to think on it!" Richard quelled his rebellion. The duke provided excellent guidance in a matter where Richard's thoughts were compromised by the turmoil of fear for his new family, and he needed to keep a cool head. "I apologize. Your guidance is appreciated. I will do what you recommended and start listing out suspects to investigate until I uncover the source of this threat."

Halmesbury smiled. "I hope you uncover it swiftly. If there is anything I can do to help, do not hesitate to ask."

CHAPTER
TWELVE

"Dignity in a woman commands respect and admiration."

Dr. John Gregory, A Father's Legacy to His Daughters

~

Just off St. James's Place, having failed to locate Richard earlier, Sophia wandered through the modiste shop her husband had recommended for her new wardrobe befitting the wife of an earl. Lily was accompanying her, animated in her exploration of the explosion of colorful fabrics to inspect.

"It is so exciting! You can wear so many colors now that you are wed. I am quite envious." Sophia smiled at her exuberant cousin. Lily was such a ball of energy, she never failed to lift Sophia's spirits or distract her from her worries. Worries such as the fact that one of the new Johns had joined her in the carriage for this outing.

The coachman and the customary footman had sat on the box, but the shorter of the two Johns abruptly entered the carriage behind her without so much as a by-your-leave. It was unprecedented, in her experience, to have a male servant inside the carriage. When he failed to explain himself, Sophia remained quiet and tensely observant. The only reason she had not leapt out to run back into the house was the sight of Radcliffe on the front steps. The butler had been watching closely, displaying no surprise when the footman embarked, which allayed her initial fear. Still, she resolved to talk to Richard the moment there was an opportunity.

When she had collected Lily from her home, her cousin had entered the carriage and then hesitated in dismay at the sight of a footman installed on the opposite seat, but his presence prevented her from questioning Sophia about it.

It had been a relief to reach the modiste shop and exit the vehicle, but she noted that The Shorter John, which she had taken to calling him in her mind, followed them up to the entrance and was currently visible through the front window while her cousin chattered about which colors Sophia should consider.

Turning her attention back to Lily, Sophia leafed through the fashion plates they had been provided. Thinking about her husband, her thoughts strayed to how he had known to send her to this particular modiste.

The proprietress was an elegant Italian woman, dressed in a stylish but simple gown. This was unusual because most modistes were obsequious French women, and a large majority of those were English women feigning their French accents and names in an attempt to be fashionable to their clientele.

Her stomach tightened as an unbidden pang of jealousy crept in. Had Richard brought other women here in the past to gift them with expensive clothing? Mistresses? Widows? Perhaps even lonely wives or celebrated courtesans? She forced herself to stop the train of thought before it spiraled further, her chest aching at the mere idea.

"How is it?"

Sophia looked up to find Lily's large brown eyes fixed on her. She had just quietly regaled her cousin with the events of the past couple of days, but her thoughts distracted her and she found she had lost the thread of the conversation.

"How is what?"

"Married life? Are you enjoying life with the earl?" Her petite cousin appeared to be holding her breath.

"His past has created some interesting situations to deal with."

"Pish! You knew it would. How are you enjoying him?"

Sophia hesitated, thinking. "I ... like him. He has been most considerate, making a point to forewarn me about situations. He is learning to be a generous father, and he has spent a great deal of time with me and his son since I arrived." She checked the shop to ensure no one could overhear her before dropping her voice. "I very much enjoy the kissing. Saunton is ... I do not know ... I am becoming very attached. I think this marriage may ... may ..."

"May?"

"He needs me so, and he treats me like an equal. I ... may be falling in love with the earl."

Lily clapped her gloved hands in glee. "I knew it. I knew he was the one for you. And if anyone is capable of managing such a scoundrel of a man, it is you, Sophia!"

Sophia shook her head. Her cousin was such a hopeless optimist. There was much to deal with at Balfour Terrace before she could claim her happily ever after.

But I am on my way!

She sighed. Lily's optimism was contagious, it would appear.

Over at the counter, Signora Ricci was conversing with two customers, waving her hands in the manner of the Italians. She did not notice when the bell on the door sounded, but Sophia was startled and turned her head to see who entered the shop.

Sophia recognized two women she had met at the Yardley ball, one of whom was a young widow known for her daring fashion choices. The widow's ball gowns had been so tightly fitted and cut so low that Sophia had winced at the thought of how uncomfortable her stays must have been.

Today, the woman was dressed in a striking scarlet day gown that was, to Sophia's mind, rather bold for the occasion. True to form, the bodice was cut so low that Sophia could not help but feel a twinge of concern for the woman's dignity. Surely the gown would betray her at any moment?

The pretty blonde caught her eye and arched a perfect eyebrow, fixing her cold blue eyes on Sophia. A wave of pure malevolence crossed the distance between them.

"Lady Saunton. It is a pleasure to see you out and about. I did so hope that those vicious prints circulating the *ton* about your wedding night would not cause you to hide within Balfour Terrace."

Lily gasped, but Sophia found herself impressed—the woman's dig was well played.

"Thank you, Lady Partridge. I do appreciate your concern."

The succubus narrowed her eyes with a sly smile. "And how is Richard? I have not yet called at Balfour Terrace this Season." Her companion, a finely dressed lady with an air of mischief, let out a quiet, knowing laugh at the remark.

Sophia kept her composure, but she could see Lily's delicate brown eyebrows shooting up to her hairline. The viper was not subtle. Richard was not known for holding events at Balfour Terrace, so there could be only one insinuation to draw from her remark. Lady Partridge had visited Richard's home for reasons that were quite obvious to conclude.

"He is well." Sophia offered a polite smile, all the while searching for an appropriate way to excuse herself from the conversation. Surely nothing good could come from lingering with a brazen creature of such questionable intentions.

"Please send him my regards. We enjoy a very special connection, and I am sure he will be pleased to hear I am thinking of him."

Sophia reached her limit. This ladybird was stepping far beyond the bounds of good taste with her implications. Sophia needed to mark her territory regarding her husband, or his former paramours would devour her with malicious remarks in shops across London. Let the word get around that Sophia possessed teeth and claws.

"You are a widow, if I am not mistaken?"

"What of it?"

"And the time of your ... memorable connection with Lord Saunton, you were a widow then?"

The woman scowled in confusion. "Yes, what is your point?"

"Oh, I was just thinking ... You are quite young and of childbearing age. If your relationship with my husband was so ... *special* ... then he could have proposed to you, not so? Yet, he did not. He married me after several Seasons of hunting for his bride. Why is that, do you think? I hate to state the obvious, but ... Mayhap your time together was not as memorable as you claim?"

Both Lady Partridge and her friend gasped in wounded outrage, while Sophia maintained a politely interested expression. The she-devil struggled to find a retort, apparently not quick enough to engage in verbal sparring. After a few seconds passed with her mouth opening and closing in the manner of a fish, Sophia took her cousin by the arm. "Look, Lily. I see celestial blue silk near the back wall. Shall we examine it more closely?"

Lily appeared agog over the scene she was witnessing, but she managed a nod, accompanying Sophia away from the speechless women.

"We are to remain in the shop with them?" her cousin whispered beneath her breath.

"I am in need of a wardrobe. If I depart a shop every time a small-minded bit of muslin enters the door, I will never replace these debutante gowns your mother made me wear."

"I cannot believe what you said. You are so brave."

"Not brave. Just determined to live my life without strumpets interfering."

WHEN SOPHIA FINALLY REACHED HOME, she stalked toward Richard's study. Pausing by the door which was slightly ajar, she heard his brother, Perry. "No, not him. He slipped and broke his leg over Christmas, so he is languishing at his Derbyshire estate until he recovers. It was a bad break."

"I will cross him off the list, then," Richard replied.

Sophia pushed open the door and stormed in. Her husband leapt to his feet, distracting her for a moment. He looked very fine in a green tailcoat that picked out the color of his eyes. "Sophia, you are ba—"

"Did you hire guardsmen for Ethan and myself?"

He glanced away. "What do you mean?"

"The two *Johns* in the ill-fitting livery? Both of whom are *coincidentally* recently arrived from your country estates?"

"*Four* Johns," piped Perry from behind her. She turned to find him sprawled in one of the ivory armchairs, nursing a drink in his hand.

"Four?"

Perry gave a flippant nod, lifting his tumbler to sip on his brandy with his distinctive Balfour eyes fixed on hers.

Sophia spun back to Richard. "Did you hire *four* guardsmen?"

Richard glowered at his brother. "I did."

"Why have I met only two, then?"

"Two of them are on night watch."

"And *why* have you hired guardsmen?"

She saw something in his eyes. Shame, perhaps? "No reason. I am an important man, and I now have a new son and bride in my home. It seemed best to be cautious."

She narrowed her eyes at her lying husband. He was having difficulty meeting her eyes, and he moved his hand to cover a list he had been writing when she entered.

"Are you hiding something, Richard?"

"No."

"I do not believe you."

"It is simple. You and Ethan are my responsibility, and I am taking precautions to ensure your security."

Sophia tilted her head, recalling her mention of security the day before. Was it possible that conversation had prompted him to do so? She felt slightly mollified until her attention returned to Richard, who, she noted, was fidgeting like a schoolboy caught in a lie. Then, no. Something had happened, but he elected not to inform her. Sophia flushed with resentment. He had promised that they would be honest with each other, but now, after a mere three days of marriage, he was keeping a secret.

He did not trust her! She thought they had made so much progress, but ... *He does not trust me!*

Taking a deep breath, she tried again. "Are you sure there is nothing you wish to tell me?"

Richard looked like a guilty child, shaking his head in dissent. The resentment in her chest burst into flames. She wished to claw him in her anger—the stupid, glib idiot.

"I met your dear friend, Lady Partridge, today." Richard visibly flinched. Behind her, she heard Perry choking back a laugh.

"She is very eager to renew your *special* acquaintanceship." This time, there was no concealing it. Perry laughed out loud.

Richard held out his hands in appeal. "It was two or three years ago—"

Sophia did not wait for his excuses. She was already heading out of the room, ignoring his response.

RICHARD LEFT his brother in the study to follow Sophia. When he could not find her in the library or lower rooms, he eventually tried her chambers and found her sitting on a window ledge, seething. Her eyes were directed out to the street, but he sensed she was not seeing anything, instead lost in her thoughts.

He wished to tell her the truth, but more than that, he

wanted to maintain her esteem and admiration. How could he tell her that, despite the fact she sought security by becoming his wife, not three days into the marriage, he had brought the enemy to the gates? He could not. He thought about what the duke had advised him, but he just could not bring himself to risk losing her regard.

Instead, he would need to use his well-honed charms to coax her out of her mood. A little misdirection to restore her good humor. "I apologize for not informing you about the guardsmen."

She turned her head to scowl at him.

"You and Ethan are too important. Having a family depending on me is an unfamiliar experience. I promise I am being cautious because I care about you."

His knees went weak with relief when her face softened to its normal composure. "I appreciate that. I appreciate that this is new to you."

Richard stepped closer, his gaze soft as he looked at her. "I have never known a woman like you before, Sophia. And now, a child ... such a tiny, precious child. At times, it feels like an overwhelming responsibility."

She tilted her head back to look at him, her iridescent blue eyes speculative. "This is quite a change in circumstances, is it not?"

He nodded, running a hand through his hair. "I had no idea one's life could change this much in such a short period. I had to step in when I inherited the title. But this ... this is different. This is ... real. Living, breathing *family* under my roof, depending on me to make the right decisions to keep both of you safe."

Sophia reached out a slender hand to capture his own. "I understand. I apologize for my impatience."

He looked down at their clasped hands, and something

stirred in his chest. Mayhap Halmesbury was right. Was it possible that a Balfour was developing a true depth of feeling for his wife? What horrific timing to have his emotions entangled for the first time in his adulthood, just when he needed to keep a clear head and find the source of the machinations plaguing his life.

He raised her hand to his lips and placed a gentle kiss on her fingers, relieved that he had distracted her from her suspicions.

CHAPTER
THIRTEEN

"Decorum in conduct is essential to a woman's respectability."

Dr. John Gregory, A Father's Legacy to His Daughters

~

Sophia knew her foolish husband believed he had distracted her from her suspicions, but she merely relented when she noticed the strain visible in the tense lines of his face. For a man of just seven and twenty, his worries were aging him before her eyes these past few days. If only he would share the burden with her, but the oaf was keeping secrets. Most likely because of ridiculous male pride. However, she had promised him patience while he grew used to having a partner in his life, so she would provide it. Within reason.

She set aside her suspicions and allowed herself to enjoy dinner with him. Later that night, he had shown her just how his devilish reputation had been earned, proving himself to be both attentive and entirely captivating. Her cheeks warmed as she recalled the moments of pure bliss he had given her, his tenderness leaving her in awe.

If he continued to treat her with such care and devotion, she thought with a small smile, patience would come easily.

But now it was morning. And practicing patience, fortunately, did not mean she could not take steps to investigate what he was hiding from her. Which was why she currently pressed her ear to the door of his study to eavesdrop while he discussed the secret problem with his brother.

"... the night guardsmen reported they saw a man out in the square until late who could have been watching Balfour Terrace."

She heard Perry whistle. "So, it is true, then? There is one perpetrator for your wedding night fiasco, the spiteful print, and the note?"

Note? What note? She knew it! Richard was hiding something from her.

"It would appear so. I think I should increase security. If this continues—I will do whatever it takes to keep Sophia and Ethan safe."

Just then, Sophia heard the clip of Radcliffe's shoes approaching. She straightened up in haste and smoothed her skirts before lifting her hand to knock on the study door. Her husband called for her to enter.

As she stepped into the room, she feigned surprise at the sight of Perry lounging in one of the plump armchairs. "Good morning," she said politely before turning her attention to her husband—her prideful, stubborn husband. Keeping her expression composed, she greeted him pleasantly, though she was certain her cheeks betrayed her with a faint blush at the memory of their time together the night before.

At least Richard looked pleased to see her, and the warmth in his gaze softened some of her frustration.

"I was wondering if you and I could take Ethan to the park this morning? The boy is used to living on a farm, and I think it would be good for him to enjoy the outdoors."

Richard appeared torn for a moment, clearly thinking about the threat to their safety that he refused to discuss with her. He looked over at Perry. "Would you like to join us?"

"In the park? You must be funning—" Perry stopped abruptly at the expression on Richard's face. Her husband must want an extra presence with them, but he was unable to state it with her present, so he threatened Perry with a vicious glare. "I would be ... delighted"—the younger brother grimaced—"to join you. It is high time I met my nephew."

Richard turned to smile at her. "We will all go to the park with Ethan, then."

She smiled back, her thoughts turning to how this former scoundrel of a husband had once managed to charm his way into so many hearts. She saw little evidence of the subtlety such exploits must have required. Perhaps he was losing the glibness of his former charms, or perhaps others had simply failed to notice what was happening right before them.

Sophia, however, was learning to read him as easily as a favorite book. She decided she would let him believe he fooled her, but only for small matters—such as withholding the truth about that mysterious note. Yet heaven help him if he ever considered straying from her. She would take him apart with her bare hands if he attempted it.

So it was that Sophia found herself in a very crowded carriage. Her husband and his brother sat on the bench across from her, while she, Daisy, and Ethan were jammed together on their bench. Besides the coachman and the customary footman on the box in the front, the two Johns were crammed onto the rumble in the rear.

Apparently, one woman and one small boy required six men and a nursemaid to protect them. She would be exasperated with Richard for being overly cautious, but it reminded her of how she had recently gone to extreme measures to defend herself from Leech—which had turned out to be the exact right amount of caution, or she would now be wed to the murderous lord. She could not blame Richard for being a little overzealous. Nay, she blamed him for failing to inform her of the note.

Squashed into the corner of the squabs, with a pelisse adding bulk over her walking dress and a large bonnet blocking her peripheral vision, she compared the brothers. She knew her husband was two years older than his brother, but it was hard to believe. Perry was a fraction taller and slimmer. They both possessed the artfully cut brown curls, deep green eyes, handsomely symmetrical faces, and strong jawlines, but Peregrine's face was that of a sulky, indolent spare. Richard displayed a lightness of spirit and smiled frequently, while his brother often looked cold, haughty, or sarcastic—sometimes all three at once. His immaturity was obvious to her sharp eyes.

Thinking of Richard's request on the morning of their wedding, Sophia observed that Perry's greatest issue appeared to be his lack of purpose. While Richard maintained several estates, overseeing thousands of tenants as well as several successful investments that had grown the wealth of the Balfour family, Perry had no discernible or worthwhile activities that he engaged in. Sheer boredom was likely the cause of his sour moods.

When the current situation settled down, she would mention to her husband that, despite the fashionable *ton's* ideas, Perry needs an occupation of some sort if he was going to find his way in life.

Perhaps Richard should involve him in his estates or teach him how to handle investments. It would do the spoilt young nobleman a world of good to have a greater purpose to steer his days. She had never thought much of the idle lives of most of the peerage, or their neglect of children relegated to servants' keeping.

In her experience, the most competent, purposeful members of their world appeared to be the most satisfied. Not to mention, the most interesting. Her own uncle and aunt were quite productive. She did not always agree with them, but she had observed that they conducted life with a stable, predictable character unlike her own temperamental parents who lost their lives far too young.

"Mama, which park are we going to?" Ethan's youthful voice cut into her thoughts. He was on his feet with his face pressed against the opposite window. Richard watched him closely, clearly ready to grab the boy at the slightest hint of danger. She sighed at the expression on her husband's face. It was obvious he was on edge. If only the stupid man would share his burden with her, perhaps together they could find a solution.

Perry quirked an eyebrow in sarcastic comment, presumably because Ethan called her Mama. Sophia ignored it. She appreciated that Perry was assisting her husband with recent events, but she felt she had more to contribute. She knew she would be the better choice of confidante.

Did her husband see her as a weak-minded female despite his assurances that she would be his partner in life?

Is that why she was being kept in the dark, while he conspired with his brother?

"We are headed to St. James's Park, Ethan."

"Where the *pelly-kins* live?"

She gazed at him in surprise. "How do you know of the pelicans?"

"Emma said if I was good in London, then I could ask to be taken to see the *pelly-kins* at St. James's."

"Yes, we will probably see the pelicans in the canal."

"Emma would be so jealous if she knew." Ethan's little face became mournful. Richard must have noticed, too, because he scooped the boy into his arms and plonked him down on his leg. The child giggled and squirmed in delight while Richard jostled his leg up and down to simulate riding a pony. Perry grimaced in displeasure, trying to move away but finding no room to do so. He was forced to endure the play of his brother and his nephew with his lip curled in disdain.

Not for the first time, Sophia wondered if her husband had handled Ethan's move to London in the most considerate manner. The little tyke kept bringing up this Emma of whom he was so fond, and despite making time for the child every day, she was unsure they were providing the same level of attention he had received on the working farm where he had lived amongst a large family.

Her well-meaning, hulking idiot of a husband was mishandling her, so surely he must have mishandled the situation with Ethan? She should seek details on how Ethan's familial transference had been dealt with so that she could assess what else the boy might need from them as parents.

The carriage came to a stop, and Sophia was grateful to climb down onto steady ground. The additional weight of so many passengers had made the journey rougher than usual. Richard waited for her while holding Ethan's hand, stepping forward so she might slip an arm through his free one. Together, they set off to the canal.

Perry joined the guardsmen and was scanning the vicinity, while Sophia did her best to ignore the large men, and perplexed nursemaid, following them en masse. A veritable army surrounded them to protect them on a simple walk in the park. She sighed. Richard felt it was necessary, but that did not prevent it from being irritating.

They walked along a path with rolling green lawns spread in every direction while above their heads mature trees laden with fresh spring leaves cast shade. Couples and groups of ladies passed by, and at the canal in the distance, boys were floating toy boats under the watchful gaze of their nursemaids. Nearing the canal, Ethan's excitement mounted, and he tugged eagerly on his father's hand to walk faster.

"Are those boats, Papa? Where did they get them?"

"From a toy shop, I should think. Would you like one?"

Ethan's eyes widened in delight. "My own boat? That I can put in the water?"

"If you would like. We can find a shop and return here in a few days."

"But ... I do not know how to sail it."

"Would you like me to teach you?"

Sophia listened to her husband and her adopted son chattering about sailing toy boats and skimming stones, her heart melting in her chest. Richard might be a half-wit who did not include her in his troubles, but he was a sweet half-wit who was proving to be a doting father. The stubborn ox was worth a little patience, she supposed.

Just then Ethan cried out in delight, pointing a tiny

finger at a pelican that landed in the water nearby. Both she and Richard grinned at his obvious thrill before Sophia sank back into her thoughts.

She would appreciate it if he found his way to telling her about his troubles soon. She was certain she could offer a perspective that might help resolve the situation. Not to mention, an honest conversation would alleviate the recent development of grinding her teeth in vexation to maintain her forbearance.

AFTER THEIR VISIT to the park, Ethan went upstairs to play in the nursery and Sophia disappeared into the library. The outing had been a welcome respite, even with his brother and the two Johns skulking in the background as guardsmen.

Richard was thankful that he had a wife in his home to guide him. She had instigated all the activities with Ethan over the past few days, and Richard was growing to know his son as a result. There was little doubt that without her help, he would be horribly mishandling the boy without a clue of what to do.

With this in mind, he took time from penning his lengthy list of potential enemies to pick up the small leather-bound volume of poetry the duke had gifted him. Leafing through the poems, he thought about Halmesbury's advice, to be honest with Sophia about the shameful note in his pocket.

But the note was so despicable a remark on his own character that even His Grace, Philip Markham, the magnanimous Duke of Halmesbury of legendary philanthropic works could not help but judge Richard after reading it. He had seen it on his cousin's face. On the other hand, the guilt of hiding it from Sophia was weighing on him. He thought back to how understanding she had been about everything that was occurring, and how impressed he was with her composure in the face of adversity.

Pulling the note from his pocket, he stared at it for some time while he thought about his options. Finally, he placed it back into his pocket. He must tell her. He *would* tell her—immediately after his meeting with his man of business.

Radcliffe appeared at the door, announcing Johnson's arrival. The man scurried past the butler and took a seat when Richard gestured to the chair. The trusted steward of his business affairs appeared quite nervous today. Beads of sweat dotted his bulbous forehead, and his navy eyes were evasive. He pulled out a handkerchief and dabbed at his face while Richard began to worry that Johnson was bringing him bad news, but he held his tongue while Johnson scrambled through his papers. Perhaps his retainer was harried from all the extra work Richard was giving him?

"Mr. Long and I managed to investigate all the women on the list, my lord. We still need to approach the remainder, but you will be pleased to hear that there does not appear to be any more ... offspring."

Richard exhaled a deep breath of relief. "That is something." It was fantastic news. It was a mercy he had not inadvertently abandoned more children to their fate. There was only Ethan, who had fortunately been well taken care of by his extended family, so his father's unintentional neglect had done no lasting damage.

Johnson went through the list and reported what he had found. To his great relief, Richard could complete his apologies and suitable reparations over the next few weeks and close the door on his past. He stood up, ready to end the meeting. Johnson remained seated, his eyes averted. Richard felt his heart plunging into his boots. There was more.

"What is it?"

"I was at my offices preparing my report. On my way here, I passed by those print shops ..."

Richard resumed breathing in light-headed relief. He already knew about the caricature. He waited while Johnson leafed through his leather portfolio and pulled out a page. The man's hand was shaking when he reached forward to place it on the desk between them. Richard glanced down, prepared to dismiss the man, when he noticed the illustration. It was not the same one. This was a new drawing.

His body suddenly felt quite heavy, so he dropped back in his chair. With a fortifying breath, he picked the print up to look at it closer, his heartbeat pounding in his ears.

The drawing depicted two ladies calmly sipping tea. One of the women was meant to be Sophia, colored with her unique red-blonde hair. Around them stormed a horde of children—at least a dozen curly-haired devils with green eyes and demonic expressions—over the sofa where the women were seated, running amok between the furnishings, and climbing the draperies like monkeys spawned from the depths of hell. In fine, slanting print below, there was a caption.

"Lady S., are any of these children yours?"

Richard growled, his gaze transfixed on the page. From a distance, he heard Johnson making his excuses and fleeing the room while he continued to stare down at the offensive drawing. It took several minutes to gain control, and he found himself alone in his study when he finally dropped the drawing on his desk and stood up. He walked over to the window and stood staring out at the enclosed gardens in the middle of the square, seeking a clear head. When he found out who was behind this, he was going to tear the man apart, limb from limb.

The prints were coming out too quickly to be anything else but calculated attacks. If this mysterious enemy wanted to attack Richard, he could do so. He could call him out for a meeting at dawn. He could demand reparations for Richard's sins. But there could be no excusing the blackguard for threatening his new family. Until this moment, he had believed the threatening note from the musicale was intended to target Sophia, but this print proved that the mystery perpetrator was aware of Ethan, too. Which meant the note was a warning aimed at both his wife and his son. Whoever this man was, Richard wanted his blood.

Once Richard's anger cooled sufficiently, he retrieved the print and went to find Sophia. Just as before, there could be no hiding it because she would soon learn of its existence in a manner that could wreak more havoc. He resolved to show her it to her and then inform her about the note. This situation was becoming as dangerous as he had feared when he initially read it. The duke was correct. It was time to tell Sophia the full truth, so she would be prepared to defend herself.

It took him a while to track Sophia down, but he eventually found her in the nursery, reading a story to Ethan. The boy was enraptured, staring at Sophia with a besotted expression on his young face. Richard understood how the boy felt because he, too, was experiencing it. She felt like home, with her calm presence, and her endless well of patience and concern for himself and the boy. He could not believe his fortune in stumbling onto the terrace to hear her parody of his morals. The chance encounter had changed his life, abruptly, to one worth living.

Sophia's blue eyes found him standing at the door, listening to her tale. A single blink was the only sign that she noticed something was amiss. Gently, she ended in the middle of the story and promised Ethan they would read the rest together soon before she extricated herself to exit the rooms.

Richard offered her his arm, which she took, and they walked down the stairs to the library. The room was long and narrow, with shelves of books towering up to the tall ceilings. Sophia never said a word, just waited for him to speak when they took a seat at one of several library tables.

"What is it?" she finally asked in a quiet voice when he failed to speak.

"My man of business brought me another print."

Sophia looked relieved. "Is that all? I thought something serious had happened."

Richard handed her the print he was holding. He hoped she would find the humor in it as she had done before.

She took it from him and looked down. She was deathly quiet for some time. Suddenly, she exploded to her feet in a shriek of rage, knocking over her chair. "How dare they!"

Richard clamored to his feet, rounding the table to calm her, but she broke into a storm of agitated pacing. "How dare they! He is a child. This is unforgivable!" She spun to glower at him. "You must do something! Sue them ... or ... or purchase their shop and tear down the presses!"

Richard felt panic descending when he saw her blue eyes awash with angry tears. His dear wife was frantic in her desire to protect his son, whom she had only just met days before. He felt like such a cad. He knew he could never tell her about the shameful note and how he put not only her sought-after security at risk with his past misdeeds, but he had jeopardized the safety of his tiny child with his actions, too. She was correct. It was unforgivable.

He must make it right. She could not be forced to live with the burden of fear he now carried with him while he fought to protect his wife and child. It was clear he would need to keep the note to himself, but he would hire every runner in London if he had to. He would make this right and protect them.

He hurried over to fold her in his arms. She was quivering with rage and grief, dropping her head on his shoulder and sobbing in earnest. For the first time, Richard found himself comforting *her*, which was a novel experience.

"Sophia, I will make it right," he promised in a soothing voice, gently stroking her back.

"He is a child! A tiny, innocent little boy," she wept.

"I know, love. I will take care of it. Whoever is behind this will regret it." Her gasping sobs eased and her trembling body slowly relaxed into his arms while he continued to calm her with soft assurances.

Richard felt a deep pang of guilt for the situation he had caused, but he knew he must keep his promise to protect those he cared about. The print shops selling the illustration were of little concern to him now. No, his focus was on uncovering the instigator. His gut told him this was no random scandal but a deliberate campaign of malice, driven by a single, vengeful individual.

The individual may have just cause to pursue him in this manner, but there was no excuse for attacking his wife and child who were innocent of wrongdoing. He would find the man and tear his beating heart out of his chest, before displaying it to the worthless, dying bounder.

CHAPTER
FOURTEEN

"Fortitude is a virtue that enables a woman to endure trials with dignity."

Dr. John Gregory, A Father's Legacy to His Daughters

~

Sophia felt foolish over her display of emotion. Now her husband would be convinced she was a weak-minded female and never share the details of the mystery note he was hiding from her. It was her fault for making an utter cake of herself and behaving like a temperamental child.

Why the cut at Ethan scrambled her wits so thoroughly, she could not quite say. She cared not one whit about the malicious print aimed at her, but when she had seen the one aimed at the little boy in her care, her soul shattered and it had taken several minutes of sobbing in Richard's arms to gather the pieces back together.

It would not do. She must find a method of coping with

attacks on Ethan, or the vicious gossips of the *ton* would eat her alive. Showing such weakness in elite society would leave her and the child exposed. She supposed she should be thankful that only Richard had witnessed her reaction, and that she had the opportunity to prepare her composure for contending with the contentious subject in the future. There was no doubting that eventually the subject would arise, and she owed it to Ethan to remain calm in those inevitable encounters.

The drawing had caught her by surprise. It was so willfully disparaging of Richard's child that it physically hurt to think about it. Perhaps that was the key? Perhaps she should predict the type of confrontations or snide remarks that she might find herself in regarding the boy and plan out possible responses with a clear head, so she was not caught unprepared again?

The idea had merit. Planning strategies for dealing with members of polite society and the cross-purposes of her family was precisely how she had avoided matrimony with an unwanted suitor for so many years. If one handled these matters poorly, it doomed one to re-experience them over and over again, but if she made nothing of it, like her encounter with Lady Partridge at the modiste, people lost interest in their taunting and cruel gossip. Once she made up her mind that she refused to feed the gossip, Sophia felt her composure return.

With a calm face, she peered at her reflection in the full-length mirror in her dressing room. Her first delivery of the gowns she had ordered from the Italian modiste had arrived, so she finally possessed an evening gown suitable to attend the theatre. The one she wore now was a deep blue lace with a leaf pattern over a silk slip with the longer waist of this Season's fashion. A wreath covered the bodice and the puff sleeves were ornamented with rich lace and two bunches of leaves, while the hem of the skirt appeared to be two layers of skirts due to skillful bias and lace work.

The front of her hair was dressed in loose curls to fall low to the sides of her face, while the rest of her hair was loosely fastened with a pearl comb. Signora Ricci had recommended the lace color, and Sophia was pleased with how her hair shone in contrast and the hue of her blue eyes was picked out by the shade of the gown. She did not recognize the woman in the mirror in the fine colors not permitted to debutantes. The woman in the reflection looked elegant and high-born, just like a countess. Her pulse quickened when she thought of descending the stairs to meet Richard. Would he be proud of the woman on his arm when they attended Drury Lane tonight? She knew he looked especially fine in evening clothes, which was why she had been relieved to see the gown amongst those delivered earlier that day.

She pulled on her evening gloves, and the maid assisted her with a shawl before she headed out the door while the tall case clock down in the entrance hall announced the hour.

Richard was waiting at the foot of the stairs when she descended. His jaw dropped when he looked up to find her.

"You are ... ravishing." His voice was thick with emotion. She stopped on the last step, the extra inches bringing her almost to eye level to gaze at him. Reaching out, she clasped his hand.

"I am glad we married."

A flash of pain crossed his face. "Why? I have brought you nothing but chaos since the first night."

"Because you are an honorable man who is doing his very best to change. Because of how you give Ethan your attention and make him smile. Because of ... the sweet kisses you have brought into my life."

Richard's lips curved into a playful smile at her final words. "I dare say, I excel at that particular endeavor, do I not?"

"Thank you for taking me to the theatre tonight. I think it is a good idea for us to take these moments to enjoy ourselves."

"You mean before the next crisis presents itself?"

She grinned, pressing a quick kiss to his warm lips. "Precisely."

THE JOURNEY to the theatre district included the two Johns, the coachman, and a footman. Richard informed her that the additional two guardsmen, the men she had not yet met, stayed to guard the nursery, so it was clear he was not relenting regarding security. She shrugged it off. At some point this would pass, and in the meantime, she was happy to help give him peace of mind by cooperating with the measures he was taking.

They watched the first half of the show from a private box that he maintained, and she recognized many of the chattering patrons sitting in the opposite balconies who appeared to be using their lorgnettes to observe the comings and goings of other patrons under the recently installed gaslights. On either side of where they sat, she could hear the gossip spilling from noble lips in the adjacent boxes.

Sophia always found the theatre most enjoyable. She had never understood the inclination of the *ton* to use such events to tattle because the performance always riveted her.

Consequently, when the intermission arrived, she found herself quite bemused, taking a moment to realize that Richard was waiting for her to join him for refreshments. He stepped out into the corridor ahead of her, likely to ensure her safety on the short walk to where the two Johns stood waiting, when she heard a commotion. Sophia exited the box in consternation to find Richard embroiled in an argument with another patron, a young nobleman who was vaguely familiar.

Her senses reeled with confusion when she noted that a crowd of society's most important members was forming to observe the scene. Turning to Richard, she gasped when she saw he was holding a handkerchief to his face, spotted with crimson drops. She raised her hand to his face, only to drop it when the tempestuous young man lunged forward, startling her into retreating a step back at the same moment Richard angled forward to shield her with his body.

"You stay away from Lady Partridge, you hear me?" The two Johns had grabbed hold of the man's flailing arms, preventing him from attacking Richard once more.

"Stanford, I do not know what you are referring to! I have not spoken to Lady Partridge since before my betrothal to Miss Hayward. It must be at least two years since I even spoke to the widow!"

That is it—the young man is Lord Stanford!

"Your friend informed me he saw you visiting her home in January of this year, while I was in Paris on family matters. I know your reputation, Saunton!"

"In January I was in Somerset, hosting a house party with several witnesses! I could not possibly have been seen in London because I was nowhere near! What friend told you that?"

Sophia could tell Richard was keeping a tight leash on his temper, rage glinting in his narrowed eyes and his chiseled jaw set in an angry line. Stanford refused to be placated, nor would he betray the confidence of the friend who had informed him. He finally stalked off in outrage, while Richard held his head back to stop the blood.

"We should leave. Your nose might be broken, and we need to summon a doctor."

Richard's eyes found hers, his face still tilted back and his white handkerchief spotted with red.

"Sophia, I swear I have not spoken to that woman in at least two years."

She watched him for a moment, noting the sincerity and concern in his eyes while he waited for her response. She believed him, but would he finally be honest about the threat that plagued them? "Do you think that the friend he mentioned caused this trouble on purpose? Used the facts of your past to cast aspersions about the present?"

Richard looked away, staring at the ornate ceiling. "I am sure it was a case of mistaken identity."

Sophia found herself grinding her teeth once more. Her vexatious husband must think her a cretin. It had long since become obvious that there was an imminent threat, but he continued to pretend that they were suffering from a string of coincidences. What would it take for the infuriating lummox to admit there was a problem?

BY THE TIME they boarded their carriage, the bleeding had stopped, so Richard stuffed the ruined handkerchief in his pocket. He could see the ire in Sophia's eyes and the way her jaw firmed after he brushed her concerns aside. He realized it was not working to try to fool her, but he would not reveal the note. Perhaps he could admit that he had concerns the events might be connected, which was why he was taking precautions while the matter was investigated.

He looked up to find her staring out the carriage window, but like once before, he sensed she did not see the roadway or buildings but instead was fuming about his behavior.

"Sophia, I admit I had the same thought. That the recent problems plaguing me might be related."

She swung her gaze to meet his.

"I will ask my man of business to investigate."

Her eyes fell. She looked disappointed in him.

"Sophia?"

"That is all? There is no other information? Do you suspect someone is doing this deliberately?" She would not look at him. Richard's chest tightened. His wife was an intelligent woman, but it was his responsibility to protect her. He brought this into their lives, and he would solve it without burdening her with unnecessary fear.

"I do not know, but I will have it investigated. The guardsmen will continue to protect you and Ethan until I am certain there is no further threat." He reached out a hand to cover her fingers. "Please, Sophia. I apologize you are being exposed to these situations. Know that I had a very different idea of how we would begin this marriage, and I have every intention of setting this right, so you and Ethan are safe."

What a confusing muddle of ideas. He knew he was alluding to a threat, but then pretending there was no cause for alarm in the same breath. The evening had begun as a smashing success and collapsed into disaster. His nose was throbbing, he had the metallic taste of blood in his mouth, and his temper still ran hot because he had wanted to pound Stanford into the theatre carpeting after the man surprised him with a sudden punch to the face.

He wished to take a hot bath and join his wife in her bed. It was yet another dreadful day—and night—at Balfour Terrace, and the constant fear for his family with no specific target to attack was keeping his nerves on edge. Not to mention, he was lying awake at night trying to work out the most likely source of the menace in their lives.

He did not want to talk; he wanted to cut off the endless thoughts running through his head while the investigation into the source of all this pandemonium proceeded.

Sophia turned her face back, scrutinizing him. She gave a deep sigh. "I will leave the matter to you, but know that I am here and ready to discuss *anything* you need to discuss."

He gave a nod. "First thing is to summon the doctor. Then we should rest."

She turned her hand to clasp his. "That sounds lovely."

RICHARD BATHED while they awaited the doctor's arrival. It soon turned out his face was badly bruised, but his nose was intact. He had suspected this was the case, but he allowed the doctor to be summoned as a small mercy to his wife. She appeared relieved at the doctor's pronouncement and agreed that it was time to go to bed.

He undressed with the help of Shaw before donning his nightclothes and robe to join Sophia in her chambers. When he entered her rooms and saw her lying in the bed, the light playing across her face and golden-red hair, he experienced a moment of revelation not for the first time since he had met her.

Sophia was an angel. He would do anything to defend this woman, who had come to mean so much to him. He had been a fool when he denied his love to Halmesbury, because in that moment he knew his heart would stop beating in his chest if anything happened to her because of him. Just as he knew, he was not worthy of such a woman. She brought peace and grace to his home, where he had only ever brought fallen women and pursued his own selfish pleasures.

It was no longer about hiding his shame. It had become about proving himself worthy of her so that she might one day grow to love the gentleman he aspired to be and not the rascal he currently was. One day, he would be worthy of the title husband—and father—and until that day came, he would not rest in ensuring he completed his reparations and uncovered the threat that was plaguing their household. This was his duty to take care of, and until he did so, he was not worthy of earning her love.

Mercy! Maybe he needed a drink to clear his head of these maudlin thoughts?

Stuff! No, he was reforming and this small request from his wife was the only one he could currently honor. He must bear the burden of his past actions and soldier on, one step at a time.

His wife raised her head. "Are you coming?"

To his relief, she seemed in a lighter mood than she had been since the predicament at the Drury Lane Theatre. When he approached, she drew a deep breath and blurted out a question.

"Do you think there will be another caricature of what happened with Lord Stanford?"

Richard threw his head back and groaned. "I guess that would be better than the last one. Mayhap it will distract the gossips from Ethan?"

She furrowed her brow in thought. "That is a good point. Well, in that case, I hope there is another print!"

They chuckled together while he disrobed and pulled back the covers to slip into her bed. She turned onto her side, a hand tucked under her cheek. "It is good to laugh about it. I now look forward to another illustration depicting the infamous Balfours."

Richard smiled softly, pleased to see Sophia so at ease. She had been growing more comfortable in their marriage, and moments like this made him realize how deeply he valued her presence. When she lifted a hand and traced her fingers lightly over his chin, following the contours of his jaw, Richard sighed in contentment.

Her fingers traveled over his bruised face, lingering as if committing them to memory.

Sophia's sweet tenderness, mixed with the admiration shining in her eyes, called to something deep and primal within him. He stayed still, letting her explore at her leisure, feeling a quiet sense of awe at the tenderness in her touch. This was different from any connection he had experienced before. Her sincerity, her focus on him as a man, filled a space in his heart he hadn't realized was empty.

CHAPTER FIFTEEN

"Tenderness of heart is the peculiar charm of the female character."

Dr. John Gregory, A Father's Legacy to His Daughters

It was early when a sound disturbed Richard from a deep sleep. So early that a single thread of morning light crept through a gap in the draperies.

"Richard?" It was the lowest of whispers floating through the air of the large, quiet bedroom. It sounded like Perry. Richard turned his head in awakening confusion, his eyes bleary from sleep. The connecting door to his rooms was slightly ajar, and a blurry face was peering at him.

"Richard?"

His heart sank. This could not be good. He gave a nod of acknowledgment, and the door closed.

Sitting up in Sophia's bed, he rubbed his eyes to restore his vision before easing quietly from under the covers. Once he was on his feet, he searched around for his nightshirt and robe. Dressing hurriedly, he crept from the room back to his chambers, opening and closing the door with the greatest of care. He did not wish to disturb Sophia after their distressing evening.

Perry stood at the fireplace, his forearm leaning against the mantel while he waited for Richard to gather his wits.

"What is it?" Richard was afraid to hear the answer, steeling his nerve for what new crisis his brother had come to inform him of.

"I was just returning home when one of the Johns called me into the hall. It would seem that a rock was thrown through the window of your study about thirty minutes ago. The window is shattered, but the servants did not wish to disturb you. You have an injury of some sort, from what I gather?"

Richard raised his head, staring at the ceiling in frustration. "I was at Drury Lane with the countess. When I stepped out of the box, Lord Stanford happened to be passing by. Without so much as a word, he turned and punched me square in the face, accusing me of carrying on with his ace of spades."

"Ace of spades—he is involved with a widow? Never say you mean Lady Partridge? I thought you decided to stay away from that woman when she tried to convince you to—"

"I know why I steer clear of that woman. Her preferences are far too eclectic for my sensibilities."

Perry choked back a laugh. "Eclectic! My, what a gentleman you have become."

"I would have no soul left to redeem if I followed the paths she wished to lead me down. She and Father would have made perfect companions with their questionable indulgences. But that is beside the point, because Stanford claimed a friend told him they saw me leaving her home in January."

"But we were at Saunton Park for the entire month of January!"

"Precisely. It seems the enemy I have made is not above bending the truth to stir up trouble. I visited the woman's home only once, and that was back in the Season of 1818—before I realized the nature of her tastes. Either my adversary has been digging deeply into my past, or they are using scraps of idle gossip from over the years to craft plausible falsehoods."

"Given the frequency of these attacks, I would say he is posing plausible lies. How could he have the time to do otherwise? Unless he is well-financed and has a team doing his bidding?"

"We are going about our own investigation the wrong way. It is too slow, and I need results. We should make a short list of who would be this energetic, vicious, unrelenting, and angry. Then direct the runners to investigate those men first."

"Agreed. There is no predicting what this lunatic will try next."

Richard stood hesitantly in the middle of the room. He was so weary, his body felt like it was being crushed by the weight of failed responsibility. Walking over to the bed, he dropped down and asked the question which had been haunting the dark recesses of his mind these past weeks.

"Perry, am I our father?"

"Jingo! No!" His brother's reply was so utterly vehement that Richard was distracted from his worries. "Lord Saunton—*ahem*—I mean, our father was the devil incarnate. Why would you think you are him?"

"I have spent years indulging in reckless pursuits, and now my wife and son are paying the price," Richard admitted, his voice heavy with regret.

Perry let out a hollow laugh. "Reckless, perhaps. But our father? He went far beyond recklessness before I was even born. The man had no conscience—no moral compass of any kind. I was glad when he finally passed. You, however ... I would mourn deeply if something happened to you. That is why I am helping you now. Do you think I would lift a finger to aid the fiend who sired us? Never. I would sooner be out on the street lobbing rocks myself. But you, brother, are a far better man than he ever was."

Richard groaned. "Stuff, Perry, now you provide me with new worries! Do you think, mayhap, once this is over, that I will need to determine if we have illegitimate kin out in the world?"

Perry shuddered, his head falling forward in his pained despair to rest on the forearm balanced on the mantel. "I had not stopped to think, but I would say it is almost a certainty."

One step at a time, Richard.

"Never mind that thought for now. We will settle this disaster first. Once it is done, we can discuss if we wish to investigate the sins of our father."

Perry raised his head and nodded. "I will inform Shaw to come and assist you. We can meet in your study once I find some sustenance."

KNOCKING on the door of Richard's study before entering, Sophia stopped in dismay when she saw that one of the windows facing the street was boarded up and a maid was sweeping up glass from the floor.

Perry rose when she entered and made to leave the room. "I will look into this, brother." With that, the Balfour brother left the study.

Richard dismissed the maid and came around his desk to gather Sophia's hand in his. Once the door was closed, he led her to the armchairs and had her take a seat before settling in the opposite chair.

"What happened?"

"Someone threw a rock at the window in the early hours of the morning."

Sophia's fear and irritation soared. "Are you going to continue to pretend this is not a campaign of some sort?"

Richard contemplated her for a moment. "I should have known better than to attempt to fool you. Perry and I believe this is the work of one person."

"So you finally admit it!"

"I apologize. I did not wish to alarm you while I investigated the matter. But I should have realized you are too clever to not make the connections." He looked away, his expression pained. "I feel terrible about this. My past behavior is plaguing our household, and it is not fair to you. I hope you will forgive me while I try to sort out the havoc I have caused."

"That is not what upsets me. I thought we agreed to work together, and now you finally admit that you have been shutting me out. I could have contributed to solving this situation, but instead you decided to keep it from me like I am some sort of witless fool!"

Richard brought up his hands to rub his face. She finally noticed the weariness. His lips were pinched, and he was pale. Was he sleeping, she wondered with a sharp pang of guilt at the recollection of the hours they had burned away in each other's arms. She wished to ease his suffering, but she also wanted to hit him for being dense.

"I apologize, Sophia. None of this has been about your wits. It has been my shame to visit this on you and Ethan. My dark past has exposed the two of you to danger, and I am having difficulties with my conscience. But there is no time to sort it out because I must find the culprit behind this to protect you and Ethan. What if this worsens and the attacks become more dangerous ... more lethal?"

Sophia stared at him. "We will work together to resolve this. We will increase our vigilance. Have you told me everything?"

That was when her dear, wonderful, exasperating husband looked her straight in the eye—and lied. "Yes."

Sophia ground her teeth in frustration, forcing a smile onto her face. The lying reprobate still would not inform her about the note.

"I am going for tea with my aunt and cousin this afternoon. I will take the shorter John and a footman."

Richard inclined his head. "Of course."

Sophia forced herself to endure the formality of tea with her aunt, while in the back of her mind, she continued to fume. How was she to assist meaningfully if Richard insisted on keeping secrets from her? The question could not be answered while they sipped on tea and Lady Moreland informed her of the latest *on dits*.

I do not care! My family is in danger and my husband will not talk to me, she wanted to scream. But she smiled and nibbled on dainty biscuits and sipped her tea from a delicate cup while her aunt's words flowed over her like water over a rock.

Lily gave her a light pinch. Sophia realized that the room was quiet and her elegant aunt was staring at her. "My apologies. I was woolgathering for a moment. What was the question?"

Her aunt, a handsome woman, tilted her head in bemusement. She had the same enormous eyes as her daughter Lily, and her hair was a deep chocolate brown with only a few strands of silver to mark her age under her jaunty turban. After a moment, Lady Moreland's mouth curled into a knowing smile, and she discreetly picked at her bodice with slender, graceful fingers. "I recall that I had a tendency to woolgather in the first few months of my marriage to Uncle Hugh."

Out of the corner of her eye, Sophia saw Lily wince and stick out her tongue to simulate gagging. Sophia herself did her best not to grimace at the thought of what her aunt alluded to. Her cousin cleverly interjected to change the subject. "Mama asked why you left the theatre early?"

"Oh. I was not feeling well, so Richard insisted we leave early."

"Lord Stanford punching your husband in the face during intermission was not the cause, then?"

Sophia shut her eyes in defeat. She should have known her aunt had already heard the gossip. "Yes, Aunt Christiana. That is the true reason for our departure."

"Well, not to worry, Sophia. I hear Richard has barely been seen about Town since he married you. The speculation is that the rogue has finally reformed and spends his evenings with his bride."

That was good news, at least.

"I never had any doubt, niece. You are the perfect wife

for the gentleman. I believe the earl has been bored, but a clever girl like you will keep his attentions at home where they belong."

The sentiment rather touched Sophia, who smiled in acknowledgment.

Once the tea was over, she and Lily made their way to the garden. The spring air was pleasant, and the privacy of the garden afforded them an opportunity to talk. With a little coaxing from her cousin, Sophia confided all that had happened since the wedding, including the infernal note her husband kept from her.

Lily's expression was perplexed when Sophia finished telling her of what occurred that morning, and the fact that Richard still withheld the note.

"Why do you not ask him? It is quite out of character for you to not do so?"

Sophia felt glum admitting the truth. "I suppose it was some sort of test. If he told me, I would know he truly considered me an equal and trusted me, so I could trust him."

Lily pulled a face. "That is most dishonest of you."

"What? I am not the one who is dishonest!"

"Sophia, Lord Saunton is under great strain. I do not think it is a good idea to be testing his sincerity at this moment. Inform him you were eavesdropping and you are aware of the note. Ask him why he has failed to inform you of it."

"Lily, you are most unfair!"

"I am not, Sophia. You have a terrible habit of trying to solve matters on your own without any help. Look how you suffered under the threat of kidnapping from Leech but failed to obtain assistance from your own family. You did not even tell me why you were sleeping in my chambers. In fact, you outright lied to me about that. If you want Lord Saunton to trust you, then you need to extend the same courtesy to him. Ask him about the note."

"Zooks, Lily, when did you get so demanding?"

"I care about you, cousin, and you know I speak the truth. I will not stand idly by without speaking my mind. Would you prefer I clutch your hand to commiserate and weep about the awful men of the world, or would you rather receive some useful direction on how to resolve the matter at hand?"

Sophia muttered her answer in resentment. "Useful direction, I suppose."

Lily's face lit up, her customary enthusiasm restored. "Perfect! Now you should go home and ask him about the note."

When she returned home from visiting her unsympathetic cousin, Sophia found Richard dispatching letters with his quill in hand. Smoothing her skirts with fluttering hands, she approached the desk and waited for him to complete the letter he was writing. Once he was done, his head came up, and he flinched in surprise.

"How long have you been standing there?"

"Just a few moments. You appear to be tired."

"I have had little sleep since we married. I must find the source of this threat. With your safety, and Ethan's, at risk, this cannot continue."

"Yes, that is why I am here. This morning you admitted that this is a campaign, and I asked you if there was anything else I needed to know."

"I remember."

"Why did you not tell me about the note?"

"Which note?"

"I do not know which note! That is the point! You did not tell me about the note I overheard you discussing with Perry the day we went to see the pelicans in St. James's Park with Ethan."

Richard's face was blank for a moment, then his hand went to his pocket. "That note. I would have told you about it this morning, but so much happened in the past few days it slipped my mind. It was not intentional, I assure you!"

"It was intentional not to inform me of it when you received it!"

Richard lowered his gaze. "I apologize for that. Halmesbury warned me it was not well done of me."

"So you spoke with Halmesbury about the note—and Perry—but you did not see fit to inform me of it?"

"I wanted to spare you the worry."

"Is that the full story?"

Richard's cheeks turned a ruddy shade. "And I am ashamed I have caused this situation ... and the contents of the note."

"Let me see the note, then."

Richard patted at his pockets. "I do not have it on me. I must have left it in my clothes, so Shaw will have it somewhere. Perhaps it is in my dressing table in my chambers."

Sophia huffed in irritation. The walk up to their chambers was interminable in this gigantic house, and she was too impatient to make the journey. "Well, tell me about it, then. Where did it come from?"

"Shaw found it in my coat after we returned from the Lawson musicale. Someone snuck it into my pocket when I was collecting refreshments."

Sophia blanched, her legs trembling as she reached for a

seat and sank down. That night had been so special to her, yet he had kept a secret, hiding the truth from her. The realization cast a shadow over the memories of their time together after the musicale. Her voice was quiet but filled with hurt as she asked, "You ... shared ... my bed that night, all while knowing about the note?"

Richard's consternation was mollifying. "No! I did not know about it then. Shaw gave it to me the following morning."

Sophia drew a deep, fortifying breath in her relief. "What did it say?"

"It threatened to harm someone I love."

"Me?"

"Or Ethan. The caricature of all my supposed children confirmed the scoundrel was aware of him, too."

Sophia felt empathy for her husband's plight. Since the day of their wedding, he had been grappling with one upheaval after another while knowing there was a hidden enemy planning the next disaster.

Richard cleared his throat, causing Sophia to tense. It appeared another downturn was to be announced, from the expression of discomfort on his face. "Which is why I have reached a decision to send you and Ethan to Saunton Park until this danger has passed."

Sophia jumped to her feet. "No!"

"It is best—"

"No! We are a family and we must stick together."

"Sophia, be reasonable—"

"I will not! You promised me." Sophia lowered her voice, quoting in a husky tone, "'I will allow you your freedom. As my countess, you may do anything you want and I will support you, as long as you are at my side.' That is what you said the day you visited me at my uncle's home! I will remain at your side, as we agreed that day."

Richard grimaced. "Please, Sophia, I must keep you and Ethan safe. I could not live with the guilt if something happened to either of you. I can barely live with my guilt for exposing you to this because of my shameful past."

"It is illogical, husband. If Ethan and I leave London, it will expose us while we travel for days to Somerset. Not to mention we will have to divide the men we have to split off. There is no guarantee that the villain dogging you will not observe our departure and follow us in order to ambush us. Here in London, the resources are combined, and we are protected behind the walls of Balfour Terrace. I will not leave! If you attempt to force me, my cooperation will end." She banged his desk with her open hand.

Richard's jaw fell open. "Dickens, you are a magnificent creature!"

"Do not attempt to charm me, husband."

"Sophia, you have made some fine points, but—"

"No but. I am not leaving! And I expect you to show me the note!" With a flurry of skirts, she stalked out of his study. If she remained any longer, she could not be responsible for what she might do to the infuriating oaf.

CHAPTER SIXTEEN

"A father's guidance is a daughter's safeguard."

Dr. John Gregory, A Father's Legacy to His Daughters

∽

Perry loped in to collapse with a negligent air into one of the ivory armchairs. "I thought that went rather well."

Richard picked up his empty cup and threw it at his sardonic brother, who quickly ducked so that it hit the wall behind him in a shattering spray of shards.

"My, my, brother. Your emotions are taking over."

"Quit finding amusement in my troubles or I will blacken your eye, *brother*."

"The countess made several good points. I agree with her assessment that a journey to Somerset would be fraught with peril."

"I must do *something*! This is my fault!"

"Richard, this may be easier to resolve if you have a

clear head. You may have done something to cause this situation, but a man who targets an innocent woman and child is deranged, which is beyond your control. And, thus far, nothing but gossip, threats, and minor incidents have occurred, so calm yourself."

Richard groaned, leaning his elbows on the smooth finish of his desk to drop his head into his hands in a gesture of agony. "Perry, do you not understand? It is only a matter of time before the blackguard heightens the stakes."

"Your wife is losing her patience. Be careful she does not leave our household to return to the Morelands. Currently, she is cooperating with you, but you will push her too far and complicate the threat further."

"Why do you say that? How would you know?"

"It is what I would do in her position."

Richard stared at his brother. The possibility of Sophia leaving him was … It made his heart ache in his chest and his breathing shallow. "I will think on it."

Perry left him to his thoughts, and Richard sat staring sightlessly at the street through the window, aggravated by the boarded-up window in his peripheral vision.

He felt adrift, the weight of uncertainty pressing down on him. He wanted to rant, to rage, to take action, but against whom? Who had he offended so deeply? And why now? It seemed unlikely to be tied to any recent event, as he had ended his last arrangement in December of the previous year.

For five months, he had refrained from any entanglements, determined to avoid the mistakes of his past. His failed betrothal to Annabel haunted him still, her discovery of his indiscretion in the stables marking a turning point in his life. At the time, he had naively believed marriage would allow him to continue his wayward habits without consequence. But that was before he met Sophia, the captivating minx who had turned his plans—and his heart—completely upside down.

This situation made no sense. Who could be so angry with him, yet they waited a minimum of five months to enact their revenge? Had his nuptials triggered their anger? And how had they known or reacted so swiftly? He himself only knew he would wed mere days before the event. Unless they had known about his search for a bride and been lying in wait to pounce.

Richard's head swirled with the possibilities.

Drat! He needed a drink! Not the damn tepid tea he had been sipping since his wedding day, but a real drink!

Sophia was so livid when she stormed out of Richard's study that she took herself back to the Morelands', inviting herself to dinner because her earlier visit had disclosed the family's plans to stay in for the evening.

Smiling and forcing small talk gave her a megrim. Light glinting off the silver and crystal at the dinner table caused it to worsen into a sharp, throbbing pain until she was forced to massage her neck despite her aunt's disapproving stare at her unladylike behavior.

The moment dinner was finished, she grabbed her cousin Lily by the hand to drag her to the library, where the last slivers of sunlight were visible through the windows.

"Lily, the man is so frustrating! Attempting to send me to the country to rusticate with Ethan while he remains in town. Is he trying to get rid of me?"

Lily's face showed her concern. "I do not think so, cousin. I think he fears on your behalf."

"Did I make a mistake?"

Lily's elfin face scrunched in confusion. "What mistake?"

"Should I not have married him? Did I make a mistake in my choice of husband?"

Lily sighed. "I do not think so. This situation will resolve, but you need to give it time—give Lord Saunton time to straighten it out. Why so impatient, Sophia? You are one of the most level-headed people I know."

Sophia sighed, lifting a hand to knead the stiff muscles in her neck. "I am afraid. My feelings for the earl are growing. At first, his crusade to redeem his honor was so exciting, but now I fear ..."

"What is it?"

"I worry that the only reason he married me was that I somehow represented this crusade. What am I to him, merely a talisman or a ... moral compass of some sort? An ethical lodestone, if you will? What if that is all I am to him? What if he resolves his quest and loses his interest in me once he no longer needs me?"

"Silly goose! No man could lose interest in you once you got your hooks in him! You are one of the cleverest, most interesting people I know. Your mind bends around problems to solve them. Look how you sorted out the debacle with Lord Leech. It was perfection. The man was thoroughly outwitted. Nay, your husband will only grow more attached to you over time."

Sophia shot a sideways glance at her petite cousin sitting beside her on the library sofa. "Truly?"

Lily snorted inelegantly. "Of course. When will you inform the man that you are in love with him?"

Sophia stiffened in ire. "What do you mean?"

"You are independent and do not care a whit about

other people's opinions on how you should live your life. But here you sit, lamenting about what you mean to the earl, and will he lose interest in you? Clearly you have fallen in love with the man, just as I predicted."

"No ... it is not true. I merely care about him ..." Sophia squeezed her eyes shut in agony. Her cousin was correct. She did love her stupid husband. It had been inevitable from the moment he had expressed his desire and will to change. When he stated his admiration and admitted how she had inspired his crusade to redeem his honor, she was smitten with the daft man.

She admired his courage and his drive; and she appreciated his fine looks and his sense of humor. He made her feel safe when she had never allowed herself to rely on anyone because of the havoc her parents had wreaked on their lives. And his affection for his son, whom he acknowledged without hesitation despite the scandal it brought into his life, was commendable. Richard accepted the mantle of responsibility without complaint, and even now worked tirelessly to find a solution to their troubles.

And he does not trust me to assist him.

It saddened Sophia that he would not accept her help, but she admitted her cousin had made a good point earlier that day. She must accept his help if she expected him to do the same. They needed to engage in a proper discussion.

Lily prodded a sharp elbow into her side, causing Sophia to yelp in pain. "But enough about you and your woolgathering. I have a problem of my own."

"You shame me, cousin. I have forced my problems on you for days now."

"Do not be ridiculous. There was no force. But this is about me, so are you ready to stay silent and listen to my troubles?"

Sophia gave a nod. Lily settled deeper into the sofa and sighed. "Mama is relentless. Now that you are married, she has turned her full attentions to me. If she had her way, I will be married to a gentleman I barely know by the end of the week. I am not strong like you, Sophia!"

"Stuff and nonsense!"

Lily wrinkled her nose to stare up at Sophia, who felt like a veritable giant towering over her delicate cousin.

"Do not be daft. You just doled out advice to me throughout the day. You forced me to go confront Richard about the note and just persuaded me I was in love with the man, despite my resistance to the news. You have plenty of backbone."

"But ... I want to find a genuine connection with a man. I do not wish to be pressured into marriage, but I do not know how to stand up to Mama without hurting her feelings. She wants what is best for me, but her ideas are old-fashioned and too rooted in society's expectations."

"Uncle Hugh will never force you to marry a man you do not want. Just stay strong and wait for the right gentleman."

"I am not as wily as you, cousin. She will get the best of me."

"This is a silly conversation. Lily, you are just as clever as I am. Just prepare yourself to contend with her demands. Think of what her arguments are and prepare counter-arguments. When dealing with Aunt Christiana, I usually find that distraction is the best technique. You have observed me doing just that for three Seasons. Lord Francis Bacon once wrote that knowledge is power. You must use your knowledge of Aunt Christiana, but do not engage in direct debate with her because it invariably does not work."

Lily's mouth hung open in astonishment. "How did you discover all this?"

"I read a book by a Chinese general that was translated into French. Would you like me to find it for you?" Sophia gestured toward the annex behind them where the shelving was laden with heavy tomes.

Lily nodded, an expression of awe on her face as Sophia scrambled to her feet to search for the volume. "You were applying military tactics to my mother? You are such a bluestocking, cousin."

"Nay, I study what I need to know. I am not interested in study for study's sake. I must have a question to answer before I will plow through these sedate books. I found *L'Art de la Guerre* in my first Season when the pressure to marry was causing me distress." Sophia looked back to find her cousin's face pinched into a puzzled frown. "It means *The Art of War*, Lily. You will need to brush up on your French if you wish to employ military strategy, but your instincts are excellent. I will find a dictionary to assist you."

She mounted the library steps to pull leather-bound books from the shelves, then set them on the table for her cousin to read.

Shortly after that, they said their goodbyes. Sophia stood outside near to the family carriage that had brought her from Balfour Terrace. She hesitated on the steps of the Morelands' home and stared at the Saunton coat of arms gilded on the carriage door, thinking about the current state of her relationship with Richard.

Lily was right. It was time to make an effort at a proper discussion. She needed to stop playing games and tackle their issues directly. This was a marriage they were building, and it would not do to use wily misdirection and military tactics with her husband, or pose tests without his knowledge.

Sophia hovered on the steps in a state of bemusement, hugging herself in the chilled night air. She admitted to herself that she had brought the accumulated disappointments of her past and laid them at Richard's feet while he struggled to protect her and his son. Every time her charming father had made a promise—only to break it when he disappeared for days into his gambling hells to fetter away their income—in those reoccurring moments, she had realized she could not trust her beloved father, and that his words were empty of intent. Those final days, she had decided to grow up far too young and accept that he was irresponsible and would never change. And then came the night they were informed of his untimely death while sitting at a card table. All had taken residence in her mind, taunting her, challenging her to devise tests to disprove Richard's sincerity.

"Milady?"

Her husband was mostly blameless. He was ashamed that his past was haunting their present and had withheld some information to protect his pride and ease her worries, and in return, she had set him a test without his knowledge to prove to herself that he would fail.

"Milady?"

Sophia chewed on her lip, lost deep in the memories. She had not intended to compare her husband to her glib father, but she had done it all the same. It was not well done of her; the earl did not know what—or whom—he was being measured against, which meant Lily was right. She was being dishonest with him.

"Milady?"

Sophia returned to the present to find her footman

gazing at her with perplexed concern. She realized the liveried servant had attempted to gain her attention several times.

"I wish to return home. To Balfour Terrace."

The footman appeared puzzled by this specification, but Sophia paid no heed. She had reached a decision.

I shall sit Richard down and talk to him honestly. Share my concerns, so we can reach an understanding.

Her mind made up, she gathered her skirts in one hand and accepted the gloved hand of the footman with the other to step up through the open door of the carriage. When the shorter John climbed in behind her, she accepted it without resentment. Her husband was taking strenuous action to defend her, and it was time she acknowledged the concern he was displaying. They would need to talk and come to terms, but this time she would not get frustrated with him. She was confident that if they worked together, they could find a solution to navigate the danger they were living under.

RICHARD VISITED with Ethan in the nursery and read him a story, then returned downstairs at dinnertime to wait for his wife, until Radcliffe informed him that her ladyship had left for the evening. He had not expected to be so disappointed by this news, but it was the first time since they married that they were not taking their evening meal together.

Sitting in his study, nursing a fragile china cup of tea—*blech*—he thought about what she had said earlier that day. Perry concurred with her conclusion that it was safer for her and Ethan to remain in town rather than undertake a long journey.

Perhaps she had a point. Mayhap he had not involved her sufficiently, and treated her like a coddled child. But he had never confided in a woman before. This was all so new to him. Perhaps she needed to be more patient with him.

He stared down into his murky tea, wishing it was a fine French brandy, and admitted to himself that perhaps he was not making the effort that he should. If she left him to return to her family, as Perry suggested, he would be utterly lost. Why this was, he could not fathom. They had known each other for less than three weeks, but he grew mawkish at the thought of her absence. He did not want to send her away, truth be told. He wanted to eat dinner with her in the evenings before joining her in her bedchamber. The decision to send her to Saunton Park had been reached because, more important than his time in her company, he wanted her to remain alive.

He could not believe how much he missed her at this moment, merely because she had abandoned him to dinner on his own. The only conclusion he could draw was that he now looked forward to the nightly ritual in her company, only to have it yanked away because of his own failure to include her.

When she returned home from her family, *if* she returned home, he would do better. And if she did not return home, he would haunt the Abbott household every moment of every day until she agreed to come home.

BANG.

A loud thud shuddered the wooden floor beneath his feet, causing him to flinch in surprise. Richard sprang up to find out what had been dropped, but when he reached the study door, he hesitated when he heard a loud, agitated voice he did not recognize. He cocked his head to listen closer, but he could not quite make out what was being said. He only knew it was not a member of his household sounding off.

The commotion was coming from the vestibule. Briefly, he hoped Sophia had still not returned home. His body was on high alert while eerie calm descended over his mind. Instinct told him that, as he had predicted earlier to Perry, the stakes had just heightened and it was time for him to act. He finally had something—someone—specific to address.

Bending down, he removed his boots, concluding that his stockinged feet would allow him to investigate what was happening without announcing his presence. Stealthily, he crept into the corridor outside his study and moved toward the disturbance. When he reached the vestibule, it surprised him to glimpse a well-dressed couple facing away from him toward the grand staircase.

Richard stopped short, noting the thickset gentleman who appeared to be embracing a vaguely familiar woman. She was slumped at an awkward angle, and Richard could not make out her face until her head fell to hang forward. With dawning horror, he realized the gentleman was not embracing, but clutching Richard's former entanglement, Lady Evaline Wood, around her waist with her arms pinned under his, and she appeared to be swooning.

Richard caught sight of the shorter John behind the Woods, lying in a heap at the foot of the stairs and bleeding. Radcliffe stood to one side of the stairs with his hands raised outwards at an odd angle, as if he had been instructed to show them.

"That is when my wife decided that what is sauce for the goose is sauce for the gander, and in a fit of spite, she engaged in an improper liaison with *your husband!*" Lord Wood bellowed, his face red with fury.

Richard's heart skipped a beat. Sophia was here? Of course! That was why the shorter John was unconscious on the floor.

"But"—the man whirled on Lady Wood, shouting directly in her face—"you are not a *goose!* Men may stray, but women are expected to *behave!*" he roared, his voice echoing through the room.

Lady Wood seemed unresponsive, her expression frozen as though she had slipped into a state of shock.

Suddenly, Richard's perspective shifted, allowing him to see past the couple's clasped figures, now slightly parted. Standing stoically on the bottom stair, Sophia came into view, her gaze fixed not on the furious Lord Wood, but on the ornate dueling pistol clutched in his hand.

Blood thundered in Richard's ears and his eyes riveted to the pistol Lord Wood waved about while he ranted at his pale wife. With sharpened focus, he noted that the lord's bloated index finger rested on the side of the barrel, not the trigger, which meant Richard could attempt to disarm him.

One step at a time, Richard.

"Fortunately for me, a friend informed me of what was happening. Did you know that Lord Saunton was reportedly seen sneaking into my home last evening? All that talk of the rogue being reformed—nonsense, pure nonsense! Men may stray! It is simply what we do!"

He puffed up indignantly, his voice rising with each word. "We marry respectable women to bear our children, and we visit others for amusement. It is a system that has stood the test of time! It *works!*"

The man's ranting was despicable. Despite the danger of the moment, Richard could not help but be repulsed that he had once thought of women and relationships with a similar disgusting attitude as this vile reprobate who aimed a weapon at innocent people. Never had it been more clear that walking away from his past immorality was the correct decision. The only decision.

Slowly, Richard inched forward. If anything happened to Sophia because of his own debauched behavior with the unhappily married Lady Wood, he would find no redemption for his wicked soul. Damnation, what if his wife was killed tonight believing that he had engaged in an illicit affair *after* their wedding, rather than six months before he had even met her? He must save her because Ethan needed her. *He* needed her. He must save his wife!

Richard approached the dimly lit spot behind the couple. Lord Wood was in the midst of shaking Lady Wood, whose cracked lip was bleeding from an earlier blow.

Radcliffe's eyes flickered, noting Richard's arrival. His wonderful, clever butler imperceptibly straightened and lifted his chin, clearly steeling his nerves and preparing to divert Lord Wood's attention.

"My lord, perhaps a calm discussion might—"

"SHUT UP!"

"But, I assure you—"

"You speak again and I will end you, you insufferable *serf*!"

Radcliffe's ploy to distract the irate husband from Richard's approach succeeded as he crept up behind the couple. Fortunately, the angle of the light thrown by the chandelier above was in his favor, so no shadow announced his arrival. At this proximity, the raving nobleman reeked of hard liquor, which offered some explanation for his unbalanced behavior.

Verifying that Lord Wood's finger was still resting on

the barrel, Richard spoke behind his ear. "I believe you are looking for me?" Simultaneously, he swung his clenched fist down on the man's pistol-wielding right arm. Sophia immediately swung herself around the curving banister and dropped to her haunches behind the staircase. Radcliffe stood hesitant, plainly unsure whether to retreat or leap forward to help, while Lord Wood was so startled that he released his wife. Lady Wood crumpled into a heap but still possessed enough presence of mind to crawl away to where the butler hailed her toward him.

All of these events occurred in mere seconds, but Richard observed the scene with the same eerie calm, perceiving the position of every actor in the unfolding melodrama concurrently with the heightened focus that descended on him when it was time for him to spring into action. He fought for control of the weapon now pointed down between them in Lord Wood's hand, while Richard gripped the barrel. He was younger and fitter, but the beefy lord he was wrestling had the advantage of mass and a large, powerful grip. Lord Wood was renowned at their pugilistic club for packing a devastating punch—Richard knew he must avoid the man's club fists while fighting for control of the firearm.

If the unthinkable happened and he lost ... the damned weapon would only be loaded with one bullet, so Radcliffe and Sophia could protect themselves in the event of his demise.

Perry will take care of my family if he must assume the title, was his last coherent thought as the two of them stumbled and Richard took a ringing punch to the side of his head, holding on to the barrel of the pistol like his life depended on it while his vision spotted from the blow.

CHAPTER SEVENTEEN

"The most sacred friendship is that which is formed between persons of different sexes; the tender and delicate union of love and friendship."

Dr. John Gregory, A Father's Legacy to His Daughters

~

A shot rang out.

Sophia screamed in fear and clamped her hands over her ears. Then she scolded herself for being a scared little mouse, stiffened her resolve, and carefully peered around the curving banister of the staircase, which afforded a little protection.

Both men were prone on the floor, Lord Wood on top of her beloved Richard. *Please*, she prayed, *please let Richard be unhurt*. Neither man moved. Were they both dead? Panic clawed at the thought that her wonderful, foolish husband might be gone.

Slowly, she reached behind her onto a table to grab a vase as an impromptu weapon and then, crouching down, she scampered over to where they lay. Lord Wood rolled off Richard, and Sophia panicked, her eyes filling with tears until she realized it was Richard who had pushed the large man off, causing him to roll as if he were still alive.

She wept in relief, taking in Lord Wood's sightless eyes and blood seeping through the gold brocade of his waistcoat.

Richard scrambled to his knees to grasp Sophia in a hard embrace while she sobbed out her relief into his shoulder, the vase she held in her hand trapped uncomfortably between their bodies.

Sophia gasped. "You are hurt!" she exclaimed, touching his blood-soaked jacket.

"Nay, it is Lord Wood's blood. Sophia, my love, I must take care of Lady Wood. Can you be strong for me while I check on her?" Sophia realized she was still sobbing. Calming herself, she nodded.

He let her go and crawled over the few feet to where Lady Wood lay near Radcliffe, who had collapsed in a stupor. His butler noticed Richard's arrival and exhaled in deep relief. "My lord."

"Are you all right, Radcliffe?"

"Just a little dazed. I will collect myself back together, my lord."

"Take your time, Radcliffe. This is not a typical evening."

The butler bobbed his head, drawing in a deep breath while Richard turned his attention to the slight form.

"Evaline?" He touched the trembling woman on her shoulder and she flinched, cowering in a huddle.

"Evaline? Are you all right?" She shuddered and then looked up at him.

"It is over?" she whispered, her eyes unfocused and her face as pale as a white sheet.

"Yes," Richard assented. "But, my lady, Lord Wood ... I am afraid ... he is no longer with us."

She stared up at him with empty eyes until, in a hollow voice, she replied, "I could do with a strong drink, if I may?"

"I will take you to my study in a moment, as soon as I check on John over there."

Sophia watched her husband move over to the shorter John, carefully turning him over from the position he had fallen in after Lord Wood surprised him with a blow to the head with the pistol. The guardsman mumbled, to her relief, opening his eyes to look up into the earl's face. He bore a nasty gash on his temple that was bleeding profusely, and his gaze skittered about.

"Your lordship?"

"Yes, it is I. Radcliffe is calling for a doctor." Richard glanced over to the servant, who gave a quick nod and clamored to his feet.

Sophia dried her eyes, taking pride in the man she had married. Her heart had nearly stopped when her husband hurled into Lord Wood, but he had succeeded in his heroic antics and now ensured the well-being of each person, despite the ordeal he had just faced.

Richard had just saved her life.

And killed a man.

Richard placed his wife and Lady Wood in a carriage to

return to the Woods' residence, promising to follow the two women later.

Then he dispatched footmen to dig Perry out of whichever club he was gambling in that evening in his bid to gather intelligence.

Finally, Richard sent for the authorities.

When the Bow Street Runners arrived, he informed the grim-faced strangers that Lord Wood and himself had been playing cards together the day before and that Lord Wood had shown up that evening to accuse him of cheating before attempting to shoot him. Richard had been forced to wrestle him for his pistol, and the man was killed in the ensuing struggle.

Fortunately, Richard outranked the dead peer who had a reputation for drinking, an irascible temper, and violence with his fists. He recalled hearing of the man brandishing a pistol at a prize fight sometime in the past year, so he had high hopes that his version of events would protect Evaline over the coming days.

Radcliffe told the same story, forgoing any mention that the two women had been present and altering the accusations the lord had thrown to mumblings about a game of cards. Richard knew he could trust the longtime family servant to never speak on the matter.

The shorter John had been unconscious from the moment Lord Wood knocked him out with a crack to the head with the pistol the peer brandished after the couple had gained entry to the entrance hall. When the runners questioned the undercover guardsman, he corroborated that Lord Wood had been out of control upon gaining entrance to Balfour Terrace.

Richard worried if his story was weak, only having had a half hour to prepare it and gain Radcliffe's cooperation, but the runners appeared to accept what he said. Apparently, they were aware that Lord Wood was infamous for routing and fighting. The decoy tale was the least he could do to aid Lady Wood.

Perry arrived moments before the coroner. His brother was pale when he stepped through the front door, his eyes resting on the corpse before he strode over to Richard and grabbed him into a firm embrace.

"You daft cretin, you nearly got yourself killed!" His younger brother's sardonic ennui was not in evidence, his voice gruff with distress.

"Just think, you could have inherited an earldom tonight." Richard's jest was halfhearted, his tone sounding thick to his ears.

"Faugh, that would have been awful! Please promise me you will sire an heir soon. I have no wish to shoulder the responsibilities you carry. How will I find time to spend my allowance and frolic my days away?"

Richard chuckled, releasing his brother. "I am working on it."

They sat on the stairs while the coroner investigated the scene. Richard answered his questions and then, finally, the body was removed and his brother joined him in the study.

Perry made for the sideboard, poured two drinks, and walked back to where Richard sat in one of the plump armchairs to stare sightlessly into the hearth.

"Here, drink this."

"No, I am no longer drinking."

"Make an exception. You have just taken a man's life, and you look dreadful."

Richard hung his head, bringing up a hand to rub his face in despair. "I killed a man."

"Drink, brother. You are in shock."

Richard took the tumbler and downed the brandy in a few gulps. Warmth spread through his chilled body, and he noticed Perry was correct. Shock had rendered his limbs cold and sweaty, while his pulse fired too rapidly and his breathing was too shallow. As the spirits spread through his system, his body eased and he became more aware of his surroundings.

"I killed a man," he whispered.

"I only pointed that out so you would accept the liquor. I think you should focus on the fact that you saved someone's life tonight. That bullet was inevitably going to find its way into one of the people present. All things considered, the right person was on the receiving end of that shot."

"I doubt his wife would agree."

"I am certain his wife would agree. Lord Wood was notorious for using his fists to settle disputes. Do you not think his wife suffered under his temper as well? Nay, I believe she turned to you last year for a reason, and you may have freed her from the confines of a difficult, perhaps even unbearable, marriage. Is he the one behind all your troubles?"

Richard's hopes soared at the possibility before sinking like a stone into a pond.

"Nay, when I first arrived on the scene, he ranted that a friend informed him they saw me sneaking into his residence last night."

"He claimed you are currently carrying on an affair? Good heavens! I can scarcely recall a time you have left Balfour Terrace since you married the countess. I must say, I am thoroughly impressed with Lady Saunton's resilience. Any other woman would be utterly exhausted by now."

Richard glared at his brother, who threw up his hands

in surrender. "I shall not mention the countess or her resilience again, but clearly your hidden villain has struck once more. What are we doing to end this living nightmare?"

Richard leaned forward, his elbows on his knees, and dropped his head into his hands to ponder the question. "Lord Stanford knows the man's identity. He refused to name the scoundrel out of misguided honor."

Perry sprang to his feet, his jaw set with determination. "I will find Lord Stanford and compel him to reveal the identity of this troublemaker—even if it means dragging him out of Lady Partridge's den of impropriety and beating it out from him."

Richard thought about it, then nodded. "Take one of the barking irons with you." He gestured to the carved walnut box that housed his pistols on a top shelf.

Perry frowned in puzzlement. "I was not planning to kill the man or call him out."

Richard groaned. "For protection, you bird-wit! You will carry one and I the other until we settle this matter."

"Oh, that makes more sense." Perry flashed him a cheeky grin. "I am glad you are still with us, brother."

He ducked the cushion Richard hurled at him, his laughter trailing as he crossed the room. Taking down the box, he set it on the desk and opened it to retrieve one of the pistols. With careful precision, he prepared and loaded the weapon, then slipped it into the pocket of his overcoat.

With a quick, playful salute, Perry turned and left the room, leaving Richard alone with his thoughts.

After a few minutes contemplating the terror of this night, he stood up to make his way over to the Woods' residence, his carriage waiting for him when he exited the front door.

When he reached the Mayfair home of Lady Wood, he found Sophia waiting for him alone in a drawing room with an untouched cup of tea on the table in front of her. She jumped up when he entered the room, running over to fling herself into his embrace.

Richard wrapped his arms around her, grateful that she was safe and alive while he rested his cheek on the crown of her head and breathed deeply the scent of roses.

"Richard, I cannot believe what you did. My heart stopped when the two of you tumbled to the floor. I thought you were dead!"

"Who would bring trouble into your life, then?"

Sophia pulled back to look up at him. "The trouble does not concern me. I need you alive."

Richard let her go, pulling back to walk over and drop onto one of the rickety, elegant sofas, which juddered under his weight. "I do not see why. I have brought nothing but pandemonium and peril into your life. You were more protected before you married me."

His heart squeezed in agony at the deep silence following his pronouncement. After many moments, he heard her light footsteps approaching. She sat down on the sofa beside him and reached out a hand to cover his.

"We are both exhausted and I can no longer think straight, husband. But please know my relief that you survived is most profound. Could we go home to rest and then we can discuss things in the morning?"

Richard bobbed his head. He could not deny that in the aftermath, his body was heavy with weariness. He had forgotten to rid himself of the jacket, and the smell of blood aggravated his senses.

"How is Lady Wood?"

"She had a strong drink to steady herself, then confided

in me," Sophia said quietly, her voice faltering. "She showed me bruises hidden beneath her garments. Before retiring, she asked me to thank you. She believes you saved her life tonight. Lord Wood had not allowed her to leave their home without him for weeks—she has been trapped in that townhouse since March. Some of the bruises ... they were older, and ..."

Sophia broke off, her composure wavering under the weight of what she had witnessed.

Richard grimaced, his jaw tightening, and drew her gently into his arms, offering comfort as she fought to steady herself.

"Do not fret, Sophia. I will visit Lady Wood and ensure she is well taken care of. And I will have Johnson look into her circumstances to ensure that proper provisions were made for her. Hopefully, her father negotiated good terms for the eventuality of her bereavement."

Tears welled to slip down her smooth cheeks. She turned her head into his shoulder and flung her arms around him in a tight embrace. "I am such a watering pot tonight."

Richard gave her a squeeze and rose to his feet, holding out a hand to her. "Let us go so we can get some rest."

∽

Sophia clung to Richard the entire night. Each time he stirred, he found her form draped over him in different angles as if she could not bear to let him go. It warmed the depths of his soul where he still sought to come to terms with the fact that he had taken the life of a man he barely knew. Nothing could prepare a man for such an event. However, if he had to do it again, he would not hesitate to protect the woman who was lying in his arms, emitting a bleating snore from the awkward angle her head tilted so that she could nestle into his shoulder.

Carefully unwrapping her arms, he eased her onto her side, ensuring her neck was not cricked. He curved his arm around her sleeping form and went back to sleep, content to lie in bed with Sophia for the entire day if he could.

It was early afternoon when Richard and Sophia finally arose. Dressed in their nightclothes and robes, they ate breakfast from trays at the table near Sophia's window, too wrung out from the night before to bother with dressing or going downstairs to break their fast.

Once Sophia had swallowed down her eggs, sipped on her tea, and sat quietly contemplating the garden from her window, she broke their deep silence.

"May I see the note now?"

Richard huffed in mild amusement. He swallowed down his toast—he was surprised how ravenous he had been when the meal arrived—before rising to walk into his rooms.

After several minutes of searching, he found the note folded neatly with his things in a drawer of his bureau and returned.

Sitting down across from his wife, he stared at her for a while. She looked beautiful with her tousled red-blonde hair, her large eyes weary but prismatic with striations of light and dark blues reflected in their depths. And, more importantly, she was beauty itself because she was *alive*.

"I planned to talk with you when you returned last night. I wanted to apologize. Now I find I have more to apologize for."

"Apologize?"

"I thought about what you said, and I realized you were

right. I should have included you in what was happening. Instead, I treated you like a child."

"More like a weak-minded female."

"From the moment I overheard you on the terrace disparaging society, I knew you were strong and independent. I admire you greatly, and I have never thought of you as weak-minded. Only a fool would overlook your presence of mind and strength."

She gazed at him, a smile of joy playing on her lips. "Thank you."

"I should have told you about the note. Halmesbury told me I should tell you about the note. I was foolish to hide it from you, but it had nothing to do with my thoughts on you and everything to do with how I felt about myself. I was ashamed to have exposed my wife and my son because my selfish nature angered someone to this degree. And the note does not cast me in a favorable light." He grimaced. "Not that I deserve to be cast that way."

Sophia nodded. "I understand. I was on my way to find you and apologize, too."

Richard felt his jaw drop in astonishment. "What could you have to apologize for?"

"My cousin Lily had the audacity to point out that I had been testing you rather than be honest. Most men in my life have been a source of disappointment. I agreed to marry you with the best of intentions, but proceeded to be cautious and guarded with you. I did not confront you, but rather stewed in my anger that I was proven correct. Lily asked me if I would prefer we complain together about how men are terrible, or for her to advise me to take control over my situation. She made fine points. You are not comparable to my father. Look at what you did on behalf of our household. You were present, and you acted. You asked me to be patient with you, but I was not."

Sophia was flushed with the force of her opinions. She looked magnificent.

He coughed into his hand, unsure how to respond. "I cannot say I agree. Perhaps I need to understand more about your family history. I appreciate the thought you have put into ... us, I guess."

Her lips curved into a smile. "Thank you."

Richard glanced down at the note in his hand. "Please do not think less of me." He held the note out for her to take, then dropped his gaze down to stare at his hands. Working up his nerve, he finally said what had been in his heart for the past few days. "I have come to realize that marrying you was the most important decision I ever made. Sophia, I ... I love you."

Deep silence followed. He waited, but she had nothing to say.

I made a mistake! I told her before she is ready!

More silence continued. Finally, he found the courage to look up and confront her reaction to his proclamation, but he found Sophia frozen, white as a sheet, staring at the note in her hand.

"What is—"

The door to the hall flung open, banging on the wall as Perry rushed into the room. "Brother! Lord Stanford gave me the name of the man who lied to him about your attachment to Lady Partridge! It is Cecil Hayward."

"Cecil? I do not know any Cecil."

"But you do know a Hayward." Perry jerked his head in the direction of the woman sitting behind him. Richard's brow furrowed, and he turned around to find his wife staring at him with wide, shocked eyes.

"The note ... it is written in my brother's hand. He has attempted to disguise it, but ... Cecil ... he is sly but not intelligent. Too many years of hard drink have addled his brain. He used his customary stroke through the o. The trouble plaguing your household ... I brought this to your doorstep. This is all my fault!"

CHAPTER
EIGHTEEN

"In conversation, avoid too much eagerness to tell an anecdote."

Dr. John Gregory, A Father's Legacy to His Daughters

∽

Sophia felt like she had exited her body and observed the events in the room unfolding from a distance.

From the moment she had taken the note, she ceased to hear or see anything but the handwriting on the page, realizing that *she* had been the cause of the danger. Richard could have been killed. Even Ethan was in danger because she selfishly sought safety in the Balfour household and inadvertently brought her troubles with her.

Richard blamed himself for everything that had happened since the day of the wedding. He was so certain he was the cause that Sophia never stopped to observe the patterns. The bully tactics of the caricatures. The alteration of facts that caused angry paramours and husbands to target Richard. Even the rock through the window of

Richard's study carried the mark of her brother's hand, but she had failed to see it. Failed to inform Richard of the danger she represented.

She rushed back into her body with a crash. Her hand dropped the note, and she crumpled over in anguish, sorrow and regret coalescing to slash through her soul. Emitting a wail of deep despair, she dissolved into a blubbering mess. Richard's arms engulfed her, but she tried to wrench herself away. She did not deserve his solace because she had risked everything the man held dear to protect herself. And she had not even warned him of the danger.

Sophia had underestimated how vindictive her brother could be.

~

RICHARD GATHERED Sophia into his arms. She tried to pull away, but he was not having it. He hugged her closer, attempting to soothe her. It was devastating to see her anguish, his strong woman, who brought peace into his household, reduced to heaving sobs.

"Calm yourself, Sophia."

"It is all my fault!"

"Sophia, I need you to calm down. Please, my love. Whatever this is, we will sort it out."

"I could have caused your death!"

"My love, Lord Wood could have caused my death. And your brother might have put him up to it. But you did not do this, Sophia. Please, calm yourself."

Sophia sobbed in his arms with such gut-wrenching pain, he wanted to hunt down Cecil Hayward so he might pound the man into the ground. He had no idea what the blackguard was about, but he did know he wanted to kill him. Meanwhile, he must be content with making soothing sounds and caressing his hands up and down her slight back while she wept.

Finally, her storm of tears eased, and her head hung limp against him.

Perry walked over to hand him a handkerchief. Richard gently pushed Sophia back and used it to wipe at her downcast, swollen eyes. She would not look at him, an expression of guilt pasted across her face.

"Why would your brother target me? Did I offend him in some way I am unaware of?"

Sophia shook her head.

"Was he targeting me?"

Again, she shook her head.

"So, the cyprians in my bed, the caricatures, manipulating Lord Stanford and Lord Wood, the rock through the window, and the threatening note—these were misdirection to hurt you?"

She nodded.

"I feel I am missing some vital information—"

"I should leave! I will go to Saunton Park, and my brother will surely follow me there! Then you and Ethan will be safe!"

Richard took her face between his hands and coaxed her to look at him. "My love, I am not leaving you vulnerable. Now that we know who is behind this, we will find him and end it. But Sophia, you have to explain what this is about."

Sophia looked at him with such guilt and pain, it tore through him. He wanted to comfort her, to make her feel safe. It was his duty as her protector, but he knew she needed to explain the situation. Not just so that he and Perry could take action, but because she carried some unnamed burden that wreaked havoc on her usual composure. His wife needed him to listen.

"Would you like Perry to leave us alone?"

She shook her head. "I put your household in danger. Perry should know what hangs over our heads."

"Why would Cecil target you in this manner?"

She exhaled in a shaky breath before pulling out of his arms. She stood and went to stare out the window.

"I am not sure how to start. Where to start ..." She paused. "Ten years ago, my father died. He was a prolific gambler, and he drank too much. I was told he died of some sort of apoplexy while playing cards in the early hours. My mother was not a strong woman, and she died from a laudanum overdose within days of his death. Cecil is my father's son from his first marriage. He was sixteen and became very angry after our father's death."

Sophia stopped, raising a hand against the glass as if she were peering into the past.

"What happened?"

"Lord Moreland, my mother's brother, and his wife took us in. Cecil is not a blood relation of the Abbotts, but they have always valued family above all else, so they took my brother in along with me. They were not aware that Cecil started drinking quite heavily. Perhaps he was drinking before my father's death. It is possible my father encouraged it when they spent time together. I ... I did not know what to do about it. He is my brother ... the only one I had left after my parents both ..."

Richard struggled to understand where the story would lead and how it related to their wedding, which had apparently set her sibling off on this rampage, but he remained silent to allow Sophia to find her way through the tale.

"Uncle Hugh gave him an allowance, which Cecil

squandered on wagering—playing cards, placing bets at less-than-reputable clubs. The Abbotts were unaware of his decline. He fooled them with his polished manners, and they are not accustomed to dealing with someone so reckless in his habits ..."

His heart skipped a beat. He did not like the direction this was going. Had the brother hurt her in some manner?

"When I turned eighteen and came out, Uncle Hugh gave me a generous allowance. Cecil needed to pay his gambling debts, and I had money. So he took it from me. When I threatened to tell my uncle, my brother ... made it clear that I would regret it if I ever informed on him."

Perry and Richard both stiffened, Perry casting him a questioning look. Richard shook his head to indicate he did not know, but he disliked the tone of her voice when she stated it.

"Sophia, my love, can you explain, how did he make that clear?"

"He hurt me," she replied softly.

Richard jumped to his feet, agitated. Sophia needed to tell him the rest, which meant he needed to stay calm and let her finish.

Perry, noting his distress, asked the next question. "How ... did your uncle not notice?"

"Cecil was always careful—he'd strike me where the marks wouldn't show, like my stomach. Evidence was minimal."

Richard ran a hand through his hair, his expression tense as he gestured for Perry to remain silent. The thought of his sweet wife suffering at the hands of someone who should have protected her tied his stomach in knots. "Has he been doing this all these years?"

"Nay, after the first few times, I started reading military texts and working on strategies to outwit him. I hid items of sentimental value I did not wish him to take. I hid pin money, too, and told him that Aunt Christiana was making me spend it all on expenses related to the Season. He eventually stopped coming to me for funds, but I believe the gambling continued."

Richard drew a deep breath. Her resourcefulness was impressive, but he would have expected it from her. His sweet Sophia was no man's victim.

"How did we get to today? Why did our wedding rile his wrath after all this time?"

"He uncovered the truth about my dowry and realized he could come to a financial arrangement with a fortune hunter. Stealing me from my bed and taking me to Scotland for a forced marriage was discussed."

Richard stared at her in horror. "Leech!"

"Leech?" Perry hissed. "The wife killer?"

Richard nodded. "I interceded that night at the Yardley ball, or she would have been compelled to dance with him. The coroners in the matter of his wives' deaths could find no evidence of foul play and the man has powerful friends, so he walks amongst us unscathed, but he must have orchestrated their deaths."

Sophia spoke in a low, sad voice. "Based on the conversation I overheard, he definitely had a hand in their deaths. He alluded to the possibility of my own."

Richard shook his head in dismay, pacing back and forth while he tried to settle his thoughts. "Is this what you meant when you said you needed protection?" Sophia nodded, her face still averted toward the window. "Botheration! I thought you meant in a general sense that a woman needed a protector, or that you had concerns about fortune hunters pursuing you. I did not know you needed *actual* protection!"

"I was uncertain how much of a threat they posed, but once we agreed to wed, I took to sleeping in my cousin's room and paid a footman to sleep in my bed. The night before our nuptials, Lord Leech attempted my abduction, but Thomas apprehended him."

Richard and Perry looked at each other, aghast. They considered their dead father to have been the worst kind of scoundrel, but yet even he possessed innocence when compared to Sophia's brother. Richard could not believe she had lived under such intimidation. He wanted to walk over to his wife and fold her in his arms to comfort her, yet he knew she needed to finish her story for her own peace of mind, so he clenched his fists and stayed rooted to where he stood.

"I was forced to tell Uncle Hugh about Cecil's involvement. I ... I thought it was safe to do so. I would marry you in the morning and then I would be beyond his reach. I did not know he would take it this far." Sophia's voice thickened with tears. "I am so sorry for dragging you into this. I hoped to spare the Abbotts, but I endangered your household instead!"

At that, Richard raced across the room to embrace her. "Hush, Sophia, the only regret I have is that I did not know. If I had known, I would still have married you." He waved his hand at Perry, who left the room and quietly closed the door behind him. "Sophia, nothing—nothing—could have dissuaded me from pursuing you."

Sophia was mortified that she had been weeping again. Since the moment she thought Richard had been killed, her emotions had been skittering out of her control. Just when she had regained her equilibrium, she discovered she was the one at fault for the jeopardy their household was in.

She had been willing to tolerate Richard's troubles because she entered their marriage with her eyes open, but to learn that she was the true cause ... Her conscience was chewing her up from the inside. She had miscalculated the risk that Cecil posed and exposed Richard, Perry, and little Ethan to his wicked revenge.

"Sophia?"

A shiver of apprehension scurried over her skin. She looked up but had trouble meeting her husband's eye.

"Sophia, I need you to look at me."

Her eyelids flickered. With reluctance etched in every line of her body, she lifted her gaze. Richard's eyes were blazing in their intensity, green with gold striations, catching her in a net of fascination.

"Sophia, you are not to blame. Your brother is a diabolical fiend, but we will take care of it. Together."

His words penetrated the cloud of guilt she was cloaked in. "You do not blame me?"

"I do not. However, I accept your apology from earlier that you were not forthright with me, now that I comprehend what you have been hiding." His lips quirked into a wry smile. Sophia chuckled despite her dark mood. It was one of the things that made Richard so special—his ability to make her laugh in even her darkest hours.

"If I knew that he would follow me here ..." She trailed off in wordless dismay.

"I know, my love."

Sophia stared at him, her beloved husband. Who was

still alive. Impulsively, she leaned forward to kiss him on his perfect lips.

"Are you feeling better?"

She gave a brief nod. "I know you must work with Perry to find my brother, but could you wait? Last night I was so terrified you had been killed, and up until this moment, the only time we have spent together is to sleep. I am weary of dealing with earth-shattering revelations. I need a few quiet moments to stop and rest with you."

Richard drew her into his arms, holding her close. "Yes," he murmured softly. "I would like that very much."

THEY SAT TOGETHER IN SILENCE, Richard picking at the remains of his breakfast while Sophia drank tea. He thought about his earlier declaration of love. Had she heard what he said? Was she pretending he had not revealed his heart to her? Or had she been too distracted to hear him?

Dealing with the emergency that Cecil Hayward created was easier to his state of mind than the nerves that assailed him at the thought that he had announced his feelings—*blech*—but she said nothing in return. Did she desire his esteem?

This was not the appropriate time to press the matter. Emotions were running too high, while shock was still wearing off after the tragic events of the night before. But the impulse to delve into it anyway was all he could think about.

"Richard?"

He looked up to find Sophia restored to her usual composure. Her blue eyes were calm, and her manner peaceful. Apparently, her request to slow things down and stand still for a moment was exactly what she needed.

"Tell me about your crusade. What have you been doing? I know you found Ethan because of it, but I do not really understand how you have gone about it."

Richard pulled a face. "Will you still like me if you know the details?"

She extended a hand to cover his own, rubbing a thumb over his knuckles. "I will like you more."

He blew a puff of air and told her. His voice was steady but tinged with regret. He told her how he had composed a list of the women from his past whom he might have wronged, detailing how Johnson and Long had investigated their current circumstances. He explained how he had met with his former companions to offer heartfelt apologies for any irresponsibility on his part, and where it was appropriate, he had provided financial assistance to help them move forward.

He also shared how he had gifted an unentailed property to Ethan's family as a gesture of gratitude for their kindness in taking in the boy after his mother's passing.

When Richard finished speaking, he hesitated before finally lifting his gaze to hers, unsure of what he might find. To his relief and astonishment, Sophia was smiling, her eyes filled with warmth and admiration.

"Your crusade is most commendable."

His spirits lifted at her encouragement. Oh, how he loved this odd female he had married. He could think of no other woman of his acquaintance who would be so gracious about his past mistakes and his clumsy efforts to sort them out. *Except for one. You know of one other.* Richard squashed the voice in his head. He did not want to think of her. Since the moment of his revelation on the Astleys' terrace, he had made a point not to think about *her*.

It was as if Sophia picked the errant thought from his head because her next question was so unnerving that his stomach heaved when she asked it.

"Tell me about your first betrothal?"

Richard sprang to his feet in agitation, knocking over the heavy armchair with the juddering force of his movement. His heart fluttered in his chest, revolting at the subject she wished to discuss. Why did she have to ruin their nice moment?

"I think we should call for the servants. It is time to get dressed and deal with this Cecil debacle, I think."

"Richard?"

He righted the armchair to distract his thoughts, desperate to find a change of topic, but his mind was a blank. All he could think about was—

"Richard?"

He rubbed his hands over his face, panic setting in before he realized that withheld information had nearly resulted in Sophia being killed last night. That he himself was lucky to be standing there breathing. If he could survive an encounter with a dueling pistol in his own home, then surely he could survive a conversation in the privacy of his wife's bedchamber about the worst mistake he had ever committed. "Damnit!"

Sophia waited for him, calm and far too understanding. Seething with—what, he did not know—just seething, he reclaimed his seat to stare at the table in front of him. Reaching up to loosen his cravat, he floundered at the recollection that he was dressed in an open-neck cotton nightshirt. He dropped his hand back to the table.

Why was he more afraid to think about what he had

done to Annabel than he had been about leaping onto an armed man the night before? It was beyond comprehension how emotions and guilt could eat at one's soul. Emotions had no force, no tangible mass. Yet they could feel more solid than the walls of a prison, despite their intangible nature.

"Earlier you allowed me to talk. To explain about Cecil. It was not comfortable, but having finally shared the burden of what I have been living with ... it helped. I will sit here and wait until you are ready, Richard. I care about you, and it is obvious you need to unburden your conscience. It is important, because we face genuine danger when we leave this room, and I think it best we leave with clear minds so we can operate effectively. For our sake, and the sake of your son upstairs."

Drat, I need a drink!

But he only needed a drink because his guilt had been tearing him in two since the night he had confronted the magnitude of his betrayal. And ever since the first inkling of guilt had presented itself less than three weeks earlier, he had desperately tried to push it down and seal it back in a box and bury it in the attic of his mind where it could not torture him.

Now it was time to unbury the box and bring it out to open it. Stuff, it was mortifying.

Clearing his throat, he finally spoke. "Her name is Annabel."

CHAPTER NINETEEN

"Sensibility is the charm of a woman's character."

Dr. John Gregory, A Father's Legacy to His Daughters

~

"Annabel is the younger sister of a friend, Brendan Ridley. We met when we were children. She is intelligent and lively, the first female I ever genuinely enjoyed spending time with outside the ..." Richard waved his hand at the bedchamber, clearly unsure how to complete the sentence. Sophia nodded her understanding so he would continue.

"After my father passed away, I rescued our estates from the brink of financial ruin. Once I succeeded, I needed to ensure that our tenants would find themselves with responsible leadership in the event of my demise. Three or four years ago, I decided it was time to do my duty and sire an heir because Perry made it clear he did not wish to inherit. I started my search for a suitable wife, but after two stupefying Seasons of meeting tame young misses whom I could not tolerate for more than five to ten minutes at a time, I realized there was only one woman whom I could marry. Annabel was rusticating in the country because her father refused to bring her to London, and I realized I had an opportunity to marry an interesting woman."

Sophia experienced a slight twinge of envy, then reminded herself that he was not married to the other woman but was sitting in her own bedchamber recounting his history. She suppressed her jealousy and forced herself to pay attention to what was important.

"The problem was, I thought I could marry a close friend and continue my pursuits concurrently."

"I take it Annabel did not see it that way?"

"Correct. I had taken up with a maid on her father's estate, someone she cared about, and Annabel discovered us kissing in the stables."

She sighed but refrained from comment. Richard flushed in embarrassment and looked down at his hands folded on his lap, stiff with tension. "I did not handle it well. She did. She let the maid go with references. She even helped the young woman find a new position. I ... I did nothing. Except when Annabel said she wanted to cancel the wedding. Then I did something."

Sophia frowned, puzzled and trying to work out what he could have done. "Never say you refused?"

Richard's head sank lower, blushing so hard his ears turned a bright red. "And I convinced her father to proceed with the wedding."

"My word!" Sophia gasped. "Oh! I apologize. I am just surprised. Please continue."

"She begged me to change my mind, but I insisted the wedding would proceed. Annabel grew desperate, so she sought my cousin, the Duke of Halmesbury—"

"And married him!" Sophia clapped a hand over her mouth. "Please, I am sorry. It is just so ingenious of her."

Richard grimaced. "That is the short version of the story, yes. The long version is that she dressed herself like a lad and risked her life to ride alone through the night from Somerset to Wiltshire to seek him out. Apparently, she asked him to intercede with me, but he seized the opportunity to win my bride from me for reasons I will explain another day."

Sophia realized she was gaping at him, quickly pressed her lips together, then said, "It was not well done of you—what you did to Annabel—but why does it bother you so much after all this time? Given that it all worked out for her in the end."

Her husband lifted a hand to knead the muscles in his neck, his expression agitated while he thought. "I suppose ... all the other women I wronged were active, willing participants in my dalliances. Annabel was different. She was innocent of any wrongdoing, and I had no excuse to betray a friend in that manner. Then I compounded it by insisting she wed me when it was clear she did not want to. When I awoke to how wrong my past behavior has been, it finally dawned on me how poorly I treated her. If you told me a man had done this to you ... I would seek them out and pound them. It was pure villainy. My father was the very worst, far past the point of redemption, but what I did to her ... it ranked as one of the worst things a potential protector could do, and then when I was caught, I showed no remorse of any kind. If she had not gained assistance from Halmesbury, I would have proceeded with the wedding and she would be trapped in a marriage to me after I proved I could not be trusted."

Richard's face displayed his self-loathing, which made Sophia's heart ache on his behalf. She could not imagine the difficulty of repairing so many mistakes of the past and having to live with the consequences in the present. This morning, she had experienced her own guilt, which had been torturous.

"Husband, might I make a bold suggestion?"

He could not look at her, but he did gesture her to continue.

"I think if you had married her, something would have happened and you would have stopped ... your indiscretions."

Richard's head shot up, amazement on his face. "What? Why would you say that?"

"For one thing, less than three weeks ago, you made a decision to change, and you have done so. That implies that it was inevitable that eventually you would decide to do so, given the right circumstances."

"That is generous of you, but it was a chance encounter with you that did it, so—"

"And that is the other thing. You had to be seeking an opportunity to change."

"What?" Richard was genuinely perplexed, clearly at a loss for words because of her audacious declaration.

"Think about it. Why would a man planning on pursuing infidelity for the remainder of his days insist on marrying an intelligent and lively woman? It makes no sense. Unless ..."

"Unless?"

"Unless he sought a strong partner who would make him change? Someone who could hold him accountable?"

Varying emotions played across Richard's face for a while. She waited for him to think it through until she finally saw understanding dawn. "I wanted to change?"

"And that is the trait I admire about you above all else —except for the courage to leap on weapon-wielding drunkards in order to save me." She shuddered at the memory of the night before. "The reason I agreed to marry you was that I grew up with two men in my life who each and every day made worse and worse decisions. They kept moving toward moral oblivion, but you—you came to me from the brink of moral ruin and decisively announced your intention to change. Not just in words, but with genuine action that you were taking. Until that moment, I was not aware that it could be done, but I saw the sincerity in your eyes and it moved me. It was ... inspiring."

"I ... inspired you?"

"More than any person I ever met."

Richard finally looked at her, his eyes filled with admiration. "You are utterly amazing."

With that, he raised a hand to cup the back of her head and gently tugged her forward to brush a tender kiss on her lips. She gasped softly, her eyes wide with surprise, before melting into his embrace. Her hands gripped his arms as if to steady herself, and she leaned into his warmth, losing herself in the moment.

It seemed somehow life-affirming to lose herself in his arms while his hand traced down to rest on the slope of her neck where her pulse beat frantically.

RICHARD FOUND Perry waiting in his study when he went downstairs. His brother stood hovering near his desk.

"I have been thinking. I went through all of the recent events, starting the day of the wedding. The only conclusion is that the countess's brother gained access to the house through the library. Remember, he was standing by the doors that face the garden during the ceremony? He could have unlocked those doors to gain entrance later."

Richard took a seat at his desk, noticing a page covered with the timeline of events in his brother's untidy hand, along with a quill dripping ink on his smooth mahogany. Perry, who was so impeccable in his dress, had always been disorderly with his work. Richard nodded absent-mindedly while he pulled out a handkerchief to wipe the ink from the surface. He hoped the housekeeper or one of the maids knew how to clean the stain off the lacquer.

Perry pressed on. "So my question is, how did he know about Ethan? In order for that caricature to appear at the print shops so quickly, he would have needed to know about Ethan's existence from the moment the boy arrived at Balfour Terrace. Unless you believe that Johnson, Long, or Radcliffe would have leaked the information?"

"Never. I trust those men implicitly. There were maids who prepared the nursery, but only that day when my son arrived."

"So how did this Hayward fellow know about your son? I thought about it, and given ... um ... your reputation ..." Perry pulled at his cravat in discomfort. "Well, I do not know how to say this, but if I witnessed a young child arriving in the family carriage and put it together with your reputation, I might assume that your illegitimate child was joining your household. And we know the scoundrel does not care for facts because of the lies he told Lord Stanford and Lord Wood, so let us assume he did not care whether he guessed correctly. His intention was to create as much trouble as quickly as he could."

"That makes sense."

"Well, how did he observe Ethan was here? The boy arrived, entered the house to eat, he spent time with you and went up to the nursery to sleep."

Richard scowled, trying to understand Perry's point while muddling through his emotions and thoughts about the discussion with Sophia regarding his former betrothed. Then, with sudden clarity, he realized what Perry was trying to point out. "He must have seen the carriage arrive with Johnson and Ethan!"

"Exactly! If he did that, then he must be consistently watching the house."

"Which means we might find him somewhere in this square!"

"Perhaps Hayward has been visiting someone here, or he is staying as a guest. Or possibly he just broke into a home that is closed up for some reason. I propose that you and I go to meet our neighbors because no one is going to refuse an earl at their front door. What do you think? Are you tired of this situation yet? Should we take action?"

"It will certainly be better than sitting here waiting for his next strike. Do you still carry the pistol I lent you?"

WHILE SOPHIA DRESSED with the help of her maid, her mind worked over what Richard had told her about his failed betrothal. She wanted to do something for him. Last night, he had saved her life. At the time, they believed the danger had been caused by his past misdeeds, but that made it no less telling of his character when, to protect his household, he leapt onto a physically imposing man wielding a weapon.

Then it came to light that she was the one who had brought the villainous machinations to their doorstep. To which her husband had responded by giving her solace without a word of complaint. Even now, he had gone downstairs to plan with Perry how to locate her brother and end the threat.

He was doing all the work. What had she done except sit around useless? She needed to contribute in a meaningful way, and an idea had come to her after Richard left her chambers. An idea that took root and she felt driven to execute. Immediately. The moment she was dressed, she ordered a carriage be brought round. While she prepared to leave the townhouse, she saw the taller John hovering close by.

"Where is the other John? Is he all right?"

"He is recovering and well today, but his lordship assigned him the lighter duties of the nursery and tasked me with taking his place."

"Good. We are going out." With that, she stepped out the front door and headed for the carriage.

A short drive to a nearby Mayfair home and then Sophia was standing in the entrance hall waiting to be shown in. She hoped the noblewoman would see her. She needed to do something useful, and this felt right. It would help Richard confront his inner demons, so he could finally forgive himself for his past sins.

The butler returned. In his unusually hoarse voice, he informed her that the duchess would see her and showed her into a lavish drawing room decorated in blue and gold.

Sophia entered to find a young woman of her own age

seated on a fine Chesterfield sofa, with a tea service laid out on the table. She had a crown of curling chestnut hair, and warm eyes the color of brandy with glints of gold not dissimilar to the light catching in said drink.

"The Countess of Saunton," announced the very proper butler in his husky tone, startling Sophia so that she flinched ever so slightly.

The duchess stood and walked over to greet her. "Your Grace." Sophia sank into a curtsy, feeling a little in awe of the elegant noblewoman.

Her hostess smiled widely before exclaiming, "Pish! My name is Annabel."

Sophia smiled in return. She could not help it. Her mouth moved in response to the young woman's vibrant energy. Richard had said she was lively, but he had not mentioned how warm the woman was. Sophia felt like she was being wrapped in a sunny Saturday afternoon in the park, her overwrought nerves relaxing into an even state she had not enjoyed in some time.

"Sophia," she acknowledged.

"I was hoping I would meet you soon, Sophia. I wanted to see what kind of woman tamed the infamous Earl of Saunton and here you are. Shall we have tea?"

Richard was right. The duchess's mind moved quickly despite the surprise of her visit. She could see a younger version of this woman haring across two counties alone on horseback to find an escape from her nuptials. Of course the duke had been immediately captivated.

She followed the duchess to take a seat, then watched as she poured another cup of tea and passed the cup and saucer to her. Sophia breathed in the delightful fragrance before raising the china cup to her lips to take a small sip.

Annabel leaned back in her seat. "What is the reason for your visit?"

"May I speak frankly?"

"I would prefer it. I am still mastering the art of polite small talk and could do without it for a spell. We have much more interesting subjects we could talk about than the weather."

"Richard told me what happened between the two of you."

The duchess raised her chestnut eyebrows. "Indeed. The duke told me he believed a singular woman had finally captivated Richard. If your husband told you about The Stable Incident, then I know it must be true rather than merely my husband's hopes on behalf of his cousin."

Sophia smiled, feeling uncertain. They had a true marriage in the sense that they were now working together. However, the duchess appeared to believe that Richard loved her, and there was no evidence of that. He had not said so. He had not promised it at any time. She feared she might just be the medium for his crusade, but it seemed dishonorable to confirm or deny it, so she said nothing.

"I was wondering what it would take for Richard to receive your forgiveness. He feels much guilt over what happened, and it would provide him peace if he knew you were no longer angry."

Annabel sighed deeply. "I am no longer angry. Things turned out well for me. I met the man I love, and I have a wonderful baby boy upstairs in the nursery. If Richard had not been faithless, I would never have met Philip—the duke—under the circumstances that we met and I would not be wed to the most honorable man."

"So you forgive him?"

"No."

"But ... you said you are not angry with him."

"I appreciate that he finally took responsibility for what he did to Caroline Brown, but he has not done what is required to make things well with me. I am happy that he and my husband have been able to resume their friendship and I wish him all the best, but I will not forgive him. He knows what I require."

"I ... is there nothing I can do?"

"You can convince him to do the right thing."

Sophia put her tea down. She had hoped this discussion would proceed well, but now disappointment was rising in her chest and her hands were shaking from all the repressed emotions. Under ordinary circumstances, she would know what to say next, but nothing about the past couple of weeks had been ordinary. "Please, could you tell me what it is he needs to do so I can assist him?"

"I want an apology."

"An apology?"

"That is correct."

"An apology?"

The duchess nodded in agreement. Sophia wondered if she was dreaming because suddenly nothing made sense to her. "Are ... are you saying ... that the earl never *apologized* for what he did?"

Annabel raised her chestnut eyebrows, which Sophia took as an affirmation.

"My daft husband was too proud? Is that it?"

"Not exactly. At the time, he insisted he acted exactly as he should, that it was essentially a man's prerogative. Since that time, if he is now struck by remorse, I would assume it is pride that stands in the way of him coming to see me."

"So all he has to do to end this matter with you is simply apologize for his faithlessness?"

"That is correct."

Sophia bit her lip. "May I ask a favor of you?"

The duchess appeared intrigued, tilting her head in agreement. "You may."

"Before I do, perhaps I should tell you about some unusual events from the past few days and the heroics of my protector."

CHAPTER TWENTY

"Fortitude is a virtue that enables a woman to endure trials with dignity."

Dr. John Gregory, A Father's Legacy to His Daughters

∽

Richard and Perry returned after several hours of tiresome introductions, endless cups of tea, and dainty biscuits, which they nibbled on to extend their visits and establish if any of the residents in the square were hosting the Hayward scoundrel. Alas, the venture had been to no avail.

Entering the vestibule of Balfour Terrace, they removed their overcoats, hats, and gloves to hand off to the footman in attendance before Perry mumbled something under his breath about needing the necessary, and Richard made his weary way to his study.

Pushing open the door, he was astonished to find the shorter John standing just inside. The older man had a raffish air, sporting a taped gash over his right temple. Richard swiveled his head to locate the man's charge, Ethan, flinching in surprise at the sight that met his eyes. His nerves were too frayed to deal with any of it.

A nursemaid he did not recognize was holding an infant, bouncing the babe whose shock of familiar chestnut hair informed him that his cousin's heir was present. The nursemaid's low humming soothed her charge as she bobbed.

His own son's nursemaid, Daisy, sat sipping a cup of tea in a seat tucked in the room's corner while Ethan sat on the floor in front of a low table playing chess with his cousin, the large blond Viking of the Markham clan. It was a confounding scene of domesticated perfection.

"Halmesbury?"

The duke looked up from his position on the carpeting. "Just a moment, please." He turned back to the table. Ethan's little face screwed in concentration. He picked up a piece with his small hand and moved it, staring down at the board for several seconds, and then raised his head in triumph. "Checkmate!"

Halmesbury chuckled. "Well done, little cousin! I told you it would work!"

Ethan beamed before leaping to his feet and racing over to hug Richard's legs. "I beat the duke, Papa!"

Richard reached down to swing his son into his arms. "Well done, Ethan. What say Daisy take you to celebrate with something from Cook in the kitchens?"

"I want to eat biscuits," his boy proclaimed before squirming out of Richard's arms to land on his feet when he lowered his son down.

Daisy and Ethan left hand in hand, the shorter John dedicated to shadowing their heels as he exited and shut the door behind them. Richard turned to find the duke seated in one of the plump armchairs by the fire, striking an imposing figure against the bottle green of the wallpaper that framed him.

"What the deuce are you doing here?"

"Your wife invited us. She said to meet her in the mews when you returned."

Richard was lost. Halmesbury never visited his home. Sophia had never met the duke, so why would she invite him and his infant son over to visit? Was this some sort of visit for Ethan? He shook his head in confusion.

"Go find your wife, Saunton." Philip's steady gaze revealed nothing. As usual, his kinsman appeared wholly composed, providing no clues to his thoughts.

Bosh, my cousin can be infuriating!

Richard turned and stomped out, heading down the passage. He let himself out into the garden and crossed over to enter the mews, where he found the taller John standing at the entrance.

How did I think I would fool Sophia into thinking these rumpled guardsmen were actual footmen?

She would need to be blind and stupid not to notice something amiss. He blamed his lack of sleep and stress for his miscalculation of not informing her he had hired additional security.

"Where is her ladyship?" he demanded of the man, vaguely noting the distant sound of men at work in the carriage house.

"Down near the end in one of the stalls, milord."

Richard's mood worsened as he looked at the dim interior to the right. What was his wife doing here, and why had he been summoned to see her? He regretted his promise not to drink. He needed one to wash the taste of conflicting tea blends from his mouth.

He stomped down the corridor toward the workrooms at the other end of the mews, where he heard a woman talking, stopping mid-sentence at the sound of his approaching footsteps. He forced himself to relax his face into more pleasant lines before walking into the stall to unearth what this summons to the stables could possibly mean.

Where he came face-to-face with the one person he had been dreading he would encounter this Season.

"Annabel!" He winced. How was he meant to address her? "I mean ... Your Grace." He bowed stiffly.

"Annabel is acceptable."

Richard pulled a face before looking around to find his wife standing to the side with a sheepish expression on her blushing face. "What is this, Sophia?"

"I asked Annabel—Her Grace—Annabel ..." Sophia ground to a halt.

"Your wife informed me of your heroics last evening, Richard. She asked me if I would visit today so you could say what you needed to say. According to her, a conversation with me would ease some of your troubles."

Richard shot a look at his traitorous wife, who was studying her slippers in chagrin. "I see."

"I thought it would help." Sophia's voice was but a whisper.

"Why in the stables?"

"If I may?" Annabel interjected with an amused smile. Richard turned back to face her, finding it difficult to meet her eye, so his gaze settled on the brick wall behind her shoulder. "I would not come otherwise. I have waited for your apology for some time now, and I thought it would be appropriate to pick up the conversation where we left off. These are different stables, of course, but I think it lends an air of authenticity to the completion of this discussion."

Shame, irritation, and resentment squirmed in his belly. He wanted to turn and run, but he would merely look foolish. Eventually, he would need to admit that he had made a horrendous mistake with the woman standing in front of him. Richard huffed in defeat.

"All right. I suppose I owe you an apology, and you are in your rights to demand the time and place, considering ..."

Sophia interrupted. "I will be standing right outside while you talk." She hastily walked out of the stall to stand a few feet away, a nervous air about her as she folded her arms to wait.

Richard turned back to find the girl whom he had known since he was a lad and who had matured into a lady of elegance. Annabel had developed into a self-assured duchess of the realm while still retaining that spirited, intelligent glint in her brandy eyes.

He thought about what Sophia had pointed out earlier that day. How could he ever have believed he could fool this woman regarding his indulgent habits if they had married? Even two years earlier, it now made sense that he had been making decisions that would eventually sabotage the unprincipled life he had led and force him to become honest. Somewhere deep in his heart, he must have sought to change his path. But what he had done to Annabel was ... There were no words adequate to describe how deeply he had betrayed the woman who was once his friend. His chest constricted with the burden of guilt he was carrying.

"I ... am ... sorry."

Richard was surprised to discover that a small piece of the weight chipped off, and he found his thoughts began to clear. "I am sorry I misled you into thinking I planned on having a genuine marriage with you."

More weight lifted, his breathing deepened, and air rushed into his lungs. "I am sorry I betrayed you with someone you cared about."

The sheer relief at his words made him feel light-headed. "I am sorry that I showed no remorse."

Finally, he shifted his gaze to look her in the eye. "My deepest apologies that I failed to respect your wishes or allow you control over your destiny when I refused to cancel the wedding."

Annabel smiled widely at him. "Admit you feel better."

Richard returned her smile, feeling ten years younger at that moment. "I do."

"Good! I am glad you did everything you did because it led me to Philip. But I also knew you needed to say this. To accept responsibility for your actions, and that is why I remained firm on the point."

She reached forward and grabbed his hands in hers. "I am so happy you found the right woman and that you finally found your way. I always knew you had it in you, Richard. You are a great man who influences many. I want you to live a long and happy life—"

"CECIL!" At Sophia's cry, Richard and the duchess froze. The sound of someone running could be heard.

Richard burst out of the stall just in time to see his wife throw herself at the legs of a groom, wrapping her arms tightly around his knees and bringing him crashing to the hard-packed earth with a loud thud.

The man, enraged, swung his arm back and struck Sophia across the face. She reeled from the blow but clung tightly to him, her determination unwavering.

A surge of fury rose in Richard's chest at the sight.

Roaring with anger, he sprinted forward, throwing himself onto the man and pinning him to the ground. "John!" he bellowed, calling for the guard as rage pulsed through his veins.

Unable to contain himself, Richard delivered a sharp blow to the man's side.

How dare he lay a hand on my countess?

He heard John's hurried footsteps approaching as his own fists continued to drive home the message: no one harms his wife without answering for it.

"Your lordship, stop! I am here. Let me take hold of the man." Richard could barely hear the guardsman as blind outrage made him pull his arm back to throw another punch.

"Richard!" Sophia's voice penetrated his frenzied haze. Richard froze. His heart beat loudly in his ears while he slowly unclenched his fist. He used that hand to push himself up and look back.

Sophia was sitting on the blackguard's legs. The sight of disheveled hair and her split lip, with a trickle of blood running down her chin, broke his heart—until he noticed that her face, her eyes, her skin were glowing. She was incandescent with unbound joy.

"Richard! I caught him! I tackled him to the ground!"

Richard reached over to wipe the blood off her chin, feeling reverence at the bravery of his young wife. He realized why she was so overjoyed—she had just bested the bully that tortured her these past several years. "You did, my love. I take it this is your brother?"

"Of course!" He forced back a smile at her wounded affront. "I do not make a habit of tackling strangers."

The taller John helped him hold the struggling man by the arms so they could turn him over. Richard reached down and pulled off the low-slung hat to reveal red-blond hair and defiant bloodshot eyes. The brother showed evidence of hard drinking, his face ruddy and his congested skin webbed with spider veins. For such a young man, his appearance was bloated and unhealthy.

Richard grinned with grim determination. "Mr. Hayward, I spent the day looking for you."

Who would have imagined that visiting his own stables to deliver the long-overdue apology would fortuitously lead to the capture of his foe? It was fitting somehow that the two events converged in such a manner. By accepting responsibility for his past, fate dictated that he solve his present troubles.

Now the scourge of their household was trussed to a chair in a little-used drawing room. The cursing man tugged at the ties in a futile attempt to leave while being guarded by the two Johns and Radcliffe.

"He certainly has a fixation on coin," commented the duke in a dry tone.

It was as if Hayward overheard the remark; the cursing increased in volume. "I do not see why that witch should receive all the money and advantages! She leaves nothing for me!"

Annabel, the duke, Perry, Sophia, and Richard stood on the far end of the large drawing room, huddled in a group to discuss what to do while pointedly ignoring the brother's spitting vitriol.

Only Perry glared at the scoundrel. "I knew it! I knew he must have been observing Balfour Terrace! Who would have thought such a spoilt young man would take a post working as a groom? He must be quite dedicated to ruining this household!"

Sophia shook her head in disbelief. "He could be angry that I tattled to my uncle about his plot. Or he is simply enraged to be thwarted in his plans to exploit my inheritance. He seemed to think he had some right to the funds, so that might fuel his petty anger."

Richard nodded in agreement. "The stable master said one of the grooms disappeared the afternoon of the wedding—hopefully because your brother paid him off and not for more sinister reasons—and that Hayward showed up early the next morning with references, which I assume are faked. Or written by his cronies. He has been right under our noses the entire time."

Halmesbury's deep baritone interjected. "Yet somehow he found the time to sneak off to rile up Lord Stanford and Lord Wood."

"How intrepid of him. If he put half that energy into making a respectable living, he would have done well for himself," Annabel observed.

"Be that as it may, what do we do now?" Sophia's question made them all pause.

Minutes ticked by without any suggestions offered. Richard sifted through ideas in his head but came up with nothing worth offering out loud.

"We could have him jailed," Perry finally ventured.

"There is no evidence that he broke the law. The only offense we can prove is he provided false references, and an assumed name, but I would not want to take my chances that he goes to prison for a short time and then returns angrier to seek vengeance for having him arrested," Richard reasoned.

"Nothing for which he could be transported, then." Perry appeared disappointed.

Sophia hissed in dismay. "Not that! The journey could kill him, especially in his current unhealthy condition. He is still my brother."

"So, burying him in the garden is out of the question, then?" Perry joked weakly. Richard saw Sophia's elbow come up to dig his brother in the ribs. It made his heart sing to observe their familial horseplay; they were becoming a proper family here at Balfour Terrace.

After a moment, Halmesbury spoke up. "If it were me ..."

Richard waited, but the duke did not complete the sentence, clearly musing. "If it were you ...?"

The duke turned his gaze to Richard. "I would want the man as far from my family as I could manage, even if I paid coin to ensure it. Say, New York or Boston. Australia, perhaps. Whatever destination he chose, I would pay for the privilege of knowing he was very distant from my family."

Richard thought. He wanted to mete justice on the brother, but more important was the need to protect his family. "I could have him accompanied. Long or Johnson could deliver him there and find a solicitor to manage an annuity. Hayward would need to present himself each month to collect an allowance. If he has to collect it every month, he will never have time to travel back to British soil and return in time for the next payment."

Sophia clapped her hands. "That could work! Perhaps his escort could ensure that the solicitor knew Cecil's appearance and even provide a miniature of him to be kept on file, so he could never pull another of his sly tricks to collect the funds while not being personally present."

"I will do it! I will escort him to the Americas!" Perry sounded committed to the task.

Richard appreciated the offer, but he preferred his brother remained in England. The errand would take a minimum of four months to complete. "Nay, brother. I need you here. Without your assistance, I would have been lost."

Perry turned his green eyes to look at him with a hopeful glint. "Truly?"

"Aye." His younger brother seemed quite pleased at the acknowledgment. Mayhap Sophia was right; his brother needed purpose to fill his days. "Mr. Long will escort Hayward along with two of the Johns because Johnson has family to care for. I want my men safe from this trickster, so it will take more than one man to complete the task."

Annabel folded her arms in contemplation and added her thoughts. "It is unconventional, but it gets the job done. Pursuing justice is not as important as the peace of mind that your family is protected from this vengeful lunatic. With his predilections, he will be geographically tied down to that source of funds. Perhaps make their payment contingent on the countess being well and alive and ensure it is enough that he will not be willing to walk away from it."

Halmesbury nodded. "One could also remind the young man that his gambling debts will no longer plague him if he remains far from British soil."

Richard looked around at his ... his—what word would best describe what was unfolding around him?

Family!

His cousin and the duchess, his brother and Sophia, they were all family.

He sighed with deep contentment. Here they stood together at his side, assisting him to solve the predicament that faced him. Appreciation and gratitude filled his being. What an incredible change in his circumstances in such a short period, all because he opened his heart. These were the true riches of his life. Perhaps he should try telling Sophia he loved her again? It seemed almost certain she did not hear him say it before.

By Jingo, he was proud of his feisty wife for tackling her horrid brother to the ground!

CHAPTER
TWENTY-ONE

"Be even cautious in displaying your good sense. It will be thought you assume a superiority over the rest of the company."

Dr. John Gregory, A Father's Legacy to His Daughters

∽

The duke offered to mediate with Cecil, which Richard accepted to Sophia's relief. Her husband's sleepless nights, the fact that he had killed a man the night before, and his belligerence toward the sibling who had laid hands on his wife suggested it was the wise choice to make.

The men headed over to parlay with the scoundrel tied to the chair, which left Sophia to show the duchess back to where her babe was waiting in the study. The duchess collected the boy and his nursemaid and took her leave when the Halmesbury carriage drew to the front.

After the duchess departed, Sophia found herself with nothing to occupy her attention. She dared not enter the drawing room where the negotiation was taking place. Her presence would only infuriate her brother, rendering him uncooperative.

She was too tense to read and too anxious to complete any tasks. Briefly, she considered visiting Lily to tell her what had happened, but cast that idea aside as premature.

Which was why she paced up and down in her bedchamber, wringing her hands. Now that the worst of the threat had passed, she had too much time to think.

Does Richard regret that he married me?

He had said she brought him peace, but today's events revealed that was not the truth. He must now live with the fact that a man had died at his hand because the infamous Haywards had entered his life.

Did I make things worse when I tricked him into meeting with Annabel?

She was having second thoughts about that decision. After the most traumatic evening of the man's life, she then deceived him into a confrontation that he perhaps was ill-prepared to handle. What had she been thinking? It seemed like such a good idea at the time, but in retrospect, it was terribly manipulative and controlling. She would be angered if he tried something similar. Hang it all, she *had* been angry when he attempted to interfere with her life by removing her to Saunton Park.

Now that he has confronted the worst, will he lose interest in me?

After all, she had raised the possibility to Lily just yesterday that she might be some sort of ethical lodestone. Richard had risen as a hero from the ashes, reconciled with his cousin's wife, and even now was downstairs to conquer her villainous brother. What role would Sophia serve now that he had uncovered his true self? Would she fade into the role of nobleman's wife with her only duty to sire his heir?

What if I want more?

Could their marriage grow into a true partnership despite her troubled past? She had returned home the night before intending to talk to him. To explain. Perhaps to disclose that she loved him. But so much had happened since she had stepped through the front door and been accosted by the inebriated Lord Wood. This morning she had hoped they would find an opportunity to talk things out, but then she had been shocked to her core to see the note—realizing that she had missed all the clues that her brother was the secret enemy working against them.

Bah!

This was harder than she had expected. Building a life with another person was quite an undertaking. Would Richard remember how she had accepted Ethan without complaint? Would that stand in her favor when they next spoke?

Sophia concluded that thinking was not the best use of her time. She was arguing herself into tighter and tighter binds. Something to occupy her attention was what she needed to find while she awaited Richard's return from the drawing room negotiation with her trussed-up brother.

Making up her mind, she left her rooms to find Ethan in the nursery. She would read him a story and discuss his day with him.

∼

TWO HOURS LATER, Sophia returned to her bedchamber, stopping short when she found Richard sipping coffee on her settee.

"I have been waiting for you."

"How did it go with Cecil?"

"Quite well. I suspect that part of the reason he took the post as groom was it gave him somewhere to hide out. Those gambling debts of his are more prolific than is safe for a man of his current financial position. When Halmesbury proposed he leave English soil, he did not demur and then, when he heard about the annuity, his relief was palpable despite his blustering to the contrary. The duke stipulated he would not be allowed to drink during the voyage, a rule which his escorts will not hesitate to enforce."

Sophia listened with only half of her attention. Her heart was pounding hard. She wanted to race into his arms and smother him in kisses, but she did not know if he would welcome them. "It sounds like Cecil has a very uncomfortable journey ahead of him, then."

"The hope is that sobriety might take hold if he is dry for such a long voyage. We can at least attempt to assist him to recover from his addictions before we set him loose."

"Where is he headed?"

"He chose New Orleans to be his new home. Perhaps he might find a wife and settle down with the allowance he will be receiving. But that is in his hands once Long sets him up. We have done what we can to give him a chance at a new life."

Sophia moved over to the settee, sitting nervously on the very edge. Her palms were moist with her anxiety, and she discreetly wiped them over her skirts as if smoothing wrinkles in the cloth. She was at a loss for words.

"Thank you ... for making such an effort. He is an utter scoundrel, but it is still ... difficult. I remember him as a young boy when he was different."

Richard reached out to take her hand, causing her to flinch in surprise, which he ignored. He gently ran his thumb over her fingers. "It is my pleasure to take care of this on your behalf."

Sophia sat in silence, enjoying his caress and wondering what came next now that the threat had passed.

Richard cleared his throat. "Sophia ... If I may?"

She turned her head to look at him only to find that he appeared to be as nervous as she felt.

"This morning when I told you that I loved you ... did you hear me say it?"

Her eyes widened in astonishment. "You love me?" she asked breathlessly.

"Of course! Your sharp tongue saved my life, and your gracious presence gave it meaning. Before our home was invaded last night, I had every intention of talking to you about it ... about us."

"Oh, Richard!" She flung herself into his arms and—*drat*—her tears started falling once more. Mayhap she was a weak-minded female, after all? She lifted herself to wipe at the tears. "I am so sorry to be weeping again! I promise this is out of character."

Richard caught her chin with his fingers to lift her face. "Sophia, I am quite aware that you are a strong woman with her own mind. Dash it, these last twenty-four hours have been so fraught with peril and potential loss, I am inclined to join you in your tears!"

Sophia laughed in surprise, batting him across the chest. "Bunkum, Richard! Do not make fun of me."

"I do not! See?" Her ridiculous husband pulled an exaggerated face, his handsome features twisted in an attempt to mimic a tearful expression.

Sophia burst into a fit of giggles, laughing so hard that

her stomach began to ache. Unable to resist, she threw her arms around him and pressed her face against the warmth of his neck, her laughter fading as she listened to the steady rhythm of his heartbeat.

In that moment, the sheer magnitude of having this man in her life washed over her, filling her with a sense of joy she could scarcely put into words.

"I love you, too," she whispered. He tensed and then slowly relaxed to press kisses to her hair.

"My love, I am so very happy to hear that," he rumbled quietly, holding her close to his heart.

EPILOGUE

"The parental affection is the first and greatest blessing you can enjoy."

Dr. John Gregory, A Father's Legacy to His Daughters

A FEW WEEKS LATER

Something woke Richard from his sleep. His thoughts foggy, he tried to take stock of his senses. He heard breathing, not from Sophia who lay sleeping to his right, but another presence. He lay still, scarcely daring to breathe and alert the intruder that he was conscious.

"Papa?" Richard's heart skipped a beat in his chest when his son spoke almost directly into his left ear. He threw a hand over his chest, while he attempted to calm his pounding heart. The boy had frightened him out of his wits.

"Shhh ... Mama is sleeping. I will come with you to talk." Richard winced when he made to rise and realized he could not pull back the covers. "Ethan, wait for me in my rooms."

The boy left his side, giving Richard the opportunity to search for his nightshirt. He felt around in the dark and found the garment, pulling it close with relief. However, when he attempted to put it on, he discovered he had merely found Sophia's discarded night rail and was forced to keep feeling around. The night rail would never fit over his broad chest.

Once he dressed, he loped carefully to his adjoining bedchamber to find Ethan sitting on the floor waiting for him. Closing the door gently behind him, he walked over and sank down beside his son.

"What is it, Ethan?"

"I was dreaming about Emma."

"Your cousin?"

"I miss her. Is she well?"

"I do not know for certain, but I did obtain a grand new farm for your family, so I know Emma is now living in Somerset near Saunton Park. Johnson told me that there are fine gardens."

Ethan smiled. "Emma likes gardening."

"See, then she must be well. The weather is very pleasant in Somerset, and I am sure everyone in your family is happy with their new home. Johnson told me the library is well-stocked."

His boy clapped his hands in joy. "Emma likes books."

"Well, then, it stands to reason she is very happy. Shall we go steal some of Cook's biscuits before I return you to your bed?"

Ethan shot to his feet. "She made York biscuits this afternoon, but she would not let me try them!"

"We will ferret them out."

Thirty minutes later, Richard descended the stairs from the nursery, having had a word with the panicked Daisy and the new governess who had awoken to find Ethan missing from his bed. Bleary from his interrupted sleep, he turned the corner to the corridor leading to the family bedrooms, only to knock into Perry on his way in.

They both panted heavily in the aftermath of the shock of encountering each other in the dark.

"Did you just get home?"

"I am a fully grown man. I do not need to account for my whereabouts, do I?" Perry reeked of wine and cigars.

"Calm yourself, brother. I was displaying interest."

"The question is, *Saunton*, why are you prowling the halls at three in the morning?" his brother drawled with a sarcastic tone.

"Ethan woke me up. I just returned from the nursery."

"The little terror woke you up again?"

"He did. He worries over his family that he left behind."

"This is what comes of having children. And now you have another on the way. Soon there will be no peace left in this household."

Richard smiled at the reminder that his countess was with child. "It is not so terrible. He is a clever boy."

"He might be," Perry begrudgingly admitted, "but he is also a cautionary tale. Since I learned about your son, I am being most fastidious in ensuring I do not wind up in a similar position. I have no wish for children of my own nor a wife."

Richard mused on his brother's words for a moment before responding. Sophia had pointed out the path to what Perry needed, and Richard was paying mind to her advice. She was correct in her assessment that Perry lacked purpose in his life, which was why as the head of this household, he planned to alter that. It was why he had not permitted his brother to accompany Cecil Hayward to New Orleans the month before. He needed his brother close to hand if he was to intercede in the direction of his younger brother's path.

"You will change your mind, Perry. When you meet the right woman."

With that, Richard turned away from his brother to rejoin his beautiful wife in bed.

∽

Next in the Inconvenient Brides Series:
Miss Davis and the Spare
Calamity is unleashed when Perry meets the mysterious Emma that Ethan is yearning to see.

AFTERWORD

Dr. John Gregory's *A Father's Legacy to His Daughters*, published in 1761, is a work offering guidance to women on conduct, education, and virtue. Written as advice from a father to his daughters, it reflects the moral expectations and gender norms of 18th-century society, emphasizing modesty, sensibility, and propriety.

Restorative justice is highly therapeutic for both the perpetrator and the victim, no matter how large or small the offense. Planned out with good judgment, it can usually be a smooth process with a lot of gains to be made for everyone involved.

During the years of my nonprofit work, I was fortunate to assist many people with their restorative journey and to reclaim their lives as a fully contributing member of society, which was rewarding, to say the least. In that time, I received many reports of the recipients of unwarranted actions being moved to tears of joy with assertions that their faith in humanity had been restored by the simple act of a person confronting them to confess what they had done, and the offer to make amends. Most times, the

AFTERWORD

amends requested was simply to make a charitable donation on their behalf. This type of activity helped both parties receive closure and restore their sense of belonging to the tribe of man.

Richard's journey was, of course, complicated by having a hidden enemy to thwart his efforts at redemption. If not for that unforeseen obstacle, the advice from his philanthropic ducal cousin would have resulted in his progress in a more orderly fashion. But then it would not have made a good story, would it?

I did not start out with a plan to write Richard's story, but as *Miss Ridley and the Duke* unfolded, I could not help thinking about what would it take for a man of his sins to change? To change so much that he could be trusted to never revert or be unfaithful to his new wife despite his troubling history.

I hope I answered that question to your satisfaction, and that you enjoyed the trials and tribulations of pursuing honor after so many dishonorable deeds littering the past.

With the dissolutely charming Richard discovering the value of integrity, it is now time for his arrogant younger brother to discover the value of love and kinship in *Miss Davis and the Spare*. Peregrine meets a very unsuitable country mouse who captures his attentions despite himself. Can the mysterious Emma Davis draw the damaged Perry out of the aloof shell into which he retreated so many years earlier?

Find out in Book 3 of Dazzling Debutantes!

Stay in touch by signing up for the C. N. Jarrett newsletter!

About the Author

C. N. Jarrett started writing her own stories in elementary school but got distracted when she finished school and moved on to non-profit work with recovering drug addicts. There she worked with people from every walk of life from privileged neighborhoods to the shanty towns of urban and rural South Africa.

One day she met a real-life romantic hero. She instantly married her fellow bibliophile and moved to the USA where she enjoyed a career as a sales coaching executive at an Inc 500 company. She lives with her husband on the Florida Gulf Coast.

Jarrett believes in kindness and the indomitable power of the human spirit. She is fascinated by the amazing, funny people she has met across the world who dared to change their lives. She likes to tell mischievous tales of life-changing decisions and character transformations while drinking excellent coffee and avoiding cookies.

Stay in touch by signing up for the C. N. Jarrett newsletter!

Also by C. N. Jarrett

DAZZLING DEBUTANTES

Book 1: Miss Ridley and the Duke

Book 2: Miss Hayward and the Earl

Book 3: Miss Davis and the Spare

Book 4: Miss Davis and the Architect

Book 5: Mrs. Brown and the Christmas Gift

The Meddling Duke: a Collection of Regency Romantic Short Stories

Made in United States
North Haven, CT
01 December 2025